A Tale of
Two Maidens

A Tale of Two Maidens

A Novel

ANNE ECHOLS

SHE WRITES PRESS

Published 2023

Printed in the United States of America

Print ISBN: 978-1-64742-543-2
E-ISBN: 978-1-64742-544-9
Library of Congress Control Number: 2023908409

For information, address:
She Writes Press
1569 Solano Ave #546
Berkeley, CA 94707

Interior design and layout by Katherine Lloyd, The DESK.
Map is courtesy of Bagwyn Books and Judith Martens.

She Writes Press is a division of SparkPoint Studio, LLC.

This is a work of fiction. Names, characters, places, and incidents either are the product of the author's imagination or are used fictitiously. Any resemblance to actual persons, living or dead, is entirely coincidental.

Note about
Joan of Arc's Name

While Joan of Arc is the saint's most famous name today, she was known by other names during her life. She signed letters and other documents that she dictated to scribes as "Jehanne" or "Jehanne la Pucelle" (Joan the Maid). In this novel, the spelling variation of her name is "Jeanne." She is mostly referred to as "the Maid," "Jeanne the Maid" or "Jeanne de Domrémy," the name of her town.

France at the Time of Joan of Arc

1. **Domrémy**—Jeanne's birthplace (b. 1412)
2. **Orléans**—Site of her first battle; a victory for the French, May 4–8, 1429
3. **Troyes**—Jeanne marches through this town on the way to Reims (early July 1429); Troyes is Felise's home
4. **Reims**—In this city, Charles VII is crowned king of France, July 17, 1429
5. **Paris**—Jeanne attempts to win Paris back from the English but fails Sept. 8, 1429
6. **Rouen**—After being captured in battle and sold to the English, Jeanne is put on trial for heresy, including witchcraft. She is burned at the stake in this city on May 30, 1431

Contents

One

The Chess Game

March 7, 1429
Troyes, France

I could not bear it a moment longer. The headpiece dug into my scalp, forming the same groove that it always did by the end of the day. As soon as we finished washing the supper dishes, I took off the stiff linen coif and unpinned my hair. I shook my head, my unruly curls tumbling across my face and down my back.

"Every evening you unpin your hair at the same time. You are just as predictable as evening bells," my sister Ameline teased.

"I would set myself free earlier, but then I wouldn't be able to see the dishes. Besides, you are predictable too," I teased back, tucking my hair behind my ears. Her own amber tresses would remain neatly in place until just before she went to bed.

"Come, let's put the game table closer to the fire."

The night was bitter cold as Ameline and I moved the table and chairs. Filled with a heaping bowl of her fish stew, I felt warm inside in spite of the wind whistling through the cracks in the shutters. The house still held the pungent scent of ginger that she used to flavor it.

While Ameline added logs to the fire, Aunt Charlotte warmed her hands at the hearth, and I set up Father's chessboard. Tonight, I would play with the ivory pieces and Ameline the jade.

A Tale of Two Maidens

I saved my favorite pieces, the knights, for last. I loved the odd way they moved: one square diagonally and the other straight. They were tricksters, especially when they worked in tandem with one another like two pickpockets. I picked up my last knight and looked at it closely. The piece was carved to resemble a knight on horseback, pressing his thighs into the flanks of a stallion that reared up on his hind legs. His face was hidden underneath a helmet, but I imagined his look of determination to control a beast twice his size.

Goosebumps rose on my flesh as I remembered what I'd heard on the streets today as I walked home from my apprenticeship.

Ameline returned from the fire and sat in the chair across from me. Her cheeks rosy from the fire, Charlotte came to the game table too and sat between us to watch us play as she did every night.

"You look as if your mind has journeyed somewhere far away," Ameline said.

I lifted the knight closer to the candle. "Today I heard that Jeanne the Maid has been outfitted with a suit of armor. Also, she's learning to ride a warhorse. I was trying to imagine what she looked like. What do you think?"

For two weeks, rumors about this mysterious peasant girl had spread throughout our town, each day with embellishments. At night, Ameline and I discussed any new tidings about her. "Father says that people from the east of France are dark-haired and stocky," Ameline replied. "Maybe her hair was dark and unruly like yours before she cut it off."

"I imagine that she is tall for a woman and strong like a man," I said, moving the queen's pawn two squares forward.

"It's her visions that I wonder about the most," Ameline said as she moved the knight's pawn. She wrapped her black wool shawl around her thin shoulders. "Does Saint Michael the Archangel have flowing white robes and wings? And do Saints Margaret and Catherine smile at her as her own mother would?"

"I would be frightened if they came to me and told me what they told her," I said. "Cut your hair and dress as a boy. Leave home. Embark on a long journey to the dauphin's court and tell him that God wants you to help him fight to regain his lands. You must help put an end to the war that has ravaged France for nigh on a hundred years."

"I suppose I would too," Ameline admitted. "But maybe I would welcome the saints' appearance after a while. Maybe she does too."

"I don't think I would ever welcome them." I shuddered and returned my attention to our game. After we had both moved half a dozen times or more, I felt a prickling of excitement as I saw a very good move. I remembered Ameline's advice and considered the consequences before moving my queen across the chessboard and placing her in a square that threatened Ameline's knight.

"Good move, Felise," she said with a smile. "It won't be long before you defeat me."

I grinned back, proud of my improvement over the past few months. "You've taught me well."

Charlotte circled her arms around my neck and hugged me. "Good move," she said, echoing Ameline in her high-pitched voice.

I hugged her back. Charlotte never remembered how to move the chess pieces, just as she had never learned to write the letters of the alphabet in spite of all the times I tried to teach her. Her mind was a child's although she was twenty-five years old.

I expected Ameline to move her knight out of danger, but she surprised me by putting my king in check at the same time. "How did you think of that move? You are clever enough with battle tactics to be a captain in the dauphin's army. You could help the Maid go to battle for him."

"Felise," she began in a tone of voice that I knew well. Today was my fifteenth birthday, and I wondered if I would ever outgrow the need for advice.

"First, you are just as clever as I am, and you will soon be able to think of such moves," Ameline said. "Second, I know you are eager for this Maid to win the dauphin's approval and lead his army into battle for the first time. But I beg you to temper your enthusiasm."

I sighed, knowing we were about to disagree about Jeanne again. Our family, as well as most of the other fine-blooded families of Troyes, supported the Dauphin Charles, the rightful heir to the French throne. My grandmother had even named Charlotte after him. The English had placed their own false king on the throne, with the help of their French allies, the Burgundians. These nobles were cousins of the royal family but were estranged from them because of a bloody struggle for power. By joining forces, the English and the Burgundians had captured most of the dauphin's lands in the northern part of France. I yearned for the Maid to bring us victory and end the war at once, but Ameline was more cautious than I was.

"You know how I feel about the Maid," she said. "And you know that I want the dauphin to win back his throne and that I desire our land to be at peace. But I do not believe that we and the other Dauphinists in our town should throw our support to the Maid when all we know of her is rumor." She fingered a pawn on the first row of her pieces. "Let us withhold judgment until we know more of the truth about her."

"Do you fear that Satan binds her to him through false visions of saints?" I asked, making a hasty sign of the cross. That was what the Burgundians said about her on the streets.

She shrugged. "Who can say? Maybe God didn't send her saints either."

"Who else could have sent them?"

"Maybe she conjures them herself."

Her boldness startled me. "So you think that she's lying about her visions?"

"I don't know. Maybe she wants to have fame and power through them. Or maybe she isn't self-serving. Maybe she believes with all her heart that she must take action to end this war. And because of her strong desire for peace, she herself conjures the saints."

I clasped Ameline's small hand in mine and stared into her clear brown eyes. "I fear what the Dauphinists would do to you if they ever heard such an idea."

She brushed back a strand of my hair that had fallen across my face and dangled onto the chess pieces. "Don't worry. I won't speak of this to anyone but you, here in the safety of our home where no one else can hear." Her voice had that tone that she always used to lift my spirits. "Jeanne is a girl like us. She has her desires, and we have ours. Instead of waiting to find out the truth about her, we should work to make our own vision come true."

"But we don't see saints as she does."

Her eyes shone in the firelight. "True, but we do have a vision."

"What do you mean?"

"Come now. We've talked about it many times."

Suddenly I realized what she meant, and my heart began to beat faster. Our vision was a dream in our minds. It wasn't ghostly like the Maid's saints but real. We had a plan.

"In the months that Father is away on his merchant journeys, we live here alone and take care of ourselves," Ameline reminded me. "We are learning to find our own way in the world, Felise, without husbands."

I stared at the glowing embers that created caves and hollows in the wood and said, "And you, Sister, can earn your living by owning a cloth shop and I by owning a bookshop. You will make beautiful clothes and I will copy beautiful books."

She took my hand and raised it skyward with hers. Charlotte clutched each of our arms with one of hers. She had taken off her coif and unpinned one side of her hair, which glowed amber in the firelight. "Me too," she exclaimed, her crescent-shaped eyes sparkling with excitement.

"You too, Charlotte," Ameline reassured her. "May God hear our prayer and allow us to live by our own handiwork."

"As *femmes soles*," I added, my eyes on the shadow of our arched hands against the wall.

"And sisters who always—"

A loud knock on the door interrupted her. It couldn't be Father because his signal was three quick knocks. Night had fallen and it was past the proper time for visits. Ameline and I looked at each other as Charlotte tried to wriggle loose from me and go to the door. But I held her tight.

Ameline reached for one of the candles illuminating our game and gripped the handle of the holder. "Who's there?"

"Pietr Wervecke of Flanders sent us," a man's voice boomed, thick with an accent that I didn't recognize. "We've come to collect your father's debts."

In Father's desk, Ameline had found a scrap of paper in his hand mentioning a moneylender named Wervecke. I shook my head, trying to grasp what was about to happen.

"Just a moment," Ameline called as she rose from the table, her eyes intent upon me. "Don't speak," she whispered. "Just do as I say."

She flung her shawl over my head, and I hid my hair as best I could, ashamed that strangers would see it tumbling down my back. As soon as she unbarred the door, a fat man with a jagged scar on his face pushed past her, followed by two other men. Reeking of ale and horses, the stench of their unwashed flesh filled the great room as they unfurled parchments.

"See for yourselves what your father owes our master," the leader announced in his harsh Flemish accent, pointing to the loan and interest amounts listed on the scrolls.

Charlotte started toward the table, for she always took commands literally. The men drew back, and the scar-faced man turned to Ameline. "See that the idiot stays away from the table," he snarled. "I don't want her looking at us with those strange eyes, in case she puts a curse on us and brings us misfortune."

Ameline nodded and he turned to me, his gaze resting too long on my breasts. "You, girl, get us some of your father's wine," he commanded. Ameline motioned that I should take Charlotte with me. I hurried over to the wine barrel with her hand in mine. "Those men smell bad," she complained loud enough for them to hear.

"At least we're not as ugly as you are, idiot," the red-haired man yelled.

"Hold your tongue, simpleton," the scar-faced man barked, "or we'll tie you in a sack and throw you in the river."

Charlotte's chin quivered, a sure sign that she was about to cry. I put my finger to my lips, and she imitated me, barely holding back her tears. After pouring wine into three cups, I carried them on a tray back to the table. Charlotte followed me, stopping when she reached Ameline.

The thin bald man leered at Ameline, and the redhead swatted me on the rump as I served him wine. "If you and your sister wore yellow knots on your sleeves, I wager you would soon earn the money to pay back your father's debts. Especially you, girl."

The other men laughed so hard that I hoped they didn't notice the blush spreading across my face at the thought of turning to harlotry. Before I could stop the scar-faced man, he had pulled the shawl off my head and stroked my hair. "Men would pay extra money to bed a girl with such beautiful hair."

I drew back, spilling wine on his hand.

"Why such a hurry to leave, girl?" he teased, yanking a strand of my hair. The others came closer and reached out their hands toward me as the first man had. I tried to get out of their way, but the redhead pinched my breast, and I yelped in pain.

"Leave her alone," Ameline commanded.

"You're feisty," laughed the bald man as he turned toward her. "Let's see what you look like with your hair down."

The three of them shoved me out of the way and strode over to Ameline. I retreated in terror to Charlotte's side and pulled the shawl over my hair again.

Ameline drew herself upright, her eyes glinting fiercely. If she was afraid, I couldn't tell. I would try my best to be like her and hide my trembling hands behind my back while Charlotte buried her face in my bodice.

The scar-faced man stood before her. He downed his wine in one go and tossed the cup on the floor, shattering it to pieces. He yanked the coif off her head and pulled out as many pins as he could find. Still, she didn't flinch. The three men stared open-mouthed as a cascade of her thick amber hair glowed in the firelight.

Ameline looked the scar-faced man straight in the eyes. Never had I seen such power emanating from her, like that of a warrior just before a battle raged. "If you touch my sister or aunt again," she said, her voice transformed into a low growl, "I won't give you a sous. If you return to this Pietr Wervecke empty-handed, you will no longer be in his employ."

The scar-faced man gaped at her and shook his head slightly as if he had awakened from dozing. His bald companion snickered as he strode forward. "It's you I want," he breathed into Ameline's ear, his eyes glinting with lust. He drew out his knife and held it to her neck, but still she held steady.

My eyes darted around the room and found the poker at the hearth. I almost ran for it, but Ameline had commanded me to do only what she said. I stood rooted to the floor.

"You can have your way with me, even kill me, and I'll curse you from beyond the grave," Ameline said, her voice filling the room, "but I won't give you the money if you harm us. And I'm the only one who knows where it's hidden."

No one moved. The only sound came from the hearth where the logs shifted in the fire.

"Damn you, whore," the bald moneylender seethed, pushing the flat blade of his knife against her neck.

The scar-faced man grabbed him by the arm and yanked the knife away. It clattered to the floor. "You fool, don't you see she's serious? Sit down."

He shoved the bald man toward the table where the redhead sat white-faced, making the sign of the cross. "She's bewitched you," he muttered to his companion, "and almost made you forget why we came here."

With his arms squared against his chest, the scar-faced man turned his body so he could keep an eye on his underlings and address Ameline.

"A pox on Henri and his whore daughters and his half-wit sister," he bellowed. "On behalf of Pietr Wervecke, I demand full and immediate payment of his debts."

Ameline directed her gaze at him. "I don't know when Father will return, but he left me with instructions," she began. "I am to pay the first half of what he owes Pietr Wervecke. He told me to assure Pietr's messengers that the second half of his debt will be paid in full by midsummer."

What a good liar she was! Father hadn't left any instructions.

"My sister will fetch the payment as soon as I tell her where it is," she continued.

She turned to face me with her back to the men. "Jewels," she mouthed.

"Even the amethysts?" I mouthed back. She nodded and my heart sank.

I forced myself to hurry to the hiding place, the oldest of the ragbags lying neglected in a dusty corner. I opened the draw-string and groped underneath the mountain of rags until I felt a satchel at the bottom, heavy with jewels, including the amethyst ring and necklace that Mama had bequeathed to Ameline and me. I wanted to take the amethysts out of the bag and hide them but knew I could not. I settled for pressing them against my heart, certain that the moneylenders were growing impatient.

As soon as I returned, I handed the bag to Ameline. "Do you have a jeweler among you?" she asked the scar-faced man.

He nodded at the bald man, who pulled out a pair of spectacles from his moneybag. "I need more light," he grunted when Ameline handed him the jewels.

She set candles closer to him as he inspected Mama's jewels. After some figuring on a scrap of paper, the jeweler turned to the leader. "Three hundred *livres tournois*," he declared.

"No, they are worth four hundred," Ameline insisted. "A jeweler in Troyes appraised the jewels for that amount and I have a receipt to prove it."

I marveled that she had thought of everything while the bald man spluttered that he wanted to see the receipt. She fetched it from Father's desk and gave it to the scar-faced man. "Four hundred," he grunted, "but that's still not enough for the first half of your father's debt. What else do you have, girl?"

She looked around the room. "Take Father's chess set," she said. "It is made of the finest jade and ivory. I've had it appraised too."

A moan escaped my lips. Not the chess set. But we had nothing else. "It serves Henri right," snickered the man with the beard. "His debts have checkmated him."

The jeweler set to work appraising the chess set and soon grudgingly admitted that it was worth a bit more than the needed amount. As the men packed the board and pieces in burlap and thrust them into a satchel, Ameline told the scar-faced man that she wanted two receipts of her payment, one for him and one for her.

"Your father taught you a thing or two about doing business, girl," he said, narrowing his eyes. "But it won't do you any good. Mark my word, we know of your father, and he won't pay his debt by July. You and your sister and the idiot will suffer a terrible fate."

I surreptitiously wiped sweat from my forehead while the leader ordered his clerk to write the receipts. After rolling up the scrolls, the men stood and raised their fists at us. They left without another word, slamming the door as if they would break it. Ameline and I collapsed in each other's arms, with Charlotte wrapping her arms around us, all of us trembling violently. It was a few minutes before I was able to speak.

"What are we going to do?" I whispered, too frightened to raise my voice.

"I don't know," she said grimly, and the terror in her voice turned my blood cold.

Two

Rose Oil

April 1, 1429

"Hide the money," Ameline bade me from her chair by the hearth. Her needle darted through the brocade, but her pale face was etched with exhaustion.

Grabbing the money pouch that held the day's earnings at the marketplace, I strode to her workroom. My belly rumbled in complaint of the bread and thin soup we had for supper as I reached the far corner and opened the ragbag that had once held Mama's amethysts and other jewels. My fury at Father burned within me again. Many years ago, when Mama lay on her deathbed, she had told Ameline to hide some of her jewels, leaving enough that Father wouldn't become suspicious. In law, all of Mama's possessions belonged to him, but she knew that he would sell the jewels she'd inherited from her mother to pay off his gambling debts.

Mama was right. The day after her funeral, Father had taken the entire jewel box with him, and we'd never seen it again. Even as a seven-year-old child, I had shared Ameline's shame and anger at Father. Because of his debts, he had severed Mama's family tradition of bequeathing jewels from the mother through the daughters to the granddaughters.

But the loss of Mama's jewels paled in comparison to what he had done now. Why hadn't he tended to his debts before he'd left us to go on a long journey? Because of him, Ameline bent over her needle from dawn until an hour past her usual bedtime. Because of him, she had dark circles under her eyes.

I stormed out of the workroom, determined to help her finish the work she had allotted for this night. It was part of the plan she had devised the day after the moneylenders had come to our house nearly three weeks before. After work that day, she had gathered us around the great room table. We had not slept well, and the day's duties had wearied us to the bone, but we had no time to waste.

"The moneylenders might return soon," Ameline said somberly. "We cannot depend on Father to repay his debt, so we must do it for him by earning extra money. Our future depends on it."

Every night since then, we had sewn long past our usual bedtime in order to make more clothing to sell. But when I returned to the great room, it surprised me to see that she had set her needle down.

"What's wrong?" I asked.

"Just a headache. Don't worry. Tonight, I need you to sew the hem of this christening gown."

From her sewing basket, she lifted out a tiny brocade gown studded with pearls. Charlotte rose from her chair to look as well. "For baby," she crooned. "I want to hold the baby."

"Soon," Ameline replied. "Remember that our neighbor Sybille will give birth to her baby any day."

"Sybille has a baby in her belly. Soon I will hold it," Charlotte said with a smile, rocking an imaginary baby in her arms. Her short, stocky body made monstrous shadows in the firelight that belied her innocence. "Whose baby will wear this gown?" I asked Ameline as I threaded the needle. Sybille wasn't rich enough to afford a garment made of such fine cloth.

"I didn't want to accept this commission, Felise, but I had to," she replied, her voice low. "A Burgundian's child will wear my handiwork."

"What?" I gasped, looking up so quickly that I pricked my finger with the needle.

Her face grew even paler as she put her sewing aside and nodded. For the first time in nine years, a Burgundian was buying a garment from our cloth shop.

We both stared at the fire, and that terrible day when the Treaty of Troyes had been signed filled my mind. It had happened a year before Mama's death. I was six and Ameline was nine when the dauphin's mother, Queen Isabeau, had sided with the English and the Burgundians by disowning her son. She had also agreed that her daughter Princess Catherine could marry Prince Henry, the heir to the English throne. Furthermore, the treaty made him the heir to France, and his sons after him. After nearly one hundred years of fighting, the English kings had finally achieved their goal of ruling our country, thus combining England and France into one kingdom.

I had known none of this history that May morning when shouts on the street outside jolted me awake. When I ran downstairs, Father, Ameline, and Charlotte were holding hands and praying. Father hardly ever prayed since he scorned our priests, believing they were greedy hypocrites. Ameline's face was drained of color. Terror rose in me as I asked where Mama was. She was always the first to rise and kindle the fire. Before anyone could answer, I heard a loud moan from her chamber upstairs.

Her labor to give birth had begun many months too early. Petronile the Midwife, and Anes, her best friend, attended her all day as her shrieks of pain continued. They punctuated the uproar on our streets as Dauphinists and Burgundians, their enemies who supported the English, fought to the death.

The firelight illuminated Father's round face, a mirror image of mine, as he enfolded me in his arms. Beneath his tunic, I felt the rounded shape of his recorder, which he always wore hanging around his neck.

Later that day, he played merry music on it to accompany the tales of his journey, trying to distract us. But he couldn't block out the screams of agony coming from inside and outside the house. Even as a child, I had known that my baby brother or sister was dying upstairs and that men were being slaughtered on our very streets. Nightmares plagued me for months.

The memory of that day flooded me until Ameline turned toward me, her face pleading in the candlelight. "I cannot change what happened nine years ago. Nor will my needlework for a Burgundian make things any worse," she said. "Besides, the Burgundian lady will pay me well. And if she likes my work, she will want me to make more garments for her family and recommend me to her ladies-in-waiting."

I strode to the hearth as tears welled in my eyes. "Everything has changed, and I don't want any of it to happen," I burst out. "I try to follow your example and accept our lot, but I can't. I want to spend our evenings as we used to spend them, laughing and playing chess and talking of our future. I don't want to worry about the moneylenders returning. It's all Father's fault."

She rose from her chair and wrapped her thin arms around my shoulders. "You're right, Felise, but we can't let our anger stop us from doing what we must. Whenever I feel distraught as you are now, I anoint my neck with rose oil. It makes me think of Mama, and that always clears my mind."

"I always wondered why you liked rose oil so much." I sighed, turning around to hug her.

"You know my secret now," she said, laughing as she used to laugh. I went to the side table and tried not to think of Father or the Burgundian child who would soon wear the gown I was hemming. I poured some of the oil onto the linen rag that Ameline kept in a bowl and dabbed it on my neck. The scent of roses filled my nostrils. I closed my eyes, imagining our courtyard garden abloom with roses.

As my mind became more settled, I walked back to the hearth, suddenly remembering the news about Jeanne the Maid. "Ameline, today when I went to buy bread, I heard that the Bishop of Poitiers had declared that God sent the Maid to us. Thus, the dauphin will allow her to fight for his cause."

She said nothing while pressing her hand against her head as I returned to my chair. It worried me, but she said it was just a headache. I had headaches, too, right before my monthly courses.

I picked up my needle again, thinking of prophecies about Jeanne. "Remember how Father told us that when he was a child, a holy woman named Marie d'Avignon had a vision in which a vast array of armor appeared before her? She pleaded with God not to force an old woman like her to don armor and fight the English and Burgundians. He reassured her that the armor was not for her, but for a maid who would come after her death."

"There's another way to understand this prophecy." Ameline spoke slowly as she did to Charlotte, especially when she wanted her to understand something important. "Jeanne could have heard it and convinced herself that she is the girl who will fulfill it."

"I know you're usually right, Ameline." I wanted to look at her, but I was almost done with the hem, and then I could help her finish another garment so she could go to bed earlier. "But this time, I feel certain that I'm right. So are the prophecies about Jeanne. Think of how much better our lives will be after she helps the dauphin win the war. No more will thousands of French knights be killed in pitched battles and sieges, like Mama's brother was."

As I made another stitch, I paused to gather thoughts for my argument. "And remember what Father told us about the villages throughout the vast countryside of France. Between battles, those mercenary soldiers, the scorchers, will no longer band together and prey on villagers, raping their wives, stealing their crops and animals, and burning their houses. Don't you see that the villagers will live in peace at last, Ameline?"

Ameline was silent as I finished the last stitch of the hem. I expected her to praise my argument even if she didn't completely agree with it. But she didn't answer. I glanced up and saw her rubbing her head again, her eyes closed, and her face contorted in pain. Charlotte had her arms wrapped around her. "What's wrong, Ameline?" she asked in a quavering voice and burst into tears.

May 8

The shadows lengthened across the great room and across my heart. After lighting a candle, I stirred the chicken broth that I had set to simmer in the morning. I ladled broth into a cup and sprinkled a handful of dried herbs over it. "May Typhaine the Apothecary's remedy work at last," I whispered.

For over a moon, she had been claiming that this mixture would shrink the tumor that she suspected was lodged inside Ameline's skull. But for the past three days, Ameline has not risen from her bed, and I feared that the tumor was growing bigger. I tore off a hunk of bread. No, the soup would help. This evening, her sickness would begin to lift. I set the cup and bread on a plate and took it upstairs.

Our chamber faced west and still held the last bit of sunlight. I stood in the doorway watching Charlotte, who sat up in the bed next to Ameline and stroked her hair. Ameline lay with her eyes closed. She didn't turn her head toward me, but I prayed that her slumber was free of pain. Setting the soup down, I lit the candles on the mantelpiece.

The bedclothes rustled. "Felise?" she murmured as her eyes fluttered open.

I grasped her hand. "I am here."

The candles illuminated her ashen face and the deep shadows beneath her closed eyes. Tears rose up within me, and I struggled to hold them back. So far, she hadn't seen them.

Her face contorted as she gasped for breath, a sure sign that her headache had returned. She tried to lift her hand to her head, but it fell against the bedclothes. I grabbed a wet linen cloth from the game table that Charlotte and I had carried upstairs and pressed the cloth to her forehead.

Charlotte looked at me wide-eyed, mirroring my own helplessness, and burst into her evening song about the moon and stars. Ameline's breathing slowed down as the spasm passed. Behind closed eyelids, she smiled as Charlotte's sweet voice floated about the candlelit room for several more verses. I took the cloth away from Ameline's forehead and massaged her temples. She sighed in pleasure, and my shoulders slackened.

When Charlotte's song ended, she yawned loudly and snuggled underneath the covers. "Good night, Ameline," she mumbled, sleep already beginning to take her.

"May you have sweet dreams, Charlotte," my sister whispered. Her eyes closed and sweat beaded around her mouth.

I grabbed the cup of broth from the mantel. "Let me help you sit up and drink some soup," I urged her.

Ameline shook her head. "The smell alone makes me feel better."

"But Typhaine said you must drink three cups a day."

"No."

I set the broth down with a thud, and it splattered onto the game table. Typhaine was a false healer. Her cure had done nothing to heal Ameline.

"You are angry, Felise," she murmured. "Read to me. It will help us both."

Breathing deeply to steady myself, I picked up Mama's old prayer book from the game table and sat down on the edge of the bed. I opened the book to a bookmarked page and began reading Ameline's favorite story. After Jesus's death on the cross, three women went to prepare his body for burial. But when they entered the place where his body was laid out, they discovered that he was gone. He had risen from the dead.

Rose Oil

A radiant smile lit Ameline's face. For the first time in many days, she looked into my eyes. Was she healed at last? I took her hands in mine.

They were still cold and damp. I rubbed them, desperate to warm them and give her a parcel of my life.

"Felise," she said, her voice trailing, "I am dying."

I clasped her hands more tightly. "No, Ameline. I will run to the street of healers. There must be a stronger remedy."

She shook her head. "Stay. I have something to tell you."

I sank to my knees, my head collapsing onto the bed. She combed her fingers through my hair. "I don't want you to go," I moaned, unable to hold back my tears.

"Nor do I, but God does. I pray that he will let me know you are happy," she whispered. "Remember our dream, Felise."

"I can't do it without you."

Her hand stopped combing through my hair, and she didn't answer. I lifted my head and saw that she had fallen into a deep slumber that I feared was the sleep of death. I rose to my feet knowing that I must run for the priest. But what if she were dead by the time I returned?

Her hair spread like an amber fan across the bolster, and I stroked it gently. It was the only part of her body not ravaged by the illness. I dipped my fingertips into the bowl of rose oil that I had brought upstairs and anointed her forehead, tears streaming down my face. *Mother of God, may her soul be at peace even if I can't fetch Père Alphonse in time.* He would form a cross with holy oil on her forehead, but I spread the rose oil in the shape of a flower.

May 11

I placed a sprig of rosemary, with its cluster of tiny purple flowers, on Ameline's breast and gazed at her closed eyelids. I would remember her forever, not like this, but like she was when we played our last chess game and pledged to live our lives as femmes soles.

A Tale of Two Maidens

As soon as I let go of the rosemary stem, Père Alphonse lifted the lid of the coffin. The flickering candles cast shadows on her body. My eyes fell on the deep needle groove on Ameline's finger, wrought by years of sewing, and her brass thimble with its top decorated by beads that formed the letter *A*. The coffin lid closed.

A lump swelled in my throat as I clutched her shawl around my shoulders. I wanted her back—singing, laughing, and talking. Why had God taken her? She was too young to die, only eighteen and barely three years older than I.

Charlotte sniffled and wiped her runny nose against the black velvet of my bodice. She tugged at my sleeve, looking up at me with her crescent eyes filled with tears. I pushed loose strands of her hair back under her coif. For three nights, I had cried myself to sleep. The only thing that helped me bear my anguish was her hand on my head, her fingers combing through my hair.

"Ameline will come back soon," she had comforted me, but her words only made me cry harder.

"Ameline has been gone long enough," she whimpered, sniffling again. "I want her to come back now."

She won't come back—ever. I stopped myself just before these words escaped my lips, but I couldn't stop myself from wishing that God had taken my aunt and spared Ameline.

How could I think such a cruel thought? I hugged Charlotte as Ameline's words echoed within me: "When Mama lay dying, she told me to take care of Charlotte for her. Now you must take care of her for me."

Père Alphonse motioned for the pallbearers to come forward. They lifted the coffin and followed the priest down the central aisle, with Charlotte and me following behind them. André the Bookseller, the owner of the bookshop where I served as an apprentice scribe, stood in the first row gazing at me. His face was contorted to resemble pity, but I didn't trust him. When his master scribes finished copying an expensive book, he never marveled in its beauty. Instead, the look on his face as he stroked his beard was that of someone calculating how much profit he would make. I was not a girl in his eyes but merchandise no different from his books. As part of a loan repayment to André, Father had appointed him my caretaker if anything happened to Ameline when he was away on a merchant trip. He had also named André to be my guardian after his death.

Across the central aisle from me, someone coughed. I turned toward the sound and saw a young man looking at me, his deep-set eyes full of concern. I had seen this young man on market days when I helped Ameline sell shirts and purses, but I didn't know his name, and Ameline and I had never spoken to him. *Why is he here?* I wondered.

I tried to dismiss him from my mind as the pallbearers reached the open doors of the church, and we walked into bright sunshine. In a corner of the churchyard, André's servants roasted chicken on spits over a fire. Trestle tables groaned under the weight of great wheels of cheese and fresh loaves and barrels of ale. André had provided the food for the sole purpose of persuading everyone that he cared for Henri the Debtor's family far more than my father ever could. The guests murmured about André's benevolence while they gazed hungrily at the funeral feast. I clenched my hands into fists. They had come for the food and cared little about Ameline's death.

The pallbearers halted at the gravesite and set her coffin down beside it. Sweat glistened on the gravedigger's forehead as he climbed out of the hole, shovel in hand. Beside it, a pile of black earth stood ready to hide Ameline forever.

Anes, Mama's dear friend, came to us and enfolded Charlotte and me in her arms. "Your sister is with your mother now, Felise," she whispered. "Take solace in knowing that."

Mama was dead, but I was alive. I needed Ameline far more than Mama did. I buried my face against Anes's shoulder. Now

I had to face whatever happens without Ameline to guide me. Would I be forced to marry or move from our house or make some other change? I was afraid, but I couldn't let Charlotte know of our uncertain future, or she would become even more distraught than she was now. I had to be strong and care for her as Ameline had cared for us whenever Father was away on a long journey.

Père Alphonse rang a handbell. "Thou art dust and unto dust thou wilt return," he intoned as he sprinkled holy water onto Ameline's grave. Lifting my head from Anes's shoulder, I watched the men lower Ameline's coffin into the earth and wept again. She would always be alive in my heart. *May she be at peace, though I am not.*

A shout rose up from beyond the graveyard, startling me. Horses' hooves thundered and grew louder as they approached. The people who were gathered around Ameline's grave turned away, murmuring among themselves. Charlotte cocked her head, curious, but my gaze remained on the gravedigger as he shoveled dirt onto Ameline's casket. All too soon, he had buried it and anchored her headstone deep in the earth. Ameline, daughter of Henri the Merchant. 1411–1429. My whole body ached.

Many people were shouting now, louder and louder until a trumpet blared. As the crowd quieted to hear the news, Père Alphonse made a hasty sign of the cross and hurried to the cemetery wall to see what was about to take place. I bowed my head, wanting only to be alone with Ameline.

The trumpet sounded again. "Hearken to tidings of great import!" a crier shouted. "The siege of Orléans is over. The Maid, Jeanne de Domrémy, has recaptured the city from the English. She will lead Charles the Dauphin to be crowned king at Reims!"

Goosebumps prickled my flesh as I remembered the last time Ameline and I had talked about the Maid. My wish for her victory in battle had come true. But I couldn't rejoice, remembering full well my sister's hesitation. That the news of the Maid's victory should arrive at Ameline's funeral disturbed me even more.

On the streets surrounding the graveyard, the jeers of the Burgundians—most of them people of the lower classes who had sworn allegiance to the Duke of Burgundy—clashed with the applause of the Dauphinists. Both factions were ruining Ameline's funeral, but I was powerless to stop them. I grabbed Charlotte's hand and strode to the quietest corner of the cemetery. Underneath the cedar trees was a stone bench where we sat, and I tried to return to my prayers.

But I couldn't. The Burgundians burst into a song about Jeanne de Domrémy and Satan. "She dresses like a man, but she is woman all the same. She spreads her legs for Satan."

I blushed. Through the trees, I saw the Dauphinists surrounding the Burgundians with their knives drawn. "Kill the traitors!" a Dauphinist shouted.

I quickly shifted my gaze back to Ameline's tombstone and pressed my hands against my ears to block out the screaming and shouting and thudding of men as they wrestled each other to the ground. Charlotte hid her eyes in my bodice. Breakfast churned in my belly. I had witnessed shouting matches and scuffling between the Dauphinists and the Burgundians on our streets, but things had never gone this far—except for the day long ago when the Treaty of Troyes had been signed.

Just then the young man I had noticed in church ran toward us, his eyebrows drawn together in fierce resolve. He drew his knife and posted himself in front of us, blocking the fight from our view with his broad back and shoulders. I withdrew my hands from my ears and wrapped my arms around Charlotte. Though I was still afraid of what would happen, I was grateful for the young man's protection.

A flourish of trumpets rose up from the direction of the north gate, and a group of armed guards rode toward us, just beyond the cemetery wall. They were in the employ of the magistrates, our town's judges and judicial officers, whose loyalty was to the dauphin.

"Disperse at once!" a crier in their midst shouted. "Fifty lashes for the men who disobey and five days in the stocks for the women!"

Amid disgruntled mumblings, the crowd disbanded, and the guards rode off to break up the brawls that surely had erupted elsewhere. The young man put his knife away and turned toward Charlotte and me. His gray eyes still scanned the street surrounding the cemetery, as if he were making certain that no one would enter the cemetery through the gate nearby. The curly brown hair framing his face softened the square shape of his jaw. His squirrel-trimmed collar indicated that he was a commoner since our town's sumptuary laws prohibited those of the lower ranks from wearing fine furs like mink and ermine. In spite of Father's debts, my family had fine blood and did not associate with people like him. I didn't understand why he was taking it upon himself to guard Charlotte and me, but I kept my curiosity to myself as best I could.

When the noise on the street quieted, I risked following his gaze toward the cemetery gate. A young man with blood smeared on his face was walking along the street just outside the cemetery wall. He stopped abruptly when he noticed the man guarding me.

"Georges?" he asked, his voice lifted in surprise. "Why are you at an enemy's funeral?"

A Burgundian was protecting us? I listened closely for his reply, but he ignored the question, merely nodding at the man. "Farewell, until the next tanners' guild meeting, Vincent."

"I hope the Maid isn't bewitching you from afar," Vincent muttered and continued on his way. Leading Charlotte, I returned to Ameline's grave. The man called Georges followed us. "You must let me take you to your house," he said as he stood behind me, his voice full of concern. "The fighting will soon start again."

The noises of the brawl echoed in my mind, and my belly churned again. "I want to stay here," I replied. In truth I yearned for the safety of my home, but I didn't want to return there. In Ameline's place, André installed his servant Marguerite, an old woman who found fault with everything Charlotte and I did.

"It isn't safe. But if you insist, I will stay here too."

I turned toward him and was surprised to catch a look of tenderness on his face. "Why are you protecting us?" I asked.

His eyes searched mine. "Do you—" Before he could finish his question, someone shouted my name. The young man and I both turned to see who it was. André hurried toward me, the blood drained from his face. His clothes were as neat as always, since he would never have joined a fight. I positioned myself behind Charlotte, knowing that he didn't like to be anywhere near "the half-wit," as he called her. Thanks to Charlotte, I hadn't gone to live at my guardian's house when Ameline died. I was grateful for that, though I felt a twinge of guilt for using Charlotte as a shield.

"Get away from my apprentice, filth!" André shouted at the tanner. "You weren't invited to this funeral."

I winced at the harshness of his words. The tanner's eyes flashed in anger. "I was protecting her from the fight. Where were you?"

"How dare you speak to me so rudely," André growled. "If you ever come near this girl again, I will see that you are clapped in the stocks."

The tanner held his gaze for a moment before turning to leave. His head and shoulders were erect, as if he weren't ashamed of the way André treated him. I wondered how he had come to be so bold when speaking with fine-blooded people.

Avoiding any contact with Charlotte, André grabbed me by the arm and pulled me toward the gate. Charlotte stumbled to keep up. I tried to help her, but André forced me to keep going at his pace.

"Please, can't I stay here and pray for my sister?" I pleaded.

"You can pray at your father's house," he snarled.

I forced myself to walk behind him, kicking rocks out of my path and cursing Father under my breath. It was his fault that André was my guardian and could tell me what to do.

"Master André," I said, hoping he would listen, "remember the letter that my sister wrote to you before she died?"

He shook his head, refusing to answer.

"If this sickness takes me, Felise," she had said the day before she stopped speaking forever, "give André a letter I wrote. It will tell him about the moneylenders' threats and ask him to loan us money if Father hasn't returned by their deadline."

Three days ago I had given André the letter, along with the receipt that Ameline told me to include with it. After reading the letter, he crumbled it up and tossed it into the fire. "By God's chin," he sneered, "your sister may have been clever enough to run a cloth shop, but I don't need her advice. I have already considered the problem of your father's debts. Not another word of it, girl."

Don't dismiss me as if I'm a child, I wanted to shout at him, but that would only have made things worse.

His boots crunched against the street, and soon we reached my house. The smell of the neighbors' dinners filled the air.

"I'm hungry," Charlotte whined. For the moment she seemed to have forgotten about Ameline.

André scowled at me. "If I hear of you disobeying Marguerite, I will punish you soundly."

I curtsied before André took his leave. The first of July was nearly two moons from now. Could I trust André to deal with the moneylenders? Or Father? I doubted it.

Where is he right now? I wondered, as I knocked at our front door. There was no way to contact him on his journey, and he rarely wrote letters. I clutched my arms to my chest when I thought about how I couldn't even write to him about Ameline's death.

I heard Marguerite sliding the bar to open the door and gritted my teeth, not wanting to enter my own house. I picked up a strand of Ameline's hair that still clung to her shawl that I was wearing and closed my eyes. *Blessed Mother, keep us safe from the moneylenders.*

Three

Watermark

May 21, 1429

André clapped his hands. "Begin the day's labor!" he shouted, his command echoing through the scriptorium.

At every sloped desk, master scribes and apprentices dipped their quills into inkpots and began to copy; everyone except for me. I looked out the window, longing to go to the cemetery and pray for Ameline.

Michel, the teacher André had appointed to oversee the apprentices, approached me with a scowl on his wrinkled face. He shook a gnarled finger at me. "Get to work at once," he whispered in his raspy voice. "The bookseller is in a foul mood today."

"Yes, monsieur," I replied, pretending to start the day's copying. Until the day Ameline took ill, I had loved everything about being a scribe, from sharpening my quill to filling the inkhorns and above all copying books with my own hand. But now, on my first day back at work after her death, my pleasure in writing had shriveled up like a dead leaf. As soon as Michel went to another apprentice's desk, I breathed deeply and prayed that my joy in writing would return. Since childhood, when Père Alphonse had taught me how to write the alphabet, I'd loved everything about writing and books. Once I understood that a scribe copied entire books—letter by letter, page by page—I knew that I wanted to become one.

When I was twelve, Father asked André if I could become an apprentice at his bookshop. After seeing a sample of my script, the bookseller agreed to give me a try. The first day of my apprenticeship, my heart raced in anticipation as I dressed in the garments Ameline had sewn for me: a black underdress and a skirt and bodice made of bright blue, my favorite color.

As I walked into the scriptorium that day, it seemed that I had entered a magical palace, so vast that four of Mama's cloth shops could fit inside it. The radiant morning light that streamed through a tall bank of windows cast a glow on the white walls and gray tile floor.

I took my seat with the five other apprentices in the small alcove where I sat now. I was thrilled to have this sloped writing desk and straight-backed chair. Eager to begin the day's work, I touched the sheaf of paper on my desk. To my amazement, it felt alive beneath my fingers. That first morning, Michel had taught us about watermarks. I hadn't taken the time to find one in years, especially after I progressed to writing on parchment instead of paper. But today I felt the urge to find a watermark, hoping for a sign to direct me back to a task with promises of hope. I had to risk a scolding.

While Michel had his back turned, I held up a sheet of paper so that it caught a ray of sun streaming in through the windows. There was the watermark, a design that the paper maker set onto the sheet. It was a swan, graceful and long-necked, gliding across the sea of paper.

I shivered in wonder. What if people had watermarks too, indelible marks hidden inside that would one day come forth when a light shone upon their souls? I put the paper down and sharpened my quill with my knife, imagining what mine would be. A bird did fit me, though not a swan, for swans spent little time in flight. It needed to be a bird that could soar freely, high above the earth. Setting my knife down, I ran my finger against the feather quill, imagining the hawks that nested in crannies near the cathedral spires. A hawk—that would be my watermark.

A Tale of Two Maidens

André strode toward the apprentices, furious about the supplies wasted in his absence, and I quickly returned to work. We all knew the real reason his temper was flaring. His recent trip to solicit new orders for books had been unsuccessful because the Maid and her army had disrupted his business.

I forced myself to work steadily on the last section from a book of sermons, long rants that denounced everyone as sinners. One thing that I shared with Father was my hatred of such sermons. "Your soul is crawling with worms." I copied this sentence and the rest of the page as quickly as possible.

Michel set out a new exemplar for me and opened it to the place where I was to begin copying. A picture in the upper left-hand corner showed a vast battlefield. The soldiers were all women in armor. Never before had I seen a picture like this. Had it really happened?

I stared at their leader, a girl who looked about my age, and thought about Jeanne de Domrémy. At this very moment, she and the dauphin and their army were marching toward Troyes. I still didn't know whether Ameline's hesitation about her was justified. No one knew whether the Duke of Burgundy would let them enter our town peacefully or if he would close the gates to them, thus provoking them to attack. Many of our neighbors, fearing a siege like the one at Orléans, had stocked up on dried food and water.

The dinner bell rang. All around me scribes headed for the great room, but I decided to stay and ask my teacher about Jeanne and the women warriors. Unlike the rest of the apprentices, I wasn't afraid of him. He was gruff, but I often stayed to help him and ask him questions about books and other matters. The scribes told me he owned a large library and burned many a candle reading late into the night.

I helped him refill inkhorns that were less than half full. "Monsieur," I began, "is the book I am to copy after dinner about a girl like Jeanne the Maid?"

"Yes. In fact, the section you are copying is a legend about a whole tribe of women warriors called Amazons, who lived over a thousand years ago."

"But most of the books that I copy are about men. And not about warriors but learned churchmen and saints."

"True," he replied, looking pleased at my curiosity. "The difference is that a woman wrote this manuscript. She is the Lady Christine de Pisan. Her husband died, leaving her with his debts and the care of their children. This lady was thus forced to earn her own living by means of her quill."

Wonder filled me for the second time that day. "I never knew it was possible for women to earn their bread by setting down their own thoughts and stories in writing."

"It is rare," Michel replied. "Some of Lady Christine's ideas are also unusual, even bold. She writes that women's nature is noble, and that has led some men of the church to claim that her book is heresy. Even so, our bookshop often receives commissions to copy her writings. Mostly from women, I suspect."

While Michel locked the ink back in its cupboard, I touched Lady Christine's book and closed my eyes. Maybe I could live the dream that Ameline and I had shared without her here to guide me. In my bookshop, I could do more than copy men's books. I could write the stories—Father's and mine—that were locked inside me!

As Michel and I walked to the bookseller's great room, I felt as if I were carrying Lady Christine's manuscript with me. It made my heart glow with hope.

A week later, André's servant Barthélemy escorted me home as he usually did in the evening. He was so clumsy that his gangling arm often knocked into mine, and once he had stepped on me with his impossibly large feet. Still, I would rather be outside walking with him than at home. Marguerite had taken over our house, and whenever I was disobedient or surly, she informed André. The worst part was seeing the empty chair where Ameline used to sew by the hearth. I couldn't bear to look at it and feel the emptiness within me.

In the main square, the scent of freshly baked bread rose from the public oven. My stomach rumbled, but there wasn't any money in my purse to buy a loaf. A group of rowdy young men crowded around the baker, clamoring for raisin loaves. They didn't have to go to a lonely house and do women's work. They were free to roam the streets all night if they wanted, with or without an escort. Their soft caps didn't dig into their scalps like my coif. I pushed a loose strand of hair back under it, wishing I could take it off.

"Felise," someone called from behind.

Wheeling around, I saw Georges the Tanner approaching, his face flushed from working close to the fire all day. His clothes smelled of leather, an acrid smell that I disliked. He greeted me with a nod and reached into his purse for a handful of coins. "Go and get us a loaf," he told Barthélemy, thrusting the money toward him.

"But the bookseller told me not to let this girl out of my sight," the servant said.

"She's still in your sight. Go, before the fresh bread is sold. I'll share it with you."

Barthélemy licked his lips, eyeing the fresh loaves stacked in the baker's stall. "Promise that you'll stay here," he said.

"Of course," the tanner replied. Barthélemy grabbed the coins and hurried to the oven.

As soon as he was gone, the tanner turned to me, his gray eyes filled with intent. No man had ever looked at me thus, and I shifted my gaze to my hands, spotted with ink. I wanted to be back at the scriptorium where I would be spared having words with a young man whose purpose I knew not.

"I heard that André is away delivering books to his customers in Auxerre," he began, his voice deeper than I remembered it.

Just because the bookseller was gone and the tanner didn't have to worry about being thrown in the stocks, it didn't give him the right to approach me. I turned and walked away from him, knowing it was rude but unable to stop myself.

"Wait, I have something important to tell you," the tanner continued, his voice coming from close behind me. "I promise you no harm, and the servant can go with us. But I want you to walk with me and hear me out."

I halted but kept my back to him. His boldness appalled me. "How could a Burgundian, my enemy, have a message for me?" As soon as these words burst out, I clapped my hand over my mouth. *Sweet Virgin, when will I learn to think before speaking?*

He strode around to face me, and I flinched, not knowing if he would strike me or lambaste me with words. Instead, he was silent, his arms squared against his chest. I wanted to read the look on his face, but I didn't dare. "Don't think that I am not aware of our differences," he retorted. "Put them aside to hear tidings that concern your future."

What did he know? I looked up, searching for a clue on his face. The strong intent was still stamped upon it, but his furrowed brow showed anger and confusion. Barthélemy returned with a loaf, and the tanner divided it into three portions. I picked off a morsel of the warm crust, churning over what to do. "Tell me your news," I said in a low voice, glancing at the servant to see if he heard me over the baker's noisy customers. He didn't look up from devouring his portion of bread.

"It can't be spoken of amid all these people," the tanner replied. "I will tell you on a quieter street."

My curiosity grew as I ate the bread. "I will hear what you have to say in the graveyard where my sister is buried. First, you must let me pray for her soul."

"As you wish," he said. We set out walking side by side, with Barthélemy lagging behind. Lowering my gaze from the bright sun, I noticed the tanner's rolled up sleeves and his bare arms made strong from pounding his mallet against cowhide all day long. His arm was bronzed in the sunlight and looked as if it would be smooth. He was close enough for me to touch it.

I shifted my gaze to his hand. The knuckles were raw from scraping hide all day long, and the top of his hand was laced with scars and crested with a dome-shaped blister.

"You should wear gloves. That burn looks like it hurts." My face reddened in embarrassment that I had allowed myself to speak with concern to an enemy.

"We tanners get used to burns," he said with a shrug. "Just as you scribes get used to your quill marks."

I cast a furtive glance at my hand. There was a distinctive groove in my first finger and thumb, not as deep as my teacher's or the groove in Ameline's finger made by the pressure of the needle, but I had a quill mark, nonetheless.

We approached a tavern where knives were piled at the front door. Tavern keepers forced customers to leave them there in an attempt to keep peace these days. But the shouting and curses flying through the open window sounded like a fight was about to erupt. The feuding between Dauphinists and Burgundians had been escalating ever since the day of Ameline's funeral when we first heard the news that the Maid and the Dauphin Charles were leading their army toward Troyes.

I was glad that the tanner quickened his pace until we passed the tavern. "If the dauphin loses the war, your family will have no choice but to support the duke," he said. "From all reports, the dauphin's army is starving, and his soldiers are ragged and barefoot."

I turned to glare at him. "The dauphin's fortune is rising. Jeanne de Domrémy brings him good luck."

"She is mad. They say she speaks to people who aren't there."

"She isn't mad. That is what you Burgundians say because you fear her power," I argued, cloaking my own doubts. "Her saints inspired her to lead the dauphin's army to victory at Orléans."

"It wasn't her doing that the siege was lifted," he said, his mouth set in a smug line. "It was the other captains."

"How do you know that?" I crossed my arms and realized that I was almost as tall as he was. "You weren't there."

"Neither were you," he replied, turning to me. He wasn't angry at all.

Instead he smiled slightly, as if he enjoyed sparring with me.

What a brash young man he was. I strode a few paces ahead, but he caught up with me and soon we reached the graveyard.

"Don't stay long," Barthélemy warned, patting his stomach. "That morsel of bread just made me hungrier for supper."

The tanner reached in his moneybag for a handful of coins. "Take this for your trouble," he told the servant.

Barthélemy grinned as he counted them. "More money for gambling tonight."

He sat on a bench, just inside the graveyard wall, and took out his bone dice to practice his lucky rolls. I went to kneel at Ameline's grave while the tanner crossed the graveyard to where the commoners were buried. Their headstones were smaller and plainer than those of my family. I kissed Ameline's headstone and thanked God that he had found a way for me to visit her, even if I had to endure the tanner's company.

He soon returned and stood guard as he had at Ameline's funeral. But this time, he was probably watching for anyone who might report him to André. His feet crunched against the ground as he shifted position. Whenever Charlotte accompanied me to Ameline's grave, she made more noise than the tanner with her singing and clapping; still I could always attend to my prayers for Ameline's soul. Why then was I so distracted by the sound of his boots?

I turned toward Mama's grave and my little brother's. *Marie Ameline, wife of Henri the Merchant. 1389–1421.* My beautiful mama with pale red hair like Ameline's and Charlotte's. This was the very place where I had stood eight years ago with Ameline and Charlotte and Father on the day we laid her to her rest. I had cried for Mama to come back, and for my stillborn baby brother too, who lay in the tiny grave beside hers. *I pray you are with Mama and our brother, Ameline.*

My gaze shifted to the headstones of the other members of Mama's wealthy family: her mother Felise, for whom I was named, and who had died giving birth to Charlotte when Mama was a child. Mama's father rested next to her. I barely remembered him. He used to give Ameline scraps of cloth from his great warehouse where he worked as a cloth merchant.

The tanner started to pace back and forth, but I ignored him and tried to quell my curiosity about his purpose. Mama's brother Nicholas lay in the grave next to Grandfather's. He had been only a young man when the English slaughtered him at the Battle of Agincourt, along with thousands of other French soldiers. I clenched my fists, thinking of how horrified Mama would be if she could see me standing at her brother's grave with a Burgundian.

"I can delay no further," the tanner said abruptly. "The book-seller's servant woman is probably wondering why you are late coming home." He knew about Marguerite. I had almost forgotten.

Barthélemy was still practicing dice on the bench as the tanner led me to the farthest corner of the cemetery. We didn't speak, and I sensed him glancing at me from time to time. I wished that we were back on the crowded streets sparring again.

He broke our silence, his voice filled with urgency. "I will get right to my news. André is hard at work to secure a husband for you."

My stomach lurched. That explained why André always looked as if he were measuring my worth. I smoothed my skirt and tried my best to feign calmness. "How do you know this?"

"One of my customers, Thibaut the Dyer, was bragging about a marriage contract he was about to conclude with André. He mentioned you by name and said he hoped that soon after you married, you would bear him a son."

I gripped the cemetery wall, not wanting to believe that his words were true. The tanner stood close to me, his hand on the wall too. "Don't you remember me from when we were children?" he asked quietly.

I stared at him in surprise. How could I have met a Burgundian boy when I was a child?

"Your mother brought Charlotte and you with her when she came to my mother's silk shop to buy thread," he said.

We used to go to a tiny shop in which threads of all the colors of the rainbow hung on hooks from the ceiling. While we were there, Charlotte and I always played hide and seek with a curly haired boy. After Mama died, we never went back there because Father always brought Ameline her thread and cloth.

"The boy in the thread shop was you?" I asked.

"Yes." His hand on the wall lifted as if to touch mine but he quickly withdrew it. "I saw you often in the marketplace before your sister died. I noticed how the two of you took care of each other and Charlotte too. And then after Ameline got sick, you sold her cloth work by yourself. You cloaked your worries about her as best you could and never let anyone cheat you. You stood firm with your prices, and you held your head high when the gossips needled you about your father's debts."

I drew back from him, bewildered by his revelations and frightened too. "You've been spying on me without my knowledge?"

"Not for ill intent," he replied quickly. "I want to help you. Please, hear me out, Felise. André and Thibaut have almost settled the terms of their contract. For the dyer, marrying you is nothing more than a business arrangement and a way to secure the son that his first wife never bore him."

I covered my face with my hands, feeling light-headed as I tried to absorb this news. "How could you possibly help me? Only my father—who will return any day now—can put an end to André's plans."

"We must go soon," Barthélemy called.

"Just a little while longer," the tanner said.

He stood directly in front of me, so close that I could hear the sound of his breathing. "I don't want to tell you the rest of my news, but I must be honest with you. Last winter, your father and I were about to sign a marriage contract. He was going to sell you to me for a large sum of money."

How could a mere tanner have such a sum? Yet when my eyes met his, I knew he was telling the truth.

"Your father had to leave on a journey, but he promised me he would seal our contract when he returned," the tanner continued.

I clutched my arms against my chest, his news echoing in the space between us. "But Father promised me that I could remain a femme sole like Ameline—" My voice broke.

"Your sister was a skilled seamstress, and you are only an apprentice," the tanner reminded me. "You won't earn your living for a long time. You need—"

"I need nothing," I interrupted, darting away from him. "Trust me," Father had said. Yet he had betrayed me and planned to enslave me to an enemy, destroying my dream of becoming a femme sole.

A strand of hair fell onto my face as I ran away. I yanked the coif off my head, hairpins flying everywhere, and threw the headpiece to the ground. I stomped on it, grinding the black earth of the cemetery into the white linen.

Barthélemy came running and grabbed me by the arm. "Stop that!" he shouted, pulling me off the coif and snatching it from the ground.

"I'll never let you speak with her again," Barthélemy growled at the tanner, who pressed his lips together, his face suffused with regret.

I stormed after Barthélemy with tears streaming down my face.

That night after Charlotte fell asleep, I flung the covers off and strode to the mantel. I picked up a seashell that Father had brought me last year. He knew how badly I wanted to see the ocean for the first time. Bigger than my hand, the shell was shaped like the conical hats that the duke's womenfolk wore on festival days.

When Father had given me the shell, he told me about an ocean-dwelling unicorn with a spiraled horn that had surfaced near his ship. He said it looked directly into his eyes before plunging back into the water. As he handed me the shell, Father looked deep into my eyes, as if remembering the sea creature. I leaned my head against his barrel-shaped chest and listened to the steady beating of his heart.

I wrapped my fingers around the whorled shell, clenching it as tightly as I could, wanting to crush this token of a father who loved his dice more than he loved me. But the shell was too hard to break, and I thrust it back on the mantel.

The next morning as I was hard at work, Thibaut the Dyer arrived at the scriptorium. A groan escaped my lips, and the apprentice nearest me turned to see what the matter was. I shook my head and clenched my jaws.

The dyer's ermine cap domed above a painted screen next to André's desk. The two men talked so softly that I couldn't hear a word. I stared at Lady Christine's words, trying to forget what was taking place behind the screen. "Our land was never better ruled by any man," she wrote in praise of Queen Blanche, who ruled France many years ago.

After what seemed like hours, André and Thibaut emerged. I quickly set to work copying the lady's next word, "warrior." To my dismay, André led Thibaut over to the apprentices' alcove. No one dared to look up, but I sensed everyone's curiosity prickling the very air.

The two men stood right behind me, so close that I smelled the garlic that clung to their clothes. I forced my quill to keep moving.

"Look at that fine script. She's my best apprentice," André

bragged. "I would be happy to keep her in my employ after you wed her."

My quill wobbled and the "r" trailed off below the line.

Thibaut grunted. "She would already have to be a master scribe, to help defray the price you demand for her."

"In addition to this girl, I will buy dye for my book covers only from you. And I will sell your wares at all the courts where I sell my books," André reminded him. "Enough of business for now. Before you go, would you like to touch her face?"

"Gladly," Thibaut sighed.

He reached out a fat hand to stroke my cheek. The quill dropped from my hand, spilling ink all over the paper, but he said nothing about my clumsiness. His fingers were moist with sweat, and I flinched as revulsion rippled through every part of me. I stared at a fly on the corner of my desk, trying to ignore his touch. But I could not.

Behind me I heard him murmuring in delight. "Her flesh is so soft and supple. I know she will bear me a son."

His damp fingers clamped to my cheek like leeches. After what seemed an eternity, André cleared his throat. "On the morrow I am certain that we can reach an agreement, Thibaut," he said with confidence.

I jumped to my feet, releasing myself at last, and kept my back to the men.

"I like the girl's spirit," Thibaut chuckled. "It's more than my wife ever had."

As soon as they left, the other apprentices barraged me with whispered questions. Ignoring them, I grabbed a wet rag and scrubbed my face where the dyer had touched me.

Four

The Scroll

June 18, 1429

What could I do? I had to find a way to stop Thibaut from touching me with his sweaty hands again. I slouched and kept my head down in case he was also attending Anes's son's wedding as I was.

Handbells rang to signal the beginning of the ceremony. The church doors opened, and everyone cheered for the bride and groom as they turned to face Père Alphonse. He flipped the pages of his prayer book to find the wedding ceremony. *Surely, he should have committed the words to memory by now.* Aside from Lent, it seemed as if there were a wedding here every Saturday. Mama had been forced to wed at this very place. I clenched my hands behind my back. *Not I.*

Women in front of me gossiped that Mathilde's family was wealthier than they suspected, judging from her magnificent gown. I remembered it well. It was the last gown Ameline had sewn before her death. To prepare for the moneylenders' return, she had forced herself to finish it despite her terrible headaches.

After the exchange of rings, the newly married couple turned to face the crowd. Ignoring his bride, Guillaume smiled at her father, as if to thank him for her large dowry. Mathilde's father returned the groom's smile, his arms folded across his chest with confidence that he had chosen well. The two men sickened me, especially Guillaume. He was nigh on thirty and had nose hairs curling out of both nostrils. Worse than that, all he ever talked about was money. For many years, Anes had tried to persuade Mama to let Ameline marry her son. After all, Guillaume would inherit his father's goldsmith shop and Mama and Anes would share grandchildren.

Mathilde looked at the ground, her shoulders hunched. The bodice of her wedding dress must have bound her while the high-waisted skirt had so much cloth it seemed to anchor her to the ground and prevent her from running away. She looked uncomfortable and unhappy, standing there on display for all to see. Even worse, I saw her cringe when Guillaume leaned forward to kiss her. I shuddered, imagining Thibaut's lips leaning toward mine. *Never*, I vowed.

Hand in hand, the bride and groom walked down the steps and into the crowd. Women exclaimed that this was a fine match indeed. Men wagered on how many moons would pass before she was with child. I pressed my lips together. I had to escape before they made the same wagers about me. The bells of Saint Madeleine clanged to mark the end of the ceremony. They might as well have rung, as they often did in this season, to announce that a storm was approaching.

Thank God Thibaut wasn't at the wedding feast. I steered Charlotte away from Marguerite, who had joined the people milling around the barrel of bride's ale. I looked for a quiet spot where I could plot my escape.

"Pears!" Charlotte exclaimed, pointing to a trestle.

I hurried to the table and grabbed her some dried pears with ginger sauce, but my appetite had withered since the day Thibaut touched me. She crammed them into her mouth. She would eat delicacies at my wedding too, but she would never be forced to wed.

When Charlotte was finished eating, she had a ring of ginger sauce around her mouth. I had forgotten to bring a handkerchief so I couldn't wipe it away. *Help her stay neat and clean*, Ameline had said.

As we walked past the roundelay, the men and women wove their way underneath arches made by other dancers' arms. Everyone but the bride looked happy. "Let's go," I said to Charlotte.

"I want to stay here," she whined.

"Last week you found a coin over there by the tree. You might find another one today." God forgive me for deceiving her, but I couldn't bear to look at Mathilde's unhappy face any longer.

Charlotte nodded eagerly and followed me to the tree where she stooped down to look for another coin.

"There aren't any treasures here," Charlotte broke into my thoughts. "I want to dance."

She swayed back and forth to the music of the roundelay and sang in her high-pitched voice.

"I can't think with you singing," I snapped.

She gave me a hurt look and stopped singing as a ray of sunlight filtered through the leaves, moving across the earth in the wind. A man dancing at the edge of the roundelay smiled at me as he spun his partner around.

The tanner had said he wanted to help me. But if I went to him, I would just be settling for the lesser of two bad choices. No, I must remain free from any man's clutches, a femme sole writing my own stories in my own bookshop.

But how? When I checked on Charlotte, I saw that she was dancing in a wider circle, moving out from the tree and toward the roundelay. Usually, I kept her away from other people, but why shouldn't she be free to dance like everyone else? Why shouldn't I be free to remain unwed?

"Get away!" a man shouted. Charlotte had collided into the blacksmith's journeyman and his wife as they danced. He stormed over to me, and Charlotte followed him with tears streaming down her face.

"Keep the filthy half-wit away," he snarled. "Those evil eyes are the mark of sin."

"Gladly will I keep her out of your reach," I cried out as

Charlotte clung to me, "lest you infect her with your cruelty and ignorance."

"Girl, the magistrates will clap you in the stocks for your vile tongue," he shouted.

Charlotte bawled, and people turned to scowl at her. Some even made the sign of the cross. Anes hurried over and wrapped her arms around Charlotte.

"Dennis, don't you say another word against Charlotte," Anes warned, shaking a finger at the smith's journeyman.

Glaring at me, he retreated into the crowd.

"Felise, what is wrong?" Anes asked. "You usually take better care of Charlotte than you did today."

"My stomach hurts," I lied. "It is the time of my courses. I want to go home and rest."

Anes gently unfurled Charlotte's arms from around her waist and came over to embrace me. "Things will soon be more settled for you," Anes soothed. "André is working hard to complete his arrangement with Thibaut."

My belly knotted into a tight coil as Anes scanned the crowd. "Ah, there is Marguerite," she said. "I will fetch her to escort you home."

"Is there anyone else who could do so?" I asked quickly. "She has been looking forward to your son's wedding feast for many days."

"Herluin the kitchen servant," she replied after a moment's thought. "Charlotte can stay here with me. Rest well and promise me that you will bar the door and stay inside."

"I promise," I said as she took Charlotte's hand and hurried off to fetch the servant.

When Herluin and I reached my house, I unlocked the door with the key in my purse. I barred the door as soon as I entered. I had an hour to be alone with my thoughts, an hour to decide what to do.

Whatever my choice, I needed money. I rushed into Ameline's workroom to see how much of our cache for the moneylenders was left. Bright sunlight streamed in through the glass windows, the only ones in our house, and illuminated bits of cloth dust floating in the air. I strode to the ragbags in the corner. As I groped around inside the shabbiest bag, I felt something made of velvet. My hand trembled as I pulled out a green bag and opened it. It was my seal, etched with the letter *F*, a gift from Mama when I first learned to write my name. I held it tightly and ran my finger over the grooves of the *F*, feeling the current of some invisible power that coursed through my body.

I closed my eyes and remembered the day Mama gave me the seal. Father was away and Mama's belly was round with another baby that would be born any day. On the walk back from church that morning, Anes had tried to convince Mama that Ameline should marry her son Guillaume, who always sat hunched over his ledger books. As soon as we got home, Ameline burst into tears.

Later that afternoon, Ameline, Charlotte, and I strolled with her in the courtyard garden. The day was warm, and the sun shone on the silvery lavender bush. When Mama grew tired, she and Ameline sat on the bench while Charlotte and I had plopped down on the stone pathway, watching an ant carrying a twig ten times its size.

"I have important things to tell you," Mama began quietly.

Her somber voice caused me to slide on the ground closer to her and wrap my arms around her legs. I wished she were telling us a fairy story.

"I know it must be difficult to listen to your father and me arguing about his debts." Mama continued. "We didn't argue at first. From the beginning of our betrothal, he was kind, as I saw full well in the way he cared for my sister Charlotte. As part of our marriage contract, he even agreed to let her live with us. Not many suitors would consent to such an arrangement."

"Brother." Charlotte smiled as she spoke her nickname for Father.

"As a young man, your father brought me gifts from faraway places," Mama said, her gaze resting beyond the garden wall. "He also brought me wondrous tales with his laughter and songs that he played on his recorder. I myself had never traveled very far outside the walls of Troyes. He brought me the whole world with his stories."

I clapped my hands. "Me too! Someday I will go on journeys and have adventures like Father."

Mama smiled at me as she ran her fingers through my hair, but the smile faded quickly, and tears welled up in her eyes. "Daughters, I want to tell you something that I have not told anyone else, not even Anes," Mama said. "Will you promise to keep it a secret?"

"Yes," Ameline and I replied. I leaned closer to hear over Charlotte's song about Father.

"Before I was betrothed to your father," Mama began, "something unexpected happened to me. I met a young man of my age called Bertrand, who was a member of my father's merchant crew. We would walk in the garden while my mother sat sewing on this very bench. I enjoyed talking with him about all manner of things and saw nothing wrong with it. Before we knew what was happening, we had fallen in love."

I had glanced at Ameline, wondering if she knew what love meant.

She was listening intently and didn't turn to look at me.

"My father had already arranged my marriage to your father," Mama went on. "I tried to persuade Papa to let me marry Bertrand instead, but he lacked riches, and besides, he was too young. My father would not hear a word of my *petulance* as he called it."

Mama had opened her *aumônière*, in which she kept coins for the poor. She took out a brass thimble, set with beads to form the letter *A*, and gave it to Ameline. Then she gave me the seal. "Let's join hands," she said solemnly.

Grinning, Charlotte had joined our circle. "We play a game?" she asked.

"No, Sister," Mama replied. When she turned to Ameline and me, the fierce look in her eyes frightened me. "I will do everything in my power to keep you both free from unwanted marriages. I know it will be difficult, but I want you to promise me by these gifts, that you will remain femmes soles, unless something very rare happens and you find men whom you truly love."

Ameline gave her promise first in a clear voice, then Charlotte in her high-pitched voice. Just as I had done that day, I closed my eyes. Mama and the baby had both died within a week, but I vowed to keep the promise I made to her that day, many years ago. I clasped the seal. Mama had said it was rare to find true love. Instead of searching in vain for it, I would try my best to remain a femme sole.

Opening my eyes to the sunny workroom, I remembered that Father's mounting debts had saved Ameline from the unwanted marriage. I couldn't depend on his debts saving me too. I needed money to put whatever plan I devised into action. As I resumed my search for it, a loud knock at the door startled me. I pressed myself into the corner of the room where no one could see me through the windows. Someone—no it had to be two people—beat on the door with all their might. It was too early for Marguerite and Charlotte to return, and the noise was so loud that it must be men making it.

My heart pounded against my chest. Hours seemed to pass before the knocking finally stopped. Still I waited so long that my fingers, squeezed between my body and the wall, fell asleep.

I drew them out and moved them back and forth until the tingling stopped. Then I tiptoed back into the great room. All was still, and I crept closer to the front door. Wedged in the crack between the door and the floor was a parchment scroll.

Merchant's Daughter, we cannot wait until the first of July to secure the money that your father owes us. Jeanne the Maid approaches Troyes, and your town may well be under siege

*by that time. Thus, we arrive a week early on Midsummer's
Eve, the twenty-first day of June. If you don't repay the rest of
your father's debt in full, we will sell you and your sister and
the half-wit into servitude.*

In three days, the moneylenders were coming to seize Charlotte and me. I collapsed to the floor, hugging my knees to my
chest. They were going to bind our hands and feet and throw
us onto a cart. After a long journey, we would be sold into
slavery or prostitution in a faraway land, at the mercy of a cruel
master.

If I fled to André's house with Charlotte, the bookseller
would rescue me from the moneylenders, but he would have no
qualms about handing her over to them.

André was going to proceed with his plan of binding me in
marriage to Thibaut. At the thought of the dyer's massive body
shoving against mine, I groaned in revulsion.

I could flee to Anes's house, but I knew what she would do:
pay off Father's debt and support my marriage to Thibaut. And if
I went to the tanner . . .

I rose to my feet. I would not give in. I would keep my promise to Mama and Ameline, but mostly to myself. I paced back
and forth.

Only one choice would allow me to remain free. Charlotte
and I had to run away. I stood in the middle of the great room,
looking around at the familiar possessions. I had to leave my
home and set out on a journey at last.

I trembled as I strode to the hearth. Stirring up the embers, I
held a corner of the moneylenders' letter to them. I watched as a
flame emerged and the scroll caught fire, destroying the message
so that Marguerite would not report it to André.

I had to leave very soon with enough money to provide
for Charlotte and me. I returned to the workroom and groped
around in the ragbag for the money that Ameline had earned.

Only twenty livres tournois remained after paying Typhaine the Apothecary for her useless remedies. I needed more, far more.

Returning to Father's desk, I yanked open the drawers in search of loose coins. My search yielded only a few sous hidden under papers. But in the bottom drawer I found the key to his warehouse. He might have valuable goods there.

Running to the door, I opened it and stopped in my tracks. Marguerite and Charlotte were standing just outside.

I was under Marguerite's watchful eye the rest of the day and Sunday too. When she wasn't looking, I picked up every stray coin that I saw on the streets. I also pilfered the pile of coins that Charlotte had hoarded under our bed. If she could understand everything I had to consider, I knew she would forgive me.

For two nights I slept fitfully, my mind spinning over everything I had to do in order to keep Charlotte and me safe. I decided to leave Monday night after midnight. A chill came over me.

Tonight . . . I was leaving tonight. I wiped my sweaty hands on my sleeves and forced myself to write. I made many mistakes.

André was still away on his journey, and Michel the Scribe was too preoccupied to notice my mistakes. None of the scribes paid attention to work, as a riot on the street assailed us through the scriptorium windows. Immersed in my thoughts, I didn't know what caused it. I put my quill down and listened to the other apprentices talking excitedly about the latest tidings.

I learned that Jeanne the Maid, the Dauphin Charles, and his army had nearly reached Gien, a town loyal to him and not far from Troyes. Our town's magistrates, who favored the dauphin, declared that they would surrender Troyes to him when he reached our gate.

Philippe, the Duke of Burgundy, as an ally of King Henry of England, was doing everything in his power to thwart the dauphin and the magistrates. This morning the duke's men had captured a group of the dauphin's spies on the road to Troyes.

In retaliation, the magistrates decreed that the people of Troyes must help the dauphin by paying the ransom to release his spies from the Duke of Burgundy's prison.

"Kill the spies!" the Burgundians roared outside on the street. "Down with the dauphin!"

"Victory will be ours!" the Dauphinists cried, drowning them out.

The sounds of fighting broke out amid the shouting match. Scribes swarmed toward the door, pushing each other aside in their haste to join the fight or flee to their homes. Michel and another scribe went to close the windows, but before they could finish, a rock soared into the scriptorium and knocked over an inkhorn of red ink. It splattered onto the tile floor.

I stared at the red ink. Was it an omen of bad fortune, warning me not to run away? No, I couldn't let anything stop me now. I jumped to my feet, grabbed Ameline's shawl, and ran to find Barthélemy in the throng of scribes by the door. He had clearly forgotten his duty to escort me home, for he had jostled his way to the front of the line. A barrier of many scribes separated us. I didn't want to face the rioters without him, but what if he refused to take me to Father's warehouse? I had to risk going there alone. I clutched the shawl around my shoulders and pushed my way outside, into the crowd.

I hurried down an alley, avoiding the mob that grew bigger as more people joined in. At the end of the alley, I was forced to stop because I could hear the mob approaching. I withdrew into the shadows, panting to catch my breath.

Carpenters and shoemakers and barrel makers passed the alley. They thrust hammers and shovels toward the sky, their makeshift weapons glinting in the afternoon sun. A band of silk spinners wielded their distaffs and chanted their hatred of the dauphin.

Next came Georges, leading the tanners and armed with a large mallet. I stared at him from the shadows, my heart racing as he passed the alley. This time it wasn't the fire that made his face red, but frenzy. "Drive the dauphin and the witch from our walls!" he shouted in a hoarse voice. "Victory to Philippe, Duke of Burgundy!"

His men took up his cry while my mouth opened of its own accord. When we had argued about Jeanne a short while ago, he had hidden this wrath from me. In the moment when he passed the alley, it was unleashed before my very eyes, so powerful that I feared what he would do this day, and what he would incite the others to do. What would he do to me if he saw me now? I drew back farther in the alley.

Once the mob was out of sight, I ran the rest of the way to Father's warehouse. I made sure no one was watching as I fumbled with the key. As a child, I always looked forward to the warehouse's pungent scent of cloves and to our game, which we called "Princess of Cloves." Father was my royal merchant, and he brought me treasures. His wares—cloves and other spices, bolts of cloth, and saddles—were my props and playthings, full of magical powers.

I stepped inside, staying in the ray of sunlight that sliced the room in half. Not the smell of cloves, but a stench like rotten eggs assaulted my nostrils. I had no idea what it was.

A hasty search revealed that Father's usual clutter of goods had vanished completely. Nothing other than a few loose coins, rusted tools, rat droppings, and the nasty smell remained. I kicked a shovel to the ground, fuming that I was now the Princess of Nothing.

Upon reaching home, I barred the front door and entered the great room where dirty dishes drew flies to the table.

"You are late, girl. No supper for you," Marguerite hissed as she poured herself a cup of wine. "Wash the dishes at once."

As I did her bidding, the sounds of the riot assaulted my ears while my thoughts turned again to a slave's life. A cup fell from my hand and shattered on the floor. But by now, Marguerite had drunk too much wine to notice.

At last, I heard her rising to her feet. "You are to mend my apron before you go to bed," she slurred, pointing to a pile of clothes lying in a chair.

As soon as she stumbled up the stairs, I poured rose oil into a bowl of water and anointed my face and hands.

Where could I go? In the villages around Troyes, I would be easily found. My hiding place needed to be bigger. Gien . . . it was a city nearby. The dauphin's army would soon be there if they weren't already. The vast horde of soldiers would serve as a shield to hide me from my pursuers.

A chill came over me. I could not escape; I would be caught as soon as I fled. My plan was too bold for a girl.

Charlotte sang louder, distracting me from my thoughts. I wheeled around and cried, "Stop!"

Her face crumpled, and she burst into tears. I rushed to her and held her tightly, hoping that Marguerite couldn't hear. "Please don't cry, Charlotte. I'm sorry."

Little by little she grew quiet. Maybe I should leave her here with Marguerite, since her outbursts would draw attention and endanger us. But if the moneylenders seized her, she would be worth a good price on the slave market. With her beautiful voice and small stature, she could be sold as a court performer, like the dwarves who entertained the Dukes of Burgundy. André would be glad to be rid of her that easily.

Sniffling, she lifted her head and looked at me forlornly. Her headpiece was tilted down over one eye, and I lifted it up to brush crumbs from around her mouth. I could never leave her here to suffer such a fate. I loved her and had promised Ameline to take care of her.

"We'll sleep downstairs by the fire tonight," I told her, taking her by the hand.

The Scroll

Charlotte nodded without saying anything about how strange it was not to sleep in our room upstairs. She seemed to have completely forgotten that I made her cry.

"Stay here while I fetch some blankets," I told her. "We'll sleep in our clothes."

The moment she finally fell asleep, I lit a candle and went to Father's desk, remembering the knife I had seen there. It would afford me some protection against man and beast, but was it enough? I looked down at my dress. It would draw attention to the fact that I was a young woman traveling alone. I thought about Jeanne the Maid on the night she decided to leave her village and travel to the dauphin's court. It was said that her saints gave her the idea of dressing as a boy. Her male clothing had helped her on her journey and helped her now as she traveled with the army.

No one would look twice at a man traveling alone, especially one wearing dull and ragged clothes. Holding the candle, I crept to Ameline's shop, to the shelf where she kept clothes that needed mending. From the pile I pulled out Father's torn, rust-colored tunic and a pair of old breeches. I imagined myself wearing them instead of my clothes. Was it dangerous and wrong, the doing of shapeshifters and sinners?

But you have to do it, a voice inside urged. I started, never having heard this voice before, and tried to calm myself by closing my eyes and breathing deeply. I didn't know what Jeanne the Maid looked like, but I tried to picture her as she dressed as a boy for the first time. It was night, and she was alone. She believed that dressing as a boy was a sin. Her saints appeared to her and told her that God would forgive her for doing what she had to do. She gathered courage and started untying the stays to her bodice. I bowed my head, imagining her saints appearing to me and commanding me to put on Father's clothes.

My hands trembled as I untied my bodice stays. Goosebumps rose up on my breasts. I couldn't let them reveal my secret.

Grabbing Ameline's sewing shears, I cut rags into long strips and used them to bind my breasts as tightly as I could endure.

I donned Father's tunic and leggings, which smelled strongly of horses and reminded me that we needed a horse. Charlotte would tire quickly, and, though short, she was too heavy to carry. I quickly cut a belt out of burlap cloth. After looping Father's knife and a leather pouch through it, I tied the belt around my waist. Father's breeches were so long that they mostly hid my shoes.

I picked up the looking glass that Ameline kept here so that ladies could see the backs of their gowns. I looked like a frightened urchin boy . . . except for loose strands of hair brushing against my cheek. Jeanne had cut her hair and I must do so too.

It was as if someone else's hands plucked out the hairpins, and my hair tumbled down around my face. Clutching a handful of it, I picked up the scissors and snipped it off. The sound was harsh and foreboding, but I kept going until it was all cut. After donning Father's ragged hood, I swept the shorn hair into a pile and rolled it up in a rag. I had to take it with me or else everyone would know I had disguised myself as a boy. Grabbing two burlap satchels, I packed a blue work dress, blankets, food and water, Charlotte's things, and all the money I had collected.

Somehow, I contained myself in the house until the midnight bells had finished ringing. I shook Charlotte's shoulders several times and called her name. Her eyes opened. "Pears," she mumbled groggily, as if she were dreaming of them. Thankfully, she was too sleepy to notice the change in my appearance.

It took forever to get her to stand up and, leaning heavily against me, hobble to the door. I opened it and stood in the doorway. The moon had not yet risen, allowing night to shroud the empty street except for a pool of light around the streetlamp. Father would not be afraid of the dark, nor would Ameline. She would sometimes go out alone at night to care for a sick neighbor or a member of her guild who was giving birth. Picking up the unlit lantern that we kept by the front door, I looped the handle around my arm and draped the satchels over my shoulder on the same side.

The noise of the mob rose up in the distance. My heart beating fast, I waited until I was sure that people weren't headed toward us. "Be quiet and follow me," I whispered to Charlotte.

"Where are we going?" she asked, her voice more alert. "Where are your clothes?"

"Hush—we are going on a journey," I said, grabbing her arm. "Come."

She yanked it back. "I don't want to go."

"But we have to."

"No," she insisted loudly.

"You will wake up the neighbors," I hissed and pulled her along.

"Stop," she shrieked, as I clapped my hand over her mouth.

"Do you want me to go away like Ameline and never come back?" I knew I had frightened her cruelly, but I couldn't risk someone hearing her.

Her eyes widened and she shook her head.

"Then you have to be quiet and come with me. Do you promise?"

She nodded, and I walked farther down the street, passing the streetlamp. A shutter creaked in the wind, and we ducked into a doorway until I was certain it was safe. At last we reached the stable. As I set the satchels on the ground, I listened for the night watchmen. Maybe they were patrolling a neighborhood that was loyal to the Duke of Burgundy, like the tanner's street. They might have even thrown him into jail for leading the tanners.

"Wait here with our things," I whispered to Charlotte. "I will be right back."

"I want to go with you," she moaned, clutching my hand.

I resigned myself to taking her with me, even though I feared she would alert the ostler to our presence. She loved horses, and I could use that to my advantage. "You have to stay here, or we can't ride a horse," I told her.

A grin spread across her sleepy face. "Go get our horse," she said.

Creeping into the stable, I found the stable boy asleep at the far end of the passageway, a lit lantern beside him. A huge horse stood breathing quietly in the dim light of the first stall. At the next, a smaller horse whinnied and walked toward the gate as if to greet me.

As I started to unlatch it, the boy called out in a high-pitched voice, "Who goes there?"

I wheeled around to face him. He cowered on his knees, but his knife was drawn. "My master needs his horse at once," I said in my deepest voice.

"In the middle of the night?" he asked, rubbing sleep from his eyes.

"Yes, he must go at once on urgent business. He bade me pay you well for the trouble of awakening you." I reached into my purse and pulled out a few francs.

The boy put his knife away and approached me. He grabbed the coins from my hand. "Who is your master?"

I stood there, dumbfounded, not having thought this far ahead. Then I remembered the tanner mentioning that he owned a horse. I muttered his name.

With a yawn, he went to a stall and hooked his lantern on a nail. The horse inside was the biggest one I had ever seen. It stared at me with black eyes while the boy deftly put a bit in its mouth and bridled it. Its teeth must have been three times the size of mine. I looked up at the thatched roof, trying to calm myself. Father always said that a rider mustn't be afraid, for the horse could always sense it.

All too soon the stable boy had saddled the horse, and he opened the gate and handed me the rope. The horse surprised me by plodding behind me.

Outside in the cool night air, Charlotte clapped her hands in delight as she ran toward the horse. She stopped a short way from its muzzle and patted it, cooing in the same voice she used when she played with babies. The horse whinnied its greeting.

Recalling how Father prepared for his journeys, I threw a satchel across the horse's back. Thankfully the tanner's mare didn't seem to mind, so I threw the other one on. Then I used ropes to secure them to the saddle. The horse stomped her back legs, but I finished the task, remembering well Father's advice not to stand where the beast could kick me.

"Time to get on the horse," I told Charlotte. She loved to ride with Father as much as I did. Taking hold of her thick waist, I helped her stand on the mounting block and put her foot in the stirrup. Groaning from her weight, I lifted her onto the horse's back and panted, "Grab hold of the saddle."

Her arms barely reached it, and her short legs dangled off one flank far above the stirrups, yet she beamed with happiness. "I ride a horse!" she exclaimed, positioning herself in the saddle.

"Hush," I whispered, listening for the watchmen.

With the lantern in one hand and the guide rope in the other, I set out for the south gate, the closest one to our house. "Put your head down on the horse's neck," I told Charlotte, "and keep quiet."

I led the mare into the shadows. I had to throw several stones against the gatehouse door to awaken the gatekeeper. He peered through the bars on the door, his knife glinting in his lantern's light.

"By God's ear, why do you disturb my slumber, boy?" he thundered.

"My sister and I were afraid of the mob," I replied in my new voice. "We were waiting for the crowd to go home and fell asleep at the stable. When I woke up, it was well past curfew. But we must return to my father's farm, or he will flog us both."

"That would serve you right for waking me up," the gate-keeper bellowed, adding a string of curses and complaining that earlier it was the rioters who robbed him of sleep.

Just as I was losing hope, he shuffled out of the gatehouse and fumbled for the key dangling from his belt. My disguise was working! I smiled in the darkness.

It took a long time for him to unlock the gate, but at last it creaked open. I led the horse through it, and we crossed the meadow. Moonlight spilled onto it, illuminating a host of rabbits that hopped out of our way. Ahead lay the forest, and I searched for the path that passed through it. Father and I had walked along this path many times before, but it looked completely different at night.

As I forced myself to enter the forest, the moonlight vanished. After lighting the lantern, I checked to make sure we were alone. Charlotte was slumped with her head against the horse's neck—she must have fallen asleep. I resisted the urge to wake her up.

Years ago, when I was with Father, this path had seemed short and peaceful in the daylight, but now it wound forever past trees and glades. With each step, I fought the urge to return home.

The town bells startled me. The sound was much fainter than usual, marking how far I had already gone. I paused to listen, longing to take comfort in something familiar and orderly. But tonight, even the bells had changed. They tolled an urgent warning to return home.

Setting the lantern down, I clenched the horse's guide rope. What had I done? It was past midnight, and I was running away from home where I had lived for fifteen years. I had dragged Charlotte into a dark forest. We could return right now, and no one would ever find out.

On the last stroke of the bells, I grabbed the lantern. As the words "slave" and "dyer" echoed in my mind, I led the horse as fast as I could away from Troyes.

A wolf howled nearby, and I froze. The sound was coming from deep in the forest. I couldn't go any farther. I spun my body halfway around, toward home, and a branch whipped against my face, stinging my cheek. Another wolf answered the howl, closer to us. My heart leaped in my throat, and terror rooted me to the ground. But somehow, I found the strength to go as fast as I could toward home.

Five

Fleabane

June 22, 1429

I was a horse thief. At daybreak, the ostler was bound to discover my theft and alert the tanner. He would find me in these woods and drag me back to town. He hated all Dauphinists and would turn me over to the magistrates for my punishment: death by hanging.

I couldn't return home. The lantern nearly slipped from my hand.

The wolves howled again. Fangs sinking into my neck . . . that image shot an urgency to flee throughout my body. Clutching the lantern in one hand and the guide rope in the other, I dragged the horse as fast as I could toward the main road and ran for a long way.

Sweat soaked Father's tunic. Slowing down, I listened for the wolves but didn't hear them anymore. The smell of dry grass filled the air and the moon illuminated open fields on either side of the road.

The terror of the wolves and the dark forest subsided, but a new fear crept through me—in the open I could easily be discovered. Long rows of grapevines terraced the hills beyond the fields. I headed toward them, seeking protection in their shadows.

A faint whinny came from that direction, and the tanner's horse whinnied in response. Maybe a stable lay hidden behind the vineyard, a stable where I could exchange the tanner's horse for another, so that no one would discover my theft.

I led his horse as quickly as I could to a cluster of trees. After tethering the mare and lifting the satchels off her back, I grabbed hold of Charlotte. Unprepared for her weight, I fell backward and hit the ground. Her body pressed against my ribs and squeezed the air out of my lungs.

She rolled off me, and I gasped for breath. "Felise, are you hurt?" she cried.

"Yes," I groaned and forced myself to sit up, rubbing the back of my head. "I'm taking the horse up that hill to graze. Lie down here and pretend to be asleep. Then my hurt will go away."

She obeyed me at once. Turning toward the vineyard, I unsheathed Father's knife. I had only used a knife to sharpen my writing quills and I prayed that I wouldn't have to use it tonight.

As I led the horse up the hill, I stopped to listen after every few steps. It took forever for me to reach the vineyard and tie the horse's rope to a wrought iron trellis. I crept down the first row but found no horse. Halfway down the second one, the moonlight revealed a horse's white rump. I crouched down to see if someone were asleep on the ground nearby. No one lay there, but another horse stood behind the first one, and two saddles lay on the ground. I clutched the knife, expecting men to burst forth from the shadows. Not a sound did I hear, save the rustling of grape leaves in the wind.

Maybe the men slept in a hut nearby. I had to risk swapping the horses. If their riders found me, I could even offer money for the exchange. Creeping around the white horse, I groped in the darkness for the knot that tied the rope to the trellis. The knot was taut. I tugged at the rope to loosen it—

The tip of a knife jabbed my back through my tunic. I screamed. The knife lifted but a thick arm grabbed me around the chest, pinning my arms to my sides. A man dragged me down the row toward the back of the vineyard. There, another man bolted upright on his pallet and drew his knife.

"Look who I found," my captor growled. "I'm sure he meant to harm us."

"No!" I cried.

"Then why are you here?" the man on the pallet asked, thrusting his knife closer to me.

"I only wished to trade my mare for one of yours," I said. "She's very tired."

"I don't believe you," he said, rising to his feet. He slept fully clothed even down to his boots.

"Nor do I," snarled my captor. "I think you followed us here and intended to murder us in our sleep."

"No," I protested.

The other man walked over to us. The moonlight revealed his rounded cheeks and beardless chin. "It's my turn to keep watch, Pierre," he said. "I'll go with this boy and see if he truly has a horse."

"Look, Jean, we already took a big risk riding here by ourselves. We knew we could be discovered." Pierre's tone was urgent. "This boy is surely an enemy. Why don't we just cut his throat now?"

I struggled to escape but his grip tightened, squeezing the breath out of me. "Please don't kill me," I panted. "I mean no harm."

Jean's eyes locked with my captor's. "We can't kill him without proof that he intends treachery." Although his voice was neither deep nor loud, it filled the darkness around us. I knew that he expected to be obeyed.

Without a word of protest, Pierre loosened his hold. Jean turned to me, his dark eyes boring into mine, so discomforting that I had to look away. "Take me to this horse of yours," he commanded.

"I'll go with you, Jean," Pierre said. He must have been worried that I might overpower Jean as I was taller than he was and heavier too.

Jean tossed his short hair. "As I have told you many times before, brother, I can take care of myself."

Drawing his knife, he waited for Pierre to release me and grabbed hold of me with the same fierce grip. He was too strong for me to overpower. Even if I did, I could never leave Charlotte with these two.

"Where is this horse?" he asked as Pierre scowled at me from the pallet.

"On the first row of vines."

He dragged me in that direction and soon we reached the tanner's horse.

"Why are you out riding in the middle of the night?" Jean demanded.

I could ask you *the same question*, I thought. We circled around the tanner's horse as I tried to think of a likely story. He halted, gripping me tighter. "You are lying, boy," he whispered harshly in my ear. "This mare hasn't been ridden hard at all. And you are too poor to own such a fine horse. You stole her, didn't you?"

His voice had grown so powerful that it frightened me. "No," I replied quickly. "She is my master's horse, but he sent me on urgent business."

"What business?"

"I don't know. He just gave me a letter to deliver, south of my town, Troyes."

The boy jabbed the tip of the knife into my back, and I screamed. He quickly lifted it. "Tell me the truth about who you are."

"But that *is* the truth. I'm just a messenger boy. I wouldn't dare to ask my master about the message in the letter. Besides, I can't read—"

Jean burst into laughter, a hearty but high-pitched laugh of the peasants who sold cabbages on market day. I stared at him, trying to figure out what amused him so.

"If I kept asking you questions," he said as his laughter

subsided, "you would keep telling lies until the cock crows. But you can't fool me. No master would send a girl out riding alone at night."

My legs buckled. I would have collapsed to the earth below if it weren't for Jean's firm hold around my chest.

"How did you know?" I gasped.

"A boy wouldn't reek of rose oil. That was your first mistake. And then when I jabbed you with the knife, you screamed like a girl. You did steal this horse, didn't you?"

"I didn't mean to," I stammered. "Now I'll be hanged."

He spun me around to face him, his hand clutching my arm and his knife still drawn. He stared at me as he did earlier, but this time his lips were pursed together. I sensed his concern for me even before he spoke. "You are right," he said somberly. "Even women are put to death for horse thievery. An urgent matter must have driven you to do it. What was it?"

"My father is in debt," I confessed. "He is a merchant and has been gone for many moons. The moneylenders are coming tomorrow. They are going to sell my aunt and me into slavery, so we had to run away."

He glanced toward the grove where Charlotte lay asleep on the ground. "This tale of yours I believe. You and your aunt are in great danger," he said quickly. To my surprise, he let go of my arm and put away his knife. "Those moneylenders and the horse's owner will be after you at daybreak. I will trade horses with you."

"Then you would be hanged in my place," I moaned, wringing my cold hands together. "Why are you risking your life for me? You don't even know me."

Jean smiled, his gaze upon the moonlit road. "Fear not. I can hide this mare so well that no one will find her. Do you know how to ride?"

"A little, but I have never ridden alone—always with my father."

"Come, I will give you a quick lesson. We are lucky to have some moonlight tonight."

I followed Jean to the first horse I spotted in the vineyard, the light-colored one. "This mare is Fleabane," he told me. "Don't be afraid of her. She is steady but slow if you know how to control her. She is trained to follow certain commands."

He showed me how to hoist a saddle onto the mare's back. "It's heavier than I expected," I panted.

"Get your aunt to help you," Jean advised. "Or leave the mare at a stable and have the ostler tend to it. Now climb onto her back."

He got on behind me and reached around me to grab hold of the reins. He taught me how to hold them and how to command the mare to speed up or slow down. I had to keep my heels down and pull up on one side of the reins when I wanted her to turn.

He brought Fleabane to a halt and dismounted. "Show me what I just taught you."

I hesitated. The distance to the ground seemed to have grown. "Hurry," Jean urged. I lifted the reins and commanded the mare to walk.

For the first time ever, I rode a horse by myself, my legs strong and certain. Yet after dismounting, they trembled as I led Fleabane to Jean, who grinned at my success.

"There is much more I could teach you," he said, "but at least now you can control her. Make sure to water her often. A horse can die when it gets too hot."

"How often should I feed her?" I asked.

"Do you have money?"

I clutched my purse. "A little."

"Stable her when you can. If you cannot, or you suspect that the ostler cheated you out of a fair portion of food, let her graze in a meadow the next day. Remember to loosen her saddle when she eats."

"Thank you," I said, "I didn't know any of these things about horses."

A Tale of Two Maidens

We walked in silence to the road. When we reached the poplar grove, Jean helped me tie the satchels onto Fleabane's back. Then he bent down to help me lift Charlotte, who was still asleep.

"I can carry her by myself," I quickly told him.

"I doubt that," he said and laughed. "She looks as heavy as a barrel of apples."

He stared at Charlotte's face. Even with her eyes closed, it was easy to see that they were crescent-shaped.

To my surprise, Jean didn't recoil. "A simpleton," he murmured. "She is a good companion because people will shun her, and therefore avoid you too. That will help you keep your disguise."

I gaped at him, amazed again at his sharp wit. In the moonlight, his eyes had taken on a yellowish glow like a cat's. Father's tales of witches who could change into animals came to mind.

"Why aren't you drawing back from my aunt?" I whispered. "And why did you help me?"

"I am not afraid of simpletons," he said with a shrug. "There is one in my village—he is a twenty-year-old child and has never harmed anyone. As for why I am helping you, your horse is more valuable than mine. Also, I remember all the strangers who helped me on my journey."

What journey? I almost asked, but the moon was already beginning its descent behind the trees.

"You have to leave now." Jean's words echoed my thoughts. "It will be daylight in an hour, and you won't have the darkness to protect you."

Together we lifted Charlotte onto the horse's back. She moaned in her sleep as she wrapped her arms around Fleabane's neck.

"She could easily fall off," he warned. "Tomorrow by the light of day, tie her to the saddle or better yet to you. You should sit in front, to control Fleabane better."

After we finish loading the satchels onto the mare's back, Jean pointed to the road. "Follow it south until daybreak. If you set Fleabane to a trot, by that time you should reach a path that rejoins the road close to Gien. It's the long way to the town but much safer for you than the main road. The dauphin's army will soon arrive in Gien. In the midst of all his soldiers, it will be hard for your pursuers to find you."

I climbed onto Fleabane's back and, with his help, Charlotte was settled behind me. "Are there scorchers in those woods?" I asked. Father had told me terrible tales about the mercenary soldiers hired by the English and the French, who hid in forests and preyed on villagers and travelers when they weren't fighting in battles.

He shook his head. "They scattered when they heard that the army was close by. But there are wolves aplenty. Do you have a weapon?"

"My father's knife," I replied, putting my hand on the hilt.

"Good. Wash the rose oil off when you come to a stream. Henceforth, act like a peasant boy. Speak in a deeper voice, eat sloppily with a hearty appetite, and take longer strides. Above all, act with confidence, as if you were used to commanding a horse from dawn to dusk. Farewell, girl."

"Thank you," I told him. "I wish there were something I could do for you in return."

"There is something. You said that your home is in Troyes. Is it safe to go there?"

His request surprised me, but I quickly told him of the dangers on our streets, about the daily fights between the two factions, and how things had worsened after the dauphin's victory at Orléans. "No one knows which side will win," I told him. "When the dauphin's army is at our gate, it will be decided once and for all."

"Thank you for these tidings," Jean said somberly. "Tell no one about my brother or me. Now go."

Why do you want secrecy? I wanted to ask but kept the question to myself. Fighting my dread of being alone in the darkness again, I wheeled Fleabane around and urged her into a trot. She carried us southward as the moon was setting behind the trees. It was so dark that I could hardly see the road. Again, I wondered why Jean had risked his life for a stranger and why he and his companion were camping in a vineyard. When they spoke of the enemy, did they mean the Dauphinists or the Burgundians or someone else?

Would they ride away like ghosts in the night? I was fully awake, yet it all seemed like the stuff of dreams.

As the sun rose higher, the fields around me were bathed in a pinkish light. I felt uneasy in the open and kept turning around to see if anyone was following me. Soon I came to a path—it must have been the one that Jean described—and gave Fleabane the signal to turn onto it. It was so overgrown that I had to slow the horse and watch for overhanging limbs.

By full daylight, we came to a stream that crossed the road. Fleabane lowered her neck to drink while I dismounted, my thighs sore from gripping them against the mare's flanks. As I splashed water on my face and arms, I studied her back and realized how she must have earned her name. She had a grayish coat mottled with darker spots that looked like masses of fleas. In the summer, Ameline and I would sprinkle dried fleabane flowers on the floor to ward off fleas. What would she say if she could see me now?

Through the trees, a ray of sun gleamed against Charlotte's hair. She lifted her head and looked all around at the strange surroundings and then at me. "Where is our house?" she asked.

"Far away. We are going on a journey."

She stared at my breeches. "Where is your skirt?" she asked.

"In the satchel. I don't want to get it dirty."

Her brows furrowed as she tried to understand. I was glad that my hood covered my shorn hair. But her amber hair was showing; surely the moneylenders would remember it.

I walked back to her and drew her hood over her hair. "See how my hair is covered in my hood?" I told her. "Yours has to be covered too."

"But it's hot," she whined.

"I know. It's hot for me too, but we have to wear our hoods, both of us."

For all her trouble understanding simple matters, Charlotte always understood what Ameline and I were feeling and mirrored it back to us. Her chin quivered as she nodded. "I need a chamber pot," she said.

Looking all around, I listened for people as I helped her down. "My legs hurt," she moaned as I tethered Fleabane to a sapling.

"There's no chamber pot here," I told her. "You have to go behind that tree, and I'll help you lift your skirt."

When she was done, I handed her our bread and water. "I'm going behind the tree too," I told her.

It was very strange to pull down the breeches instead of lifting my skirt. It was much easier to relieve oneself as a boy.

While we continued on our way, Charlotte amused herself by making up a "forest song." Many years ago I made up songs with her about the things around us, like the crackling fire or the wind blowing against the shutters. As I warned her to sing more softly, I longed for that carefree time when we were safe together in our house.

The smell of wood smoke wafted toward us. Fearing that the fire could be coming from the moneylenders' camp, I hushed Charlotte and listened intently. In the distance, I heard a man's voice and the faint laughter of a woman; perhaps they were lovers alone in the forest. I blushed while recalling the sound of the tanner's breathing as he stood close to me in the cemetery.

Had he discovered that I had stolen his horse yet? I urged Fleabane to a faster pace, remembering the frenzied look on the tanner's face as he led the rioters. My only hope was that the magistrates had thrown him in prison and he wouldn't find out that his horse had been stolen for a long time. As the day wore on, the only people we passed were peasants leading their mules.

Their eyes were filled with curiosity, even suspicion that a peasant boy could afford a horse.

By nightfall, my thighs ached from gripping Fleabane's flanks and my neck, from craning around to watch for my pursuers. Exhausted, I could only think of finding a safe place to rest.

At the narrow bank of a stream, I dismounted and led Fleabane far from the path where travelers might see our camp. Along the sandy banks, I found a place to tether the mare. After loosening her saddle, she grazed and drank from the stream while Charlotte and I devoured bread and cheese.

We made a pallet on the sand, stacking fallen branches around it to protect us from intruding animals or people. Had the two young men in the vineyard fallen asleep as exhausted and terrified as I was? Why else would they have taken shifts to keep watch, and what sort of treachery had they feared? After Charlotte fell asleep, I listened to the stream flowing over rocks. The sound of the water was far more pleasant than the fighting that often kept me awake at home, yet its noise could easily mask an intruder approaching. I unsheathed Father's knife and fell into an unsettled sleep.

When I woke up, the forest had lightened into a soft gray. A mist settled over the trees, and the birds chirped their morning songs. I rubbed my eyes, not feeling rested at all, and roused Charlotte. She looked puzzled but grinned when she saw the horse.

"We must eat quickly," I told her. "We have to go."

A hunk of hard bread was all that remained of the loaf I had packed. Breaking off the bad part, I thrust the rest at her, resigning myself to hunger to keep her from whining. I cupped my hands and filled my empty belly with water from the stream.

After covering up the signs of our camp, I threw our things into satchels and helped Charlotte onto Fleabane's back. I led the mare to the forest path and climbed onto her in front of Charlotte. Remembering Jean's advice, I tied a rope around her belly and mine before setting out to the south. While Charlotte giggled, thinking that the rope was part of a game, every muscle in my body coiled in a tight knot.

Gradually the path widened enough to set a faster pace, and soon we reached a clearing that contained a garden patch overgrown with weeds. Beyond lay a village with wisps of smoke rising above it, perhaps from a baker's oven. My stomach growled at the thought of fresh bread. It was only a little past first light, and I knew it would be a risk setting foot in the village.

The moneylenders—or even André—could have slept at an inn here last night. Then again, this village was isolated, and they had probably stopped at an inn on the main road. This might be the safest place to stop for bread. If I bought two loaves, we wouldn't have to stop again until we reached Gien.

I dismounted and led Fleabane toward the main gate. "Lie down on the horse's back and pretend to be asleep," I whispered to Charlotte.

She quickly put her head down. I pulled Father's hood over my eyes and walked into a small square with a fountain. The women filling jugs with water narrowed their eyes at me. I led Fleabane down the main street, glad to pass only women shouldering bread. While I looked around for any signs of my pursuers, the women clutched their children and stared at me, muttering prayers for the Virgin to protect them. Even though I was dressed as a boy, I wasn't strong and powerful. Never before had anyone looked at me with such fear.

Farther down the street, I came to a row of houses burned to the ground, as if a fire in one house had spread to the others. Pushing away my sadness for the people who lived there, I sniffed the air. The aroma of freshly baked bread rose up through the pungent smell of wood smoke. As I followed the scent, I kept to the side of the road, watchful for my pursuers.

Finally, I came to an inn. After tethering Fleabane to a post, I whispered to Charlotte, who still had her head down. "I will be back with fresh bread in a moment. Stay here with Fleabane."

She nodded, eager for more breakfast. *Act like a confident boy*, I silently repeated Jean's advice, opening the door and peering into the dark, smoky room. No one was there, except for a man who was throwing a log on the fire. He turned around and rose to his feet, his hand on the hilt of his knife. "What do you want, boy?" He growled.

"I mean no harm," I stammered in my new voice. "I need two loaves of fresh bread."

"To take back to your leader, the one who led the scorchers to attack our village?" The man demanded.

The burned houses, the women who were afraid of me—now I understood Father's tales and descriptions of how the villages of our land had been ravaged by war. I quickly shook my head. "I am not a scorcher, only a traveler hungry for bread."

He stared at me for a long time, measuring the truth of my words. My hands grew sweaty in Father's gloves, and I worried that my hair had slipped loose from the hood, revealing my disguise. Finally, he sheathed his knife and picked up two loaves from a stack on the table. "Ten sous. Where have you come from?"

"Saint Florentin," I lied, choosing the only town I could think of as I handed him the coins.

He thrust the bread at me. It was hard as a rock, not the fresh bread I smelled.

"Are you going to fight for the Maid?" he asked. Nodding, I turned to leave.

"Good," he said. "She will purge our land of the accursed scorchers who burned our houses and stole our pigs." He pounded his fist on the table.

This man was a stranger and a peasant who had sold me stale bread, and yet pity for him rose up in me. His wife may well have been one of the women who clutched their children when I entered their village. Outside the door of the inn, I discovered a band of urchin boys swarming around Fleabane and about to flee with our satchels. Charlotte was gone. My heart raced as I imagined the scar-faced moneylender close by, clutching Charlotte under his smelly arm.

"Put those satchels down!" I shouted at the urchins, drawing out Father's knife. "Where is the woman?"

They wheeled around, dropping the satchels and running away in all directions.

I chased the two youngest boys who couldn't flee as fast as the others. "Where is she?" I panted, drawing closer to them.

The last boy tripped on a stone and fell to the ground. I squatted beside him and shook him by his bony shoulders. "Answer me," I yelled. Every moment was precious—the moneylenders could be galloping off on their horses with Charlotte tied in a sack.

Groaning, the boy sat up and pointed toward a nearby road. I ran back to Fleabane and hoisted the satchels onto her back. After leading her down the road that the boy had indicated, I found a small square heaped with charred trestles, broken benches, and wooden chests that had been chopped into pieces. I stumbled over the rubble, calling for Charlotte, but she didn't answer.

"Charlotte," I called, forgetting to disguise my voice. I looked behind every piece of broken furniture. It was the first day and already something terrible had happened to her.

Frantic, I tethered Fleabane and turned into one of the alleys radiating from the square. I ran past every hovel, but she was nowhere to be found.

"Begone," a woman yelled, shaking her broom as I passed.

Panting, I returned to the square and set out down the next alley. I couldn't find her anywhere. In a panic, I raced back to the square and turned into the only alley I hadn't tried yet.

When I reached the end, I heard someone moaning behind an overturned trestle. I found Charlotte crouched behind it with blood on her hand. It was scraped badly—probably when she fell from Fleabane's back.

I pulled out a rag from my purse and pressed it to the scrape as we hugged each other. "Why didn't you stay with Fleabane?" I panted, trying to catch my breath and exhaling in relief. My body trembled all over as my heartbeat gradually slowed.

"The boys pulled me off her and told me to go away," she sobbed. "I want Ameline."

I held her tightly, wanting Ameline too.

I never looked back at that village as we rode away, taking the path to the south.

Many hours later, the city of Gien rose up from the plain before us, beckoning us to the safety of its walls. Relief washed over me when the guard let us pass through the gate. Along the main street, people spoke excitedly of the Maid and the Dauphin Charles's arrival. Women strung garlands of flowers along the fronts of their homes while men rolled out barrels of wine. No one wore royal blue caps for the Duke of Burgundy. Everywhere were the dauphin's colors—red, green, and white.

The cathedral square was clogged with carts of wounded and sick people and their families, waiting for the Maid to cure them. Food sellers wended their way through the crowd, hawking their wares.

"Do you know where I can find a stable?" I asked a boy who was helping his mother sell cheese.

"Over there." He pointed to a building a short way down the street. Charlotte sat up and grinned at him, forgetting her promise to keep her head down, especially when she recognized a child's voice. "See my horse," she said proudly.

He stared at her, open-mouthed, then turned to me. "What happened to her eyes?" he asked.

"I don't know, but I hope the Maid can cure her," I lied.

"And my brother too—from his fever," he said solemnly.

I led Fleabane to the stable, which had an inn adjoining it. After tethering her, I helped Charlotte dismount, and we lugged our satchels into the inn's anteroom where I set them down.

"Pretend to be asleep," I whispered into her ear. "We don't want the bad men to find us."

She quickly laid her head on the satchels and closed her eyes while I led Fleabane into a stable that stank of manure.

"Do you have any stalls for this mare?" I asked the ostler in my deepest voice.

He hardly lifted his head from repairing a saddle. "Twenty francs a night. Pay first."

That seemed a steep price, but I decided not to question it and paid for a night, even though I suspected he wouldn't feed her well. I remembered how Jean had said to let the mare graze the next day if the ostler cheated me. He took Fleabane's rope and led her to a stall.

When I reentered the inn, I found Charlotte still feigning sleep. "Good, Charlotte," I whispered, "keep pretending."

My stomach fluttered as I approached the innkeeper and his wife, who was pounding meat at a table. The smell of onions rose up from several pots that hung over a roaring fire. My mouth watered.

"Do you have a room for the night?" I asked in my male voice.

"Only the attic," the innkeeper replied, swatting flies away. "The rest of the rooms are reserved for the dauphin's men. They should be here by sunset."

"Will the Maid stay here?" I asked, hoping to see her with my own eyes.

The innkeeper's wife, a large woman with red cheeks, shook her head. "She will stay with the magistrate, and the dauphin with the lord."

"How much will the attic cost?" I asked, hiding my disappointment.

The innkeeper glanced over at Charlotte. "For the two of you, thirty francs. That doesn't include supper."

"May we eat in the attic?" I asked. "My sister is ill."

They turned to each other in alarm. "Does she have plague buboes?" the wife hissed, drawing back.

"No, she just ate too many dried pears," I replied quickly, hoping they believed my lie.

They eyed her suspiciously, and then the innkeeper returned his gaze to me.

"Five francs more for supper brought to you," he said.

I drew the money from my purse and noted that it was quickly disappearing. After paying, I went to fetch Charlotte. "Lean against me, as if you are half-asleep," I whispered.

The innkeeper led us up a narrow staircase. He opened a door, and we entered a tiny room, hardly enough room for two people. Sunlight streamed in through one window, revealing a pallet and a chamber pot. He opened the window and gazed out. "No sign of the army yet."

As soon as he left, I helped Charlotte take off her cloak. Her bodice was soaked in sweat from wearing it throughout the hot day. Chortling at the sunbeam, she followed it to the window. "Pretty," she murmured as she pointed at the clouds. I hoped that her memory of the boys had vanished.

I washed her scraped hand with a rag and ran my fingers through her matted hair, picking out twigs and bits of leaves. "Get the brush and I will make your hair pretty."

A lump grew in my throat as I brushed Charlotte's amber hair, so close in color to Ameline's. She was gone forever, but Father wasn't. I was still angry at him, but I wondered if I would ever see him again. I imagined him at this very moment settling into an inn for the night somewhere along the road. I got out the seashell that he had given me and held it to my ear, imagining the sound of waves breaking. Maybe he was at sea. I closed my eyes and sent him a silent message about Ameline and my flight from home.

Someone knocked on the attic room's door. The innkeeper's wife brought us each a bowl of stew, which smelled meaty and rich but contained mostly gristle. As we finished our meal, the wind began to slam the shutters open and shut. Rose petals from the garlands meant for the dauphin and Jeanne were swept into the attic. Lightning flashed and thunder rumbled; then a sideway rain lashed into the attic. Water started to pool on the floor, forcing me to shut the window. Almost at once the room grew stifling hot and smelly from the chamber pot. I opened the door to the hallway and set it outside, along with our empty bowls. Downstairs the innkeeper yelled at his wife and complained that the storm had robbed him of the soldiers' payment for the night's lodgings.

Charlotte clung to me as she used to cling to Ameline whenever there was a thunderstorm.

"Where's my doll?" she cried, her eyes wild with longing.

"Back at our house."

She pressed her lips together and stomped her foot. "Go get her!" she wailed.

"I can't—it's too far away."

She collapsed into a heap on the floor, her shoulders heaving, and her sobs filling the tiny room. Worried that someone would hear, I took her by the arm. "Come with me."

Whimpering, she rose to her feet and followed me. From the pile of kindling, I grabbed a stick and broke off the cap of an acorn that lay on the floor. That became the doll's hat. For her hair I tied hay underneath the cap with a bit of string. Dried leaves and rose petals became her cloak and skirt, also tied with string.

"It's the best doll I can make," I said, handing it to her. She beamed at me as she rocked it in her arms. I smiled back, pleased that I could do something so simple to soothe her.

By the time the storm passed, dusk had set in. Charlotte helped me strike the flint and light our candles, which we carried to the window. When I opened it, raindrops splashed against our faces. The moon appeared and disappeared through passing clouds and a breeze ruffled our hair. Charlotte wanted to sing her evening song, but a man was walking on the street below. For all I knew he could be one of the moneylender's men.

"Let's sing as we get ready for bed," I told her as I closed the window. "We have to ride the horse early tomorrow morning."

By the last bit of light, I started to take off my filthy clothes, but decided it would be safer to remain dressed as a boy. I opened the satchel, searching for Charlotte's night shift. Rummaging around, I found something shaped like a small pot. It was Father's inkpot, which through some miracle, was still tightly corked. I also found a pouch containing several quills and paper that I had grabbed from Father's desk.

Charlotte fixed her gaze on the quill. "I want to draw," she said.

When I was small, Father would often let Charlotte and me draw on scraps of his paper while Mama and Ameline sewed. But as I got older, I preferred to practice my letters while Charlotte continued to draw. She would sit in front of the hearth after supper, her back hunched over the paper, and make pictures for us all.

I gave her a scrap of paper and a quill that I had dipped into the inkpot. She set to work, and I glanced over her shoulder. She was drawing a horse in her own childlike way, and yet there was no doubt that the horse was Fleabane. Her drawing captured a certain look on the mare's face when her nose was being patted. As Ameline said, Charlotte might be simpleminded, but she understood many things that other people did not.

Charlotte was so intent on her drawing that I hardly heard her breathing. At the scriptorium, I must have looked like her as I copied the *Book of the City of Ladies*. Picking up a quill, I held it so that it fit inside the groove of my quill mark. Though it had been only a few days, it seemed as if that were another time and a different girl who loved to hold a quill and write beautiful letters and dreamed of one day writing her own thoughts.

Six

Horse Girl

June 25, 1429

I woke to the sun heating my face, so bright that I knew at once it was well past first light. Charlotte was already awake and playing with her new doll. "I'm hungry," she whined.

Mama's prayer book was opened on the floor, and Charlotte had drawn a tree across the page. I strode across the room and snatched it from the floor. "Don't you ever draw in a book again," I snapped. "Especially Mama's book."

"But I drew a pretty tree. For you," Charlotte said, her lower lip jutting out. She folded her arms across her chest and looked down at the floor. Ameline called this her "pout" and explained that Charlotte did it when she knew she had displeased us but didn't understand why.

Ameline would have found a way to chide Charlotte without getting angry. Guilt rippled through me as I went downstairs for water and a loaf of bread. "Are you taking the attic for another night?" the innkeeper asked. "One of the soldiers will surely want it if you don't."

I didn't know what to do but decided to pay for another night anyway. Hopefully, the few remaining coins in my moneybag would be enough to pay the ostler too. When I returned to the attic, Charlotte was still in her pout as an uproar rose from the street below. People were chanting Jeanne de Domrémy's name over and over, calling her "the Maid who will save our land."

The clanging of many bells drowned out their chanting.

"Why are the bells ringing?" Charlotte asked as she came to stand at my side. As I explained what was happening, she pulled off a hunk of bread and showed no sign of remembering her pout.

"Come to the cathedral square!" a crier proclaimed. "The Maid and the dauphin are on their way to attend Mass!"

As we ate bread, Charlotte and I stood at the window and watched people swarming toward the cathedral. Soon the street cleared except for peasant men dressed in ragged clothes, shoving and sparring with one another. Many of them were boys, and not much older than I was. Some had quivers filled with arrows slung across their backs.

These men were soldiers. Was this our army—the men who were fighting to save our land from the English? They pushed their way to a group of innkeepers who were vying with one another to be the first to fill their rooms.

"How much for the night?" a soldier demanded.

"Forty francs," an innkeeper replied. That was double the price I had just paid.

"All the rooms here in Gien are the same price," another innkeeper quickly added.

Amid the soldiers' grumblings, I noticed two men leading their horses toward them, their faces red and dripping with sweat. As they drew closer, I clenched the windowsill, gaping at one man's jagged scar—one of the moneylenders who had come to our house last March. The other man had a dark scraggly beard.

Pulling Charlotte with me, I ducked below the windowsill. My heartbeat quickened, and her body trembled as I held her tightly.

"Listen well, soldiers," the scar-faced man shouted. "We seek a runaway girl who may be hiding among you."

The men burst into laughter. "But the Maid banishes our women," a soldier replied. "This girl must be brave to defy her."

"Thirty livres tournois go to the man who finds her," the scar-faced man shouted in his Flemish accent. "Mark you well, our reward is higher than that of the other men who seek her."

I clutched my trembling knees to my chest. André or Georges or both of them?

The soldiers talked excitedly among themselves. "With such a reward the girl must be valuable," a man said. "What does she look like?"

"She's tall for a girl," the moneylender with the scar replied, "and she has blue eyes and dark hair. You can tell it's the girl we seek by her companion, an idiot woman with red hair."

"It should be easy to find an idiot," a soldier snickered. They started wagering about which of them would find me first. I wiped the sweat beading around my mouth, wishing that I had found a way to leave Charlotte safely in Troyes.

"We go now to Saint Florentin. Bring her there if you find her," the moneylender interrupted the soldiers.

After the moneylenders left, the soldiers dispersed, each still boasting that he would win the reward. I jumped to my feet to make sure that the door was locked.

"What's wrong, Felise?" Charlotte asked, her voice full of concern.

I pressed my back against the door, wishing she could help me think, but all I could hope for was that she wouldn't reveal our whereabouts. Ameline's words of advice about her echoed within me: *Keep instructing her in the same way, and she will obey.* Hadn't I seen this advice work when Charlotte kept pretending to be asleep, even after I went to talk with the innkeeper?

"The bad men are getting closer to us," I told her, my voice trembling. "We have to be very quiet, and you have to obey me. Do you understand?"

Nodding, she put a finger to her lips.

As soon as night fell, Charlotte went to sleep, her belly full of the last of our dried fruit. Downstairs, the soldiers' revelry continued. The more they drank, the more they boasted about how easy it would be to catch me, and the more trapped I felt.

At last they quieted, and I dozed fitfully with my back propped against the wall. Before first light, I awakened Charlotte, who was eager to ride the horse again. We tiptoed down the stairs past the great room. A chorus of loud snores rose up from the group of soldiers scattered across the floor.

Only a few coins remained in my purse after I paid the ostler, but there wasn't time to think about that. I helped Charlotte onto Fleabane and reminded her to keep her head down. With a fervent prayer that she wouldn't give us away, I flicked the reins and urged the mare to walk faster down the deserted street.

Outside the walls of the city, a vast sea of pallets spread across the meadow, thousands upon thousands of sleeping soldiers. In the gray light of dawn, they started to awaken, stoking up campfires and playing at dice. I stopped, clutching the reins in my sweaty hands, my eyes riveted on the soldiers.

They must know about the reward by now. I was trapped in the open, an easy quarry. More soldiers were awakening. At any moment one of them could discover who I was. My panic rose, constricting my breath into shallow pants.

I gripped the reins, knowing that I had to ride past them before it grew lighter still. But where could I go? I nudged Fleabane forward and saw the forest beyond, my only choice for a hiding place. My body trembled as I urged the mare into a walk. *Act like a peasant boy, not a frightened girl*, Jean had warned. Looking straight ahead, I ignored the soldiers whose gaze fixed on me with disapproval and led Fleabane on a slow steady course toward the forest.

"Coward," a soldier spat, his spittle spraying my breeches. "Stay and fight for the Maid with the rest of us."

"But he has a girl," another man sneered, pointing at Charlotte. "He doesn't want the Maid to strike her sword against the girl's rump."

Laughter broke out as I urged Fleabane onward, past the rows of pallets to the edge of the forest. There, families camped near carts that carried their sick and dying kin. I veered away from them, hoping that they hadn't heard about the reward too.

The soldiers who were following me pressed closer, and their curses grew louder. Rocks flew at us, thudding against the earth all around us. One of them hit Fleabane and she neighed loudly before surging forward faster than before.

"Whoa!" I commanded her, pressing my thighs against her flanks, but she only galloped faster.

I pulled back on the reins as hard as I could. The carts and trees blurred together, closer and closer. The faces of the people camped there were frozen in terror. Charlotte's arms squeezed me around the waist, but Fleabane's speed caused her body to be jerked up and down so violently that I felt her grip loosening. Unable to hold on, Charlotte screamed as she tumbled off the horse's back. Her body pounded into the earth behind me.

"The girl is ours," the soldiers roared, their footsteps getting closer.

"Run, Charlotte!" I screamed, but I couldn't steer Fleabane around to see if she obeyed. I pressed my knees harder into Fleabane's sides, trying with all my might to stop her. My efforts were to no avail. She galloped along the edge of the forest, gathering speed and jouncing me up and down in the saddle. With the ties around the horse's body loosened, the saddle slipped to the side. I struggled to keep myself astride the mare's back but could hold on no longer. I flew off Fleabane and hit the ground so hard that the breath was knocked out of me. Gasping for air, I watched in horror as the mare disappeared into the forest.

"No," Charlotte wailed. Had the soldiers seized her? I rolled over to look for her and saw her stumbling toward me, her eyes wide with panic. The soldiers were gaining on her, only a stone's throw away when they spotted me. They raised their fists toward the sky. "Come back and fight, you coward!" they shouted.

Bells clanged furiously. A band of men and women dressed in black surged out of the forest, ringing their handbells and blocking the soldiers' advance toward Charlotte and me.

I bolted upright as one of the women caught my eye. Her face had been eaten away, exposing raw inner flesh and the white of her cheekbone. I quickly turned away, sickened by the sight of her. She was a leper—they all were; their bells warned others to flee from them, for their disease was contagious.

I stumbled to my feet and hurried toward Charlotte. Grabbing her hand, I pulled her with me into the forest. As we caught our breath, I turned around and saw that the lepers were still on the meadow ringing their bells while the soldiers made a hasty retreat back to their camp. I gave silent thanks to the lepers for shielding us from the soldiers.

Charlotte and I plunged deeper into the forest, forging our way through brambles to a stream. There we found Fleabane drinking heartily, the saddle and satchels lopsided but still on her back.

"You and the lepers saved us," I crooned, wrapping an arm around her neck and resting my head against her mane. My legs trembled violently as I closed my eyes and listened to the water flowing over the rocks.

"I'm hungry," Charlotte whined later that day, her eyes on the lepers who were roasting rabbits over a fire nearby. I hoped we were far enough away from them not to catch the disease. There was hardly enough money left in my pouch for a loaf of bread or enough food to last another day.

"Me too," I told her, patting my hollow belly. "Let's keep looking."

Horse Girl

Keeping my hand firmly on Fleabane's rope, I led Charlotte along the stream bank in search of wild strawberries. I was amazed to hear music floating toward us, the joyful music of tabors and pipes and drums. In the midst of war's horrors, soldiers danced with girls on the meadow. Along the town wall, people swarmed around barrels of ale and trestles of food. As was the custom, wooden wheels were set afire and rolled downhill toward a pond.

It was the Feast of Midsummer's Eve, a celebration of the longest day of the year and Ameline's favorite feast because it was also her birthday. I ran my fingers through Charlotte's hair. Ameline would have known how to find food and how to survive; she would have taken care of Charlotte and me. If she were here, I would simply have done what she told me to do.

Charlotte grabbed my hand and pulled me toward the meadow. "I want to go there. Let's get some pears and dance."

"No. We have to stay here where no one can see us."

"Ameline let me dance," she wailed.

"Ameline is gone, and I won't let you," I told her sharply, "because I want you to be safe."

"I'm safe."

"See those soldiers—" I started to explain, but the blaring of a trumpet interrupted me.

"Jeanne the Maid is coming to attend the sick!" a crier announced.

I grabbed Fleabane's rope in one hand and Charlotte's hand in the other, surging forward with the sick people and their families. Ameline and I had spent many hours comparing our ideas about what she looked like. And the night I ran away, I had imagined Jeanne cutting her hair to inspire me to cut my own. At last, I would see her in the flesh.

But the crowd blocked her from my view, and I couldn't hear her approach over the chanting of her name. The lepers hurried toward the front of the pack, ringing their bells to warn everyone from coming too close.

"That's not fair!" a woman screamed at them as they passed. "We deserve the Maid's healing touch more than you sinners do."

The lepers ignored her as well as the others who took up her cry. They pressed forward, forcing the sick people and their families to back away. I dared to lead Charlotte and Fleabane toward the lepers, keeping the length of two horses' bodies between us.

"You fool!" a man shouted at me. "It would serve you right to catch their disease."

I continued onward, halting at the forest's edge while the lepers advanced to the meadow. A group of soldiers, maybe a dozen, headed toward the forest. The men on the outer ring held lances but the two riders in the middle did not. I craned my neck to see them better as they stopped a stone's throw away from the lepers.

"Heal us, Jeanne the Maid," the lepers pleaded, reaching out their arms toward the riders.

"Let us pray that God will heal you," a clear voice replied, a girl's voice coming from the middle of the ring. The voice, which had the accent of a peasant from the east of our land, sounded familiar. A chill ran through me.

I strained to see her, but the tall man with gray hair riding beside her blocked my view. "We must get away from these lepers," he warned her. "You cannot risk catching their disease."

"May God be with you," the Maid bade the lepers, raising her banner toward the sky. A design was embroidered upon it, but in the wind all I could see was a blue-and-green blur. "You will be in my prayers."

The lepers shouted their thanks, and the Maid and her men urged their horses forward. With my eyes fixed on the group, I kept shifting my position so that I could see the shorter of the two riders in the middle—Jeanne. When they were a short distance away, I caught a glimpse of her gloved hands controlling a spirited black horse. Standing on my tiptoes, I finally saw her eyes. Those brown eyes were the same ones that had bored into mine the night in the vineyard. Goosebumps rose on my arms as

I clutched hold of a tree to steady myself, the breath knocked out of me once again. Had her saints told her to help me that night?

My legs and feet trembled, but I remained on tiptoes to stare at her. Other than her voice and eyes, everything else about Jean—Jeanne—was different. That night I had mistaken her for a young man, but now the softness of her carriage revealed clearly that she was a girl.

I dropped my feet to rest them flat on the earth and smiled. We were both in disguise, and for the first time since I left home, I wasn't alone. That girl, who had risked her life to ride into battles and lead the dauphin's army to astounding victories, knew my secret. She had cared enough to give me advice and teach me to ride. Hot tears rolled down my face, my heart warming like a cold ember brought to flame.

Suddenly she dismounted near the sick people and their caretakers. The thin man beside her did too, scowling at the throng. The men on horseback ringed around them, holding their lances at the ready. It was clear that they would die for her. Those men weren't hired soldiers. It was love that held them next to her.

A woman with a child in her arms emerged from the crowd and approached Jeanne. The guards thrust their lances forward. "Let her come to me," Jeanne bade them. "She cannot harm me."

I heard the same lightness in her voice that I remembered well from the night in the vineyard.

"Only her—no more," insisted the man who rode beside her.

As she nodded, I wondered who he was and why she obeyed him. I could see her better now and tried to notice everything about her—her rounded cheeks and swarthy skin, the uneven cut of her hair, and her quick gait.

"Holy Maid, I heard that you brought a dead baby back to life in Lagny," the woman shouted. "I beg you, bring my daughter back from death's door."

Jeanne extended her hand to touch the sleeping girl's brow. People murmured excitedly. "I didn't heal that baby." Her voice rang out, her tone far more somber than it had been just a moment before. It amazed me that a girl, and not a man with a thunderous voice, could project so that everyone in the crowd could hear her. "We should pray to God instead that he will heal your daughter and all the sick people here."

She led the crowd in the Lord's Prayer. As the "Amen" trailed away, a hush fell over everyone, a silence like none I had ever experienced. She inspired me as well as the others to offer a true prayer that flooded us with wonder.

Something caught my eye . . . Charlotte. She had let go of my hand and was creeping forward into the open. My heart beat against my ribs. She was very still as I had never seen her before, her eyes fixed upon Jeanne as she began to hum a haunting new melody. "Horse Girl," she sang.

The wonder that kept us silent seemed to have settled on Charlotte, transforming her from the half-wit that others saw into a vision of beauty. Everyone gazed at her, her amber hair tumbling free for all to see. I forgot the reward on our heads and our desperate plight. I had been longing for a miracle and here it was, clear as water, Charlotte's tribute to Jeanne. It echoed the one that I felt in my own heart.

"What a lovely song. Horse Girl is a good name for me," Jeanne said with a wistful longing in her voice. Did she yearn for peaceful days when women could sing in joy, when swords were locked away and she could sit at ease on her horse? When being a Horse Girl meant riding freely across green meadows? Charlotte understood nothing of Jeanne's mission, but perhaps she knew her better than anyone there.

"Horse Girl!" the crowd shouted in unison. I shifted my position slightly so that I was right across from Charlotte but still hidden behind the trees. "Charlotte," I called to her, waving my arm to get her attention.

"Farewell, good people!" Jeanne shouted, her voice strong and filled with a power I had not heard before. "I will pray for you all, especially the sick among you. In return, pray for our land. Pray that one day we will rid it of scorchers and enemy soldiers and the false English king who claims the dauphin's throne. Pray that our France will be set free!"

Was it my imagination or did she feel renewed by Charlotte's song? Charlotte turned toward me, shaking her head slightly as if stirring from a daydream. "Do you like my song?" she asked, her smile radiant.

She knew her song was very special.

"Yes, but come here quickly," I said as the reality of our situation returned to me like a dark garment thrown over my face. I covered her hair with her hood and pulled her back into the forest, the branches slapping cruelly against Fleabane's flanks.

In the distance, I could hear the crowd roaring its approval. The chant, "Set us free!" sounded like something I was hearing in a dream.

At daybreak the next day, I was very hungry, but my mind was clear. I kept close to the lepers, understanding that they offered us safety. I felt myself beginning to think as Jeanne had advised me. I could trust myself a little to see danger coming and prepare for it. Again I smiled, and a pleasant warmth returned to my limbs.

Later that day, I rode between the lepers and the caravan of sick people who followed the army. The girl whom the Maid had laid her hands on rode in the center, for everyone believed that Jeanne's touch was still upon her. The power of it would radiate outward, bestowing healing grace upon the others, even the lepers. A man proclaimed that his stomach sickness had vanished. I felt a strange understanding of what a miracle was. It returned people to themselves and reminded them of who they were.

Lulled by the steady clomping of Fleabane's hooves on the earth, I remembered the picture of the women warriors and the young woman in armor who led them into battle. Lady Christine's words beneath that picture had described the women as having the strength and bravery of men. Jeanne wasn't just a picture but a real girl made of flesh and blood: a girl with a commanding voice and the dark skin of a peasant who had miraculously appeared to serve the dauphin just when he needed her most.

The sun was directly overhead when the men stopped to rest and water the horses. Hundreds of foot soldiers swarmed onto a wheat field, cutting the sheaves with their knives and devouring the grain raw. Nearly a moon ago, I had told the tanner that the dauphin would surely overcome the Burgundians. He had scoffed at me, saying that the dauphin's men were starving. He had been right.

I kept as close as I dared to the lepers, stopping when they did at a stream. I followed the stream farther into the forest while listening for soldiers. After Charlotte and I dismounted, I let her take off the hood and splash in the cool water. Fleabane lowered her neck to drink while I cupped my hands and drank too.

Soon the lepers and families of the sick people had caught every fish and frog in the stream. They were being roasted over campfires, while berries and green apples were plucked from every tree and bush around. Weak from hunger, I filled our flask with water while Charlotte searched for berries nearby.

After tethering Fleabane, I watched over Charlotte while she dozed on the sand, her face stained with berry juice. In the late afternoon, I heard a clattering of wheels across the meadow. Parting the branches of the trees, I saw a caravan of wagons loaded with a dozen or more young men, all wearing wide-brimmed hats to shade themselves from the sun. They weren't shabbily dressed like the soldiers, and I didn't see any sick people on their wagons. I drew back into the shadows, fearing that they might be my pursuers.

They unyoked their horses and started to lead them toward my hiding place. Grabbing Fleabane's rope, I roused Charlotte. "Pick up your shoes and follow me," I whispered.

The lepers saw the men too and rang their bells in warning. The men cursed them as they turned around and followed the stream in the opposite direction.

The men spoke in the accent of those of us from Troyes. Wondering if I knew them, I led Charlotte and Fleabane to the forest's edge where I could observe the men without being seen. The rest of their group had set out food on the meadow. My mouth watered at the roasted chicken and cheeses and loaves of bread. They devoured the food ravenously and quaffed from their flasks, their laughter growing louder as they drank.

They began a game of dice, and one of them pulled out a recorder. The lively song sounded familiar. Charlotte started humming along, and I realized it was a song that Father used to play on his recorder. I scanned the group in search of Father's portly figure and long black hair threaded with gray, but I didn't see him.

Three riders approached them on horses draped in the dauphin's red, green, and white colors. One of the men rose to his feet and went to greet them. The rest grew quiet, watching. The middle rider thrust a moneybag heavy with coins into the man's outstretched hand. "Give this to Henri the Merchant," he said.

My father! These men must be members of his merchant crew. Although I couldn't see his face beneath his wide-brimmed hat, the man who went to meet the riders must have been Gaston, Father's "second in command" as he called him. I had met him several times when Father and I had walked to the market. He was a small man with green eyes that darted all around, as if he were noticing every detail about his surroundings. But where was Father?

"This purse is payment for the munitions and weaponry you have brought us," the middle rider said in an accent that I'd never heard before. "We and the Maid are most pleased with Henri's delivery, but we need threefold more, especially of cannonballs. Deliver them to us as soon as possible. This purse also contains a partial payment in advance for such a shipment. Can you oblige us?"

"Gladly," Gaston replied with a bow. The three riders wheeled their horses around and rode off, raising a cloud of dust. My head spun. Father was selling arms to Jeanne the Maid! I suddenly remembered the smell of sulfur in his warehouse and realized it must have come from munitions he had stored there. And I remembered when I saw him last that he believed he had found a way to end his debts forever. Was his secret that he was a weapons procurer for Jeanne and the dauphin?

Father's crew cheered as Gaston walked back to them, grinning broadly and thrusting the moneybag toward the sky. "Henri was right," he shouted. "Jeanne the Maid is a lucky talisman. She'll make us all rich."

"By God's heart, she protected us too, just like Henri said she would," one of the men shouted.

"And she helped us escape from those Burgundian spies," another added, raising the flask of wine. "Our heads would have been impaled on posts if not for her."

As the men grew quiet, the image of Father's handsome face frozen in a mask of death filled my mind.

"Let us not forget something just as important. She turned Henri's luck at dice around," one of the men joked. I suspected he did so to lift the somber mood. "Now that was a true miracle. Remember how it was before we started working for her . . . that night in January when he lost everything but the shirt on his back?"

"He was so drunk he could hardly stand," Gaston recalled, laughing, "but he kept singing and dancing with the whores."

"He was somewhat lucky that night," another man countered. "He got the one with the big breasts."

They burst into laughter as my cheeks blazed. So this was how Father comported himself on his journeys? While he was away buying weapons and gambling and wenching, Ameline had died, leaving me to save Charlotte and myself from slavery. He had abandoned us when we needed him the most.

Disgusted, I watched Gaston distribute coins to the men who milled about him like eager children. I started to leave, but a voice within me clamored, *Wait, maybe these men could help you.* Father had betrayed me and planned to sell me in marriage, but I needed his protection from the moneylenders. His crew could take me to him.

"Charlotte," I said in a low voice as I tethered Fleabane to a tree, "I'm going to ask those men for food. Stay with Fleabane and take care of her for me. Promise?"

She nodded, rubbing her belly. "Bring me some of the chicken."

Tucking my hair underneath my hood, I waited for all the men to be paid before emerging from the forest. I blinked in the bright sunlight. I felt vulnerable out in the open and looked all around to make sure none of the soldiers were close by. A band of them was picking broad beans in a field across the road, too preoccupied by hunger to notice me.

I headed straight for Gaston, calling his name in the most confident male voice I could muster. Father's men turned to me, their mouths agape. His brow furrowed in puzzlement, Gaston rose to his feet and strode toward me. "How do you know my name, boy?" he asked in his deep voice, standing so close that I could see the chicken grease on his hands.

"I'm Felise, Henri's daughter," I whispered. "Could you take me to my father?"

His eyes opened wide as they darted over my features, so like my father's, and his ragged tunic. "But why are you away from Troyes and dressed in Henri's old clothes?" he asked.

I quickly told him about the moneylenders but decided to talk face-to-face with Father about Thibaut and the tanner. And Ameline. "Take me to him at once," I commanded, confident that he would obey his leader's daughter.

Gaston scowled as he shifted his weight and glanced over at

the men, who were murmuring among themselves. "By God's jaw, why did you have to find us, girl?" he muttered. "I have enough problems without adding a runaway girl to the pile. Wait here while we decide what to do." He strode over to the men as I clenched my fists behind my back. He thought of me as a nuisance, a mere girl, but if he tried to get rid of me without giving me what I wanted, I would threaten to tell Father.

I tried to overhear them, but they were talking too softly. After a few minutes, Gaston returned, carrying food and a moneybag, which he thrust at me. "Here, you can have these, but we can't take you to Henri. The Burgundian spies lurk everywhere along the road, lying in wait to kill us all. Even you."

This time I imagined my own head on a stake, but I quickly dismissed it as I straightened my back to stand as tall as I could. "I don't need to travel with you and the men. The spies don't know who I am, and they'll take me for a beggar boy. They would have no reason to harm me."

Gaston's brows lifted. "I see that you have a whit of your father's daring," he said. "But I can't let you go to him alone either. He would never forgive me if I caused any harm to come to his daughter."

"If you won't take me to Father, take me to a convent or another safe place."

"We couldn't risk taking you with us, even as far as the nearest town with a convent," he insisted, folding his arms across his chest. "Listen, your best refuge and your best chance to be reunited with your father is to continue traveling with the army. God willing, he and the rest of us will deliver the war supplies to the dauphin by early next month. In the meantime, I'll tell him about you. If he doesn't find you traveling with the army, he'll go at once to the moneylenders and pay your ransom."

"But where is Father?" I asked again. It seemed as if he had been swallowed up in a hole in the earth.

"I can't tell you that," he replied, a look of fear crossing his face. "God willing, may we both survive until we meet again."

Seven

North Star

July 7, 1429

It wasn't even midmorning and already I was drenched in sweat. The still, dusty air smelled of vomit and unwashed flesh. Worst of all, I was hungry again after two days of gorging myself on Gaston's food. My belly ached from a breakfast of raw berries and hard grapes.

I scanned the same fields I had seen the first morning after I ran away. Then they had been thriving and well-tended, ripening sheaves of wheat in the hot sun. Now they were trampled and stripped of every edible part. The terraces of grapevines farther up the hills, where I'd first met Jeanne the Maid, were denuded of the hard green fruit. Not a single rabbit hopped upon the meadow in the dawn. The soldiers and bands of sick people had roasted every one. We weren't scorchers, but in our hunger, we had picked the land clean and left the bones to dry in the sun.

I had slept little during the past few days. Last night someone stole food from a widow traveling with her servant and sick daughter. It was the last of her food—a good supply of dried fruits and walnuts—after which I too had lusted. Other thefts happened in the night, and rapes. Thank God, the men took me for a boy and shunned Charlotte altogether. Only the lepers refrained from turning to prey upon one another. The alms they begged for along the road sufficed. Yesterday, for the first time, I had accepted their offering because, fearing the moneylenders, I hadn't dared to enter Saint Florentin to buy food when the army marched triumphantly through the town. The lepers had speared a loaf of bread on a long stick, so as not to touch it with their hands, and left it wedged between the branches of some trees for us to take.

The leper woman with the exposed cheekbone died yesterday. Before we set out on the day's journey, the other lepers buried her in the shade of a giant beech tree. Charlotte and I were the only people without the disease to watch the ceremony from afar. The lepers wept for the woman and called her "Sister," which stirred my sorrow for Ameline.

Seated on Fleabane behind me, Charlotte pressed against my back. The mare plodded along the dusty road, her hooves settling into a rhythm, and my head began to nod. A shout made me suddenly alert, and I watched as a messenger on horseback approached, his mount draped in the dauphin's colors—green, red and white.

"We will reach Troyes by late afternoon," he cried to the band of sick people and their families. Rubbing sleep from my eyes, I tried to absorb this news. The army was traveling north to Reims where the dauphin would be crowned king. Troyes was a day's journey south of Reims and we would pass it on the way, this very afternoon. André and Thibaut had probably hired men to look for me among the soldiers. I drew Father's hood over my forehead and tucked my hair behind my ears, then hid Charlotte's hair too.

"The Duke of Burgundy and his men refuse to open the gates," the messenger continued. "The dauphin and the Maid will lay siege to the city!"

The sick people and lepers roared their approval while I stared at the messenger in disbelief. If my town, my home, were besieged, what would happen to Mama's friend Anes and my teacher, Michel . . . and to the tanner? A sick feeling erupted in the pit of my belly.

When we stopped to water the horses at midday, a man whose face was splotched with a purple birthmark joined the lepers. He cast furtive glances at my satchel, and I clutched it tightly. He would never get his filthy hands on Gaston's money. I grabbed Charlotte and helped her quickly onto Fleabane. Once seated on her, I set her to a trot, leaving him behind in the dust.

I rode to the front of the caravan of sick people and glanced back to make sure the man with the birthmark hadn't followed. I chose to ride next to a peasant family and their five children. The mother's prayers for her deaf son drifted toward me from their mule wagon. She believed that the Maid was a unicorn in the form of a girl. I understood why the woman thought of Jeanne as a magical creature. I wondered if I too would have seen her in that light, had I not first known her as an ordinary person who was kind enough to help a stranger on the road.

By midafternoon, I spotted the walls of Troyes rising up across the meadow. It seemed a very long time since I had left, and yet it could not have been much more than a week. This was the same meadow I had crossed that first moonlit night, only now it looked completely different, dry and barren and trampled. Dismounting, I led Fleabane deep into a poplar grove. All around me, the sick people talked excitedly about the siege of Troyes, their words causing my concern to grow by the hour.

Late in the day, the bells of the town began to toll. Too loud and furious to mark the hour, the bells surely rang to warn of the approaching army. Charlotte and I hid in the grove while most of the sick people gathered on the meadow to watch what was about to happen and pray that the Maid would lead the army to victory over Troyes.

"Are the bells for a wedding?" Charlotte asked, looking up from the new doll she was making. She had developed a rash on her face, and it was growing worse. Yesterday it had been a fine sprinkling of red bumps, and today the bumps had melded together into deeper red blotches. She complained that the rash itched and had drawn blood from scratching it. I feared it might be leprosy.

"No," I replied, not wanting to tell her that our town was on the verge of siege.

She knew something was wrong anyway and buried her face in my tunic. I wanted to wrap my arms around her, but I didn't dare, for fear of the rash.

Amid the tolling of the bells, a crowd poured out of the gate of Saint Quentin, the very gate by which I had fled. Peering through the trees, I saw mostly women and children pulling carts and driving dogs, pigs and chickens along with them. Their cries rose over the bells as they swarmed onto the meadow. I strained my eyes to see if I could recognize Michel or Anes among the townspeople gathered there, but there were so many of them, and they were too far away. I didn't dare go to the meadow to find them and let them know that I was safe. My throat tightened.

In the gathering twilight, the dauphin's soldiers carried logs and kindling brush to the wooden gate.

"There's Jeanne the Maid," shouted the father of a blind boy camped near me. I craned my neck to see her, but too many soldiers blocked the view. All that was visible was the green and blue of her banner flapping in the wind.

"More logs there," she commanded in her powerful voice, "and over here too."

The families of the sick applauded her. "Burn the traitors of Troyes!" they chanted in unison.

The girl who had risked danger to help Charlotte and me and who had inspired a crowd to pray with great reverence was about to set fire to my town? She was going to burn the church and cedar trees next to the graveyard where my family was buried? I did not understand how she could act in the same manner as the scorchers whom she sought to defeat. I clutched my arms against my chest.

Shouts burst out from atop the wall where dozens of men were gathered, wearing the royal blue of the Duke of Burgundy.

They were setting up cannons and pitch and barrels of oil that they would soon set afire and drop onto the dauphin's men below. Was Georges among them? I prayed not.

All afternoon, both sides continued their preparations for battle, hurling curses and insults at each other as they worked. At dusk, a trumpet suddenly blared. Carrying torches, a band of the dauphin's men entered the gates. All the preparations for battle ceased and the jeering at the wall quieted.

The families of the sick people were abuzz with speculations about what would come to pass. A siege or a truce? No one knew. The bells rang intermittently as the sun dipped low in the sky. Children from the families of the sick played in the stream, splashing and shoving one another. Their mothers sat on the bank, facing the wall and watching as I did. A group of old men passed a flask under a walnut tree, wagering on what would happen. A breeze stirred the sultry air, and the stench of sour wine wafted toward me.

As the sky darkened, Charlotte fell asleep, her cloak wrapped tightly around her. Across the meadow before me, lanterns were extinguished, and everyone grew quiet. I couldn't find sleep for a long time, so worried was I about the impending siege.

———

Before dawn, a trumpet blasted. I bolted upright and sniffed the air furiously. There was no trace of smoke. Near the gate of Saint Quentin, a man carrying a torch shouted for everyone to gather round. Dozens of guards in the dauphin's colors pushed their way onto the meadow with lances and spears.

People rose quickly from their pallets and hurried toward the messenger. I didn't dare risk someone from Troyes recognizing me, so I stayed in the forest, hoping to hear the news. Charlotte huddled sleepily next to me.

"People of Troyes!" a messenger shouted. "God has decreed that no blood will be shed this day. The Duke of Burgundy has surrendered; he and his men have fled Troyes. Charles the Dauphin reclaims Troyes. Our rightful ruler and his army will ride in triumph through the streets."

"Thank God," I said. The supporters of the dauphin threw their arms around each other and cheered while the Burgundian women and old men booed.

"Your rightful lord commands the Burgundian garrison to disband!" the herald thundered. "Do not fear, he pardons you for your forced loyalty to the enemy. Each man must sign an oath of loyalty or leave at once!"

I hugged my arms against my chest, remembering Georges's fervent hatred of Jeanne and the dauphin on the day of the riot. What would he do now?

What would I do? Charlotte and I watched the first rays of sun filtering through the trees and sparkling on the stream. I didn't know how long the dauphin's army would remain in Troyes. I wanted to continue traveling with the families of the sick, but we needed food. I didn't dare go out on the meadow, as food purveyors from Troyes were setting up stalls where lines were already forming. And I doubted I could trust one of the women traveling with the sick to take my money and buy me food. Nor could I journey alone in broad daylight along the main road.

I trembled, fighting back tears. I would have to leave tonight hidden under the cloak of darkness. I packed our things onto Fleabane's back. She had no means to complain, but I knew she was hungry too. If only I could risk letting her graze on the meadow with the other horses and mules. "Let's go, Charlotte," I said, forcing myself to sound cheerful. "We'll ride along the stream for a ways and see if we can find some grass for Fleabane and berries for us."

"I don't want any more berries," she whined, patting her empty stomach. "I want chicken and cheese and bread."

"We'll have some soon," I promised, my voice faltering as I helped her climb onto Fleabane's back.

I led the mare along the stream, heading away from the meadow and looking for ripe berries amid the foliage. I didn't know where this stream led, but I hoped it would eventually take me to a road.

I found a grassy patch and stopped for Fleabane to graze. While I searched for ripe berries, I spotted a pair of bone dice on top of a tree stump. Behind it was a pile of clothes, a man's and a woman's. I heard rustling and the crackling of branches and drew back, my heart pounding. A bare arm holding a knife parted the foliage. Barthélemy's head protruded out.

His eyes were narrowed with suspicion, but when he turned to Charlotte, a look of recognition swept over him. His gaze returned to me. "It's my lucky day, Felise," he said, grinning. "Thanks to you, I'll soon have more money for gambling."

"Please, Barthélemy, don't tell André," I pleaded, barely finding my voice.

"I'll keep your secret for a hundred livres tournois," he bargained.

"I only have a little money, but I can get the rest of it soon."

"Not good enough," he sneered.

He reached for his breeches, but they were too far away. I grabbed them and mounted Fleabane more quickly than I had ever done before. Charlotte gripped my waist, screaming for me to save us from the bad man.

"Damn you, Felise!" Barthélemy cursed, his voice coming from close behind as I urged the mare forward. But the sand made it difficult for her, and I veered her into the stream where the bottom was firmer.

Dodging rocks, I maneuvered Fleabane a good way down the stream before I dared to look around. Barthélemy was running in the sand a stone's throw behind and gaining on me, without a stitch of clothing. I jerked my head away from the sight of his manhood, but it burned itself into my mind's eye. It was the first time I had ever seen a naked man.

He splashed through the water toward me. At the desperate flicking of my reins, Fleabane set out as fast as she could, Barthélemy in close pursuit. I felt him tugging at Charlotte, trying to pull her off Fleabane's back.

A force seized me, a power unlike ever before. "You'll never take her!" I screamed. Charlotte screamed too as I urged Fleabane even faster.

An open knoll lay beyond the left bank ahead. I veered Fleabane toward it and commanded her to gallop as soon as her hooves could find firmer soil. We crossed the knoll, heading for a path in the forest beyond. "I'll find you and claim the reward!" Barthélemy shouted, his voice farther away now. Still I could hear his resolve.

I fled to the west, taking the narrowest footpath I could find along the main road to Reims. The path wended its way through a pine forest. The sun beat through the thin canopy formed by the trees' needles, and my tunic was soon soaked in sweat. By dusk, the muscles of my neck were knotted with pain from turning around so often to see if Barthélemy was still pursuing me. The only people I passed were peasants walking or riding mules in the opposite direction toward the main road. In their coarse accents, they talked eagerly of going to Reims for the dauphin's crowning. Their anticipation—that they might catch a glimpse of Jeanne de Domrémy—worked to my advantage. They hardly lifted their broad-brimmed hats to notice me.

It was dusk when we arrived at a village. I saw no one, and judging from the savory smells that filled the air, I realized that the villagers were already in their hovels eating supper. My mouth watered. I grasped my purse, feeling Gaston's coins nestled in my palm. If only I dared to knock on a door and buy food for Charlotte and me.

"Good smells," Charlotte moaned against my back. She had

dozed most of the day and her face looked worse. I had to get her to a healer soon.

I tethered Fleabane to a pear tree at the orchard's edge. At once she lowered her neck to graze on the grass below.

"Wait here," I told Charlotte after I helped her down and loosened the saddle. "I'm going to get something for us to eat."

I crept to a barnyard and heard the clucking of chickens in a rough wooden coop. Reaching through a crack, I felt around for a hen. I had never wrung a chicken's neck before, but I would do so tonight and pluck its feathers and roast it for Charlotte and me. Or eat it raw if necessary.

The hen fled from her nest, ruffling her feathers, and pecked at my hand. I withdrew it. How could I think of killing her when I knew how much it would upset Charlotte? I would bring her eggs instead. Groping around inside the coop again, I searched but found only one egg.

A door slammed and I froze in the shadows of the coop. "Come here, Graykin," a child's voice called, "I have your supper."

Through the chirping of crickets, I heard a cat meowing and the door closing as the child went back inside. I crept closer to the cat, keeping in the shadows of the hovel. I was going to eat from a cat's dish, one that the goodwife of the house never cleaned. A dish that rats and insects scurried through.

Crouching down, I listened carefully and grabbed the bowl. I gulped some of the broth so it wouldn't slop over the sides. It was still warm and flecked with beans and meat. Resisting an urge to gulp the whole bowlful, I crept back to Charlotte.

"Supper," I whispered when I reached her.

"Did you bring egg pie with cheese?" she asked, her voice sounding hopeful.

"No, but we'll have a pie soon, when we get to Reims." I tried to sound cheerful, but my voice broke.

Setting the bowl on the ground, I broke the egg into the broth and used my knife to stir it in. "Egg soup," I said, holding the bowl close to her mouth.

She gulped most of it. "It's good," she said, smiling at me in the moonlight. "Have some too."

Her kindness brought tears to my eyes. Wiping them away, I finished the soup and crept back to the hovel with the cat's bowl. When I returned, we walked Fleabane deeper into the pear orchard where I tethered her again. I gripped a long stick that I had found earlier and leaned against a tree nearby with Charlotte clinging to me. The stillness unsettled me—I had gotten used to the company of the sick and their families. The night was always filled with coughs and moans and babies' crying. Now all was quiet save for the shifting of Fleabane's hooves, Charlotte's soft breathing, and the hoots of an owl.

I dozed until a wolf's howl awakened me. Quickly tightening the saddle, I woke Charlotte and hoisted her back on the mare. Once I had remounted, I urged Fleabane toward the road again and scanned the sky looking for the North Star, the brightest star in the Big Dipper. "If you are ever lost," Father had once said as we gazed at the stars together, "use the North Star to find true north."

Eight

The Rose Window

July 16, 1429

That night was the only one we were lucky enough to find eggs and soup. For the next five days, we lived on berries and water, moving like knights on a chessboard as we made a crisscross path northward to Reims. We hid deep in the forest during the day, resting for the nights of riding. I considered swapping Fleabane for another horse in one of the pastures we passed, but she had kept us out of danger so far, and I had grown used to riding her.

During the long hours of daylight, I watched for Barthélemy as long as I could keep my eyes open. But the only people I saw from my daily hiding places were peasants traveling northward and clogging the main road. Even at a distance, I could tell that they had eyes only for Reims, where they hoped to see the newly crowned king and his maiden warrior. At the dawning of the fifth day, I finally saw the cathedral spires of Reims rising from the plain before me. I wanted to gallop into the city at that very moment but decided to wait until sundown. Then the people in Reims wouldn't be able to see us very well, and Charlotte and I could slip inside the gate among the crowd. I tethered Fleabane in my accustomed hiding place, a ways into the forest along a rivulet, and helped Charlotte down. After taking off the satchels, I tumbled onto the earth, exhausted in every part of my body, my stomach rebelling noisily from eating any more raw fruit.

"Stay where you can see me and Fleabane," I told Charlotte. "I'm going to take a nap."

"I'll watch out for the bad men," she said as she wandered toward a berry vine. She hummed in a voice that was a shadow of what it used to be, her face raw in the rising daylight. I had given up on trying to stop her from scratching it.

This very evening I would buy her a salve. I closed my eyes and remembered Father's tales about Reims. Maybe I would buy roasted chicken at the inn where he liked to stay. It was called the Golden Lion, which had prompted him to roar like a lion when he'd entertained Charlotte and me with his stories long ago. This very day, I might see with my own eyes the remains of ancient Roman baths hidden under the cathedral plaza and the statue of the smiling angel in one of the front portals. Father said that the winged angel had smiled directly into his eyes, its frankness startling him. The angel's arm bent upward, and his hand was clenched in a tight fist.

I drifted off to sleep and dreamed of the angel, who filled me with hope . . .

A noise awakened me, and I rose to my feet, grabbing my knife and looking for Charlotte. She lay on the ground asleep, berries staining her face, but Fleabane was gone. The noise that had awakened me was a loud splash. The mare was crossing the rivulet. Her rope, which I thought I had secured carefully, dangled down her flank. With a loud neigh, she galloped down the road, heading toward the city.

"Come back!" I shouted, but she kept going. I seized Charlotte by the arm and pulled her to her feet. "Help me catch Fleabane!"

"Come back!" she echoed my cry. Throwing the satchels over my shoulder, I grabbed her hand, and we ran after the mare as fast as we could, but my heart sank as she disappeared into the crowd on the road to Reims. Pushing my way through the people, I caught a glimpse of the mare's mottled coat.

"Fleabane!" I screamed, bolting toward her with Charlotte in tow.

A herald rode by, announcing that the army would soon arrive. The stewpot of noises boiled over: trumpets blaring, horses neighing, everyone cheering for Jeanne and the dauphin. Over the din, every church bell of Reims tolled in frenzied joy.

I was so close to the city that I could see the townspeople of Reims crowded along the parapet, cheering for the Maid with drunken hoots. I collided with a man who cursed me as I surged forward and scanned the crowd, hoping for another glimpse of Fleabane. A man across the street pointed at me, shouting words that I couldn't hear over the crowd. He must have known about the reward and that meant others would too. I ran faster.

"Why such haste, boy," another man called when I passed. "The dauphin isn't here yet—by God's eye, that's a half-wit. You must be the girl they're looking for!"

I sprinted along the edge of the crowd, panic spurring me onward. "Grab the half-wit," someone shouted from behind.

I jostled my way through the city gates, passing a caravan of mule carts. Our pursuers were surely close, but their shouts merged with the noisy revelers clogging the main street of Reims. Ahead of me, the spires of the cathedral rose above the crowd. Once, in the marketplace of Troyes, I had seen a thief run inside Saint Madeleine's Church to avoid being put in the stocks. Sanctuary in the cathedral was my only hope.

"Almost there, Charlotte," I panted. Her eyes were wide with terror and her face bright red from running, as well as from the rash. But she managed to keep up with me.

"Long live our true king!" people chanted as we squirmed through the crowd.

"There they are!" a man yelled close by.

Charlotte screamed as another man grabbed her by the hair. I tried to yank her away, but his grip was too strong. His gaze was fixed on my hair; my hood was down. "A girl with blue eyes and dark hair and a redheaded idiot—there's a reward for the man who finds the two of you," he crowed, sweat dripping down his bald head. "Come with me and I won't hurt the half-wit."

I started to drop the satchels and reach for my knife, but Charlotte's red face inspired me.

"Look at her face!" I shouted pointing at Charlotte's rash. "That's leprosy. I have it too on my arms and legs."

"God save me," he gasped. He released Charlotte's hair, staring in horror at his hand.

Grabbing Charlotte, I bolted out of his reach toward the cathedral, which rose like a mountain of ash-colored stone with wing-shaped buttresses. With a burst of speed I reached its plaza, searching for a door to get inside, but the crowd blocked my view. Everyone's gaze was lifted upward to the men on scaffolds who were hanging a purple tapestry embroidered with gold fleurs-de-lis. Something to my right caught my eye, a blur of coppery feathers burnished in the sun. A huge bird, a hawk, flapped its wings above the crowd. Surely it was a good omen. I followed it around the corner of the cathedral to the front facade and stood before the main door as the hawk soared to a niche behind a gargoyle.

I pulled on the door's iron handle and opened it. No one followed us inside because everyone on the plaza was too consumed with celebrating the coronation to think of prayers. For now, I had outrun my pursuers, but they could burst into the nave at any moment.

Charlotte and I hurried past the holy water font toward the altars. "Let's look at the pretty colors," she begged, pointing at reflections of the stained-glass windows that drifted across the columns.

"We can't. The bad men will seize us."

She whimpered but kept running with me until we reached the Virgin's altar, a smaller altar to the right of the main one. We collapsed on the floor behind the side that was most hidden in shadows, panting to catch our breath.

The main door creaked open, and the noise of the crowd rushed into the quiet nave. Pressing my hand to Charlotte's mouth, I listened as footsteps echoed in the vast space. They were those of a single person. Whoever it was strode toward the front of the cathedral. Had the man who seized Charlotte realized my ruse and followed us here? While straining to see who it was, I unsheathed my knife and held it tightly to stop my hand from trembling.

Georges the Tanner hurried toward the main altar. I drew in a breath to steady myself. As he came closer, I could see that his beard had grown, and dark circles rimmed his deep-set eyes. Mud splattered his tunic and breeches. With a twinge of guilt, I realized that he had probably been traveling in search of me. But had some other matter plagued him as well?

I heard voices at the main altar and shifted my position so that I could see. A group of priests and acolytes carried prayer books and candles to the altar, talking excitedly about the coronation ceremony on the morrow and what duties would be assigned to each of them.

"You should hold the archbishop's train," one of them insisted. "I'll take his staff when he anoints the dauphin."

Another priest started to protest, but the tanner interrupted him. "I must receive the sacrament of penance," he pleaded as he stood in front of the altar. "Would one of you hear my confession?"

The priests stared at him in silence. One of them stepped forward toward him. "We have no time to hear your confession now," he said coldly. "Return after the coronation. Interrupt us no more until then."

"Please, I am in great need to confess," the tanner begged.

"Your soul will have to wallow in the filth of sin for another day," the priest growled and turned back to the altar. He and the others resumed their discussion about the ceremony as if the interruption hadn't happened.

The tanner wheeled around in the shadowy light, his face

suffused with anguish. Without my bidding, I felt a wave of pity for him. What sin had he committed?

He slowly descended the altar steps, his head down, and then the Virgin's altar blocked my view of him. I quietly moved around Charlotte and peeked out the other side.

He was setting his leather satchel on the floor. I was close enough to see the trademark stamped on it, a cedar from which oil was extracted and rubbed onto animal hides. He straightened his back, his eyes turned slightly toward me, but he wasn't looking at me. Something straight ahead riveted him. A smile of wonder like a child's crossed his face, diminishing his torment.

His wonder resonated in me, and I knew, at least for a brief moment, that he had been returned to himself. I followed his gaze and my mouth opened in delight at the sight of the Grande Rose window fully illuminated in the late afternoon sun. Charlotte shifted her position to see it too, her eyes as wide as mine.

After a journey to Reims, Father told me how joyous he had been to see this window for the first time. He had explained that the window was called the Grande Rose in contrast with a smaller rose window below it. He said that the beauty of the Grande Rose, not vespers, had drawn him away from a tavern and into the cathedral late one afternoon, just in time to see the window ablaze with brilliant colors.

Father's story had inspired pictures in my mind, but now they came to life before me. The blues and reds of the window transformed into a living watermark of a rose, wrought by the union of sunlight and glass.

Georges stood very still, his wonder illuminated by the Grande Rose. I gripped Charlotte's shoulder. No longer would I flee from him. Letting go of her, I crept out from behind the altar. He didn't see me. I started to call him just as the main door was flung open and a group of men rushed inside. "I'm sure they're in here," a voice shouted. I darted back behind the altar, recognizing the voice of the man who had grabbed Charlotte.

"How can you be so sure?" another man demanded. "We lost sight of them. They could be anywhere."

"Just trust me for once."

The men's footsteps echoed in the nave as they ran toward the front. I pulled Charlotte with me to the back of the Virgin's altar and shrank into the shadows. Panic shot through me as I cupped my trembling hand against Charlotte's mouth.

"How dare you disturb God's peace?" a priest at the main altar thundered.

My pursuers ignored him and strode closer to the place where the tanner stood. "Did you see anyone in here?" one of the men demanded. The urgency in his voice made my face break out in sweat.

"No, I am alone," the tanner replied.

"How long have you been here?" another man asked.

"Only a few moments," the tanner replied. "Whom do you seek?"

Tell the tanner about me—then he'll know that I have been sighted in Reims. I urged my pursuers silently.

"An urchin who stole money from us," a man with a deep voice quickly lied. I pressed my lips together.

"And who may have given me leprosy," spluttered the man who had grabbed Charlotte.

"You're just a gullible fool," another one snarled as their footsteps grew louder, three or four of them all together. Charlotte and I could not escape from a group of that size—even if the tanner were to come to my aid. She huddled against me. Our hearts beat so loudly I was terrified that they could hear the sound.

Their footsteps stopped. The altar cloth made a swishing sound as they lifted it up. The only thing that separated us from them was a slab of marble that supported the altar down the middle. Would they dare to come around to the back, where only the priest was allowed to stand?

A Tale of Two Maidens

One of them knocked a heavy object, I guessed a candle-holder, to the floor. "Clumsy oaf," the deep-voiced man sneered. Someone else scrambled to pick it up.

A rustling sound came from behind me, and I froze. Someone was creeping toward me in the shadows. I reached for my knife, which lay on the floor beside me, but that would make too much noise. It was so dark back here that maybe the person hadn't seen me.

The cathedral bells began to toll and robbed me of my hearing. I had to see who the person was. Just then, I felt someone's breath on my ear. Terrified, I turned around.

A woman dressed in black was crouched down beside me. "Come with me," she spoke into my ear. Her words sent a ripple of fear and dread through me. Was she a leper?

Whoever she was, it was better to follow her than face my pursuers. She picked up the knife and satchels and rose to her feet, gliding silently through a tiny doorway. Charlotte and I tiptoed behind her, entering a small room, and the woman closed the door behind us. A lattice grill faced the altar. Through it, light and shadow crisscrossed the floor of the room, which contained only a pallet. I knew then who the woman was: an anchoress or a hermit who lived a life of silent prayer.

The bells ceased and through the lattice window I saw the priests gathered around the altar, their hands folded in prayer. Trembling, I listened to the men as they continued searching for me. They were so close I suspected that they were behind the Virgin's altar now, in the very spot we had just vacated.

"Let's divide up," one of the men barked to the others, ignoring the priests as they began to intone the vespers prayers. "Each of us will take a section of the nave."

It seemed like hours that they searched for me. At last their footsteps faded away, the door creaked open, and they left. Was the tanner still there? I peered out of the anchoress's grill and looked all around the nave. He was gone.

"No," I moaned, collapsing onto the floor and beating the stone with my fists, angry at God for snatching away this chance to be done with my journey and surrender at last. Didn't he know how exhausted I was from eluding pursuers and keeping Charlotte and me alive?

The anchoress touched my shoulder. I stopped beating the floor as my muscles tensed in fear. "Listen well, for I have good tidings," she said. "Your sister who died is at peace."

I sat up quickly. "How do you know?" I gasped.

Her eyes were closed and her head bowed. She showed no sign of having heard my question, so I asked again. She still gave no reply.

"Ameline," I whispered, my head dropping back to the floor. All the sorrow over her passing that I had crammed deep inside me rushed to the surface. I wept all through vespers, my tears pooling in the crevices of the stone floor. The priest swung the censer, filling the air with incense, a smell that brought back Ameline's funeral and made me cry even harder. Charlotte had been beside me then, just as she was now, her hand stroking my hair.

My tears subsided into sniffles and the heaviness drained away. Charlotte joined the priest in chanting the final vespers prayer, their song soothing as the pattering of rain.

Even after the priest left the altar, the anchoress remained deep in prayer. Someone knocked on the door of the cell. I bolted upright and crawled into the darkest corner, pulling Charlotte with me and praying that it was Georges and not my pursuers.

The anchoress returned from her prayers and drew in a deep breath as she opened the door. The candlelight illuminated a man holding a steaming bowl of soup and a loaf of bread tucked under his arm. "Two girls have taken sanctuary with me," she told him. "Please bring them supper too. And I need a salve for a rash on one of the girls' face."

"Yes, Holy Juliane," the man said with a bow.

It surprised me that she had noticed Charlotte's face, but I was too frightened to say anything. When the man returned with our supper and the salve, the three of us ate in silence. Charlotte and I gulped most of our beef broth and onions and sopped up the remainder with hunks of bread.

When we were done, I was filled with such relief as I had never felt before. Juliane dabbed the salve on a cloth and applied it to Charlotte's face. It smelled of chamomile and rosemary. Charlotte sighed in pleasure and then yawned. Juliane led her to a back vestibule with several other pallets, a pile of blankets, and a chamber pot. "For my guests," she said.

I realized how exhausted I was and considered lying on the pallet next to Charlotte. That way I wouldn't have to be alone with Juliane. I wished that she weren't dressed in black and that she would remove her veil so I could see her face. How did she know that Ameline was at peace—had she conjured up my sister's spirit? I touched my face, feeling the swollen flesh beneath my eyes, savoring the lightness of release within me.

Perhaps Juliane knew other things that would help me. I took a deep breath to steady myself and followed her to the outer cell. We sat on the floor next to each other facing the lattice window.

"Holy Juliane, you know that I am in danger," I ventured. "What should I do now?"

She didn't answer as she rocked back and forth. I could have reached out to touch her arm, but the thought of doing so frightened me. I recalled Father's tales of a holy woman who had floated to the rafters in a trance.

"Journey," Juliane muttered.

Just hearing the word made me shudder. "Is that all you can tell me?" I asked. A journey was the last thing I wanted: to take to the roads without a horse, once again starving, frightened, and alone, except for Charlotte. "Couldn't I stay here with you or go to live at a nunnery in Reims? I am an apprentice scribe, almost a journeywoman, and I could work to earn my keep. Please, you must protect me from the men who pursue me."

"Your journey is not for the seeking of refuge," she replied.

"Then what is it for? Where should I go?"

She closed her eyes and didn't answer. I wanted to shake her. She knew about Ameline . . . why wouldn't she tell me what I should do? She had given me shelter only to abandon me in her silence. My question echoed within me against my will. I crept back to a pallet beside Charlotte.

These past weeks, my only purpose had been to escape my captors and remain hidden. I had behaved like a wild beast being hunted. And now with my belly filled for the first time in many days and a pallet beneath my back, I could stop and think. I felt as I did sometimes during a chess game, when it was my move, and I didn't know what to do.

A noise startled me awake. I sat up quickly and knocked over an unlit candle, which rolled against the wall with a thud. The moonlight streaming through the lattice illuminated the cell enough for me to see that the anchoress and Charlotte weren't there. I leaped to my feet and opened the door. Moonlight shone on the black traceries and muted colors of the windows as I ran down the central aisle. "Charlotte," I called out, my voice and footsteps echoing in the cavernous nave.

I heard a song rising from somewhere at the back of the cathedral. Running toward the sound, I found Charlotte and the anchoress singing and walking hand in hand below the darkened rose window.

"I woke up and didn't know where you had gone," I scolded Charlotte. She and the anchoress both ignored me and continued singing. Juliane's low-pitched voice harmonized with Charlotte's high-pitched one and their song vaulted to the ceiling, filling the nave. It was hard to tell if Charlotte were asleep or awake.

She sometimes walked in her sleep, but she had never sung in her sleep before. I wished she were acting in her usual manner, comforting me with little gifts and taking joy in simple pleasures or even annoying me by being difficult.

The last notes of the song faded away, and Charlotte stretched her arms as if awakening from a nap. She turned to me with a grin. I hugged her tightly, but she wriggled out of my arms, distracted by a moonbeam shining on the floor. "Pretty," she exclaimed and ran to dance in its light, her body swaying slowly and her arms making moon shapes.

The anchoress's robes rustled as she joined Charlotte in her dance, imitating her movements. Charlotte giggled in delight, and Juliane smiled for the first time since I had seen her. She was younger than I had thought at first. Her veil slipped as she danced, allowing me to see her eyes at last. They too were crescent-shaped. My legs buckled as a feeling of wonder flooded me. I leaned against the stone wall to steady myself.

When their dance was over, Charlotte followed the moonbeam to the window through which it shone. I expected Juliane to follow her. Instead, she walked over to me, still smiling, and unaware that her veil had slipped back. I could even see her hair, dark and curly, with silvery threads here and there.

"Allow your companion to remain with me," she whispered. "She will be safe, and I will dedicate her to God. She will lighten my burden of praying alone for those in need and bring joy to our prayers. You can return to visit her whenever you like."

"No!" I started to walk toward Charlotte and take her away from the cathedral. And yet, in a way, Juliane's offer was the answer to my prayers. This was a safe place for Charlotte where she would be happy and well-fed, and no one would find her. I should have felt relieved, but instead the idea of accepting the offer brought an empty gnawing to the pit of my stomach. I was afraid to face the dark nights alone without her asleep beside me. I couldn't bear to continue on my journey, abandoned by everyone I loved.

"Can't I stay here too—to take care of her?" I asked.

"You are caring for her by leaving her with me," Juliane replied. "And as I told you before, this sanctuary is not for you."

I bowed my head, imagining the long days trapped in her dark cell like a coffin. Like the hawk, I needed to fly freely outside the cathedral. She was right.

"Let us ask her to choose," Juliane said.

"Don't you already know her answer?" Felise said.

She turned to me with a smile, and I noticed a dimple in her cheek. "I don't know everything," Juliane said.

I stood there trying to understand what was coming to pass. If Charlotte said yes, could I let her go? The gray light of dawn reflected against the windows on the east facade as I walked toward her. "Charlotte, would you like to stay here?" I asked, combing my fingers through her matted hair.

She looked up at me beaming. "Yes. God's house is pretty."

The rash was already beginning to heal, and her crescent eyes looked directly into mine, reassuring me in her own way of her love. I hugged her tightly as Juliane made the sign of the cross over the crown of her head. "We must return to the cell quickly," the anchoress said. "It's almost time for the coronation."

She had hardly closed the door when a group of men entered the cathedral, their voices raised in excitement as they approached the altar. They were dressed in mud-splattered cloaks. While Juliane settled into her prayers, Charlotte and I sat on a blanket, and I clasped her hand tightly. In a few hours, its plump softness would be only a memory. Already I ached for her to stay with me.

I tried to distract myself by watching what was taking place in the sanctuary. A man with a circle of hair shaved off the crown of his head placed a small silver vessel on the altar. Father had told me that this was the Sainte Ampoule, which held sacred oil that Saint Remi once used to baptize Clovis, the ancient king of the Francs. Ever since his coronation hundreds of years before, all French kings had been crowned at this very altar and had been anointed with this same oil. Even though the English had stolen other royal trappings—his crown, scepter, and orb—the sacred oil alone would suffice to render Charles our true king. If only Father were here to witness with us this moment our family had long awaited.

As the sun's rays coaxed muted colors from the gray stained-glass window above the altar, the organ filled the cathedral with joyous music that made the wooden grill vibrate. A crowd swarmed into the cathedral, their excited voices vaulting to the rafters. I tried to catch a glimpse of them, but only the altar was visible from the grill.

"Open the door," Juliane bade me. "Then you will be able to see better."

I did so and watched the crowd of noblemen and women who flocked into the cathedral, their robes threaded with gold and silver that sparkled in the sunlight. Over the organ music, a great cry rose up as peasants swarmed in the front door, shouting Jeanne's name. The guards struggled to hold them back. A few months ago, I would have done just as the nobles were doing now, pushing forward to get away from the filthy peasants. No longer. I had seen the destructive handiwork of the scorchers, and I remembered the day Jeanne had urged the sick peasants and their families to pray that our land would be set free of the English and their mercenary soldiers.

I understood now why she had nearly burned my town. She had fought for the peasants, not just for those of us more gently born. And these peasants had thrown their fierce loyalty to her and died for her cause. In their eyes, she was probably the one who should have been crowned this day.

From a side door, the archbishop processed to the altar wearing white robes and a pointed miter on his head and holding a jeweled scepter. Priests clad in snowy white surrounded him, and a tall man dressed in red, green, and white robes followed them. "Long live the Dauphin Charles," the crowd cheered, "soon to be our king!"

This gaunt man with hunched shoulders was the dauphin? I tried to convince myself that he looked deserving of a crown, but his chin quivered, and he rubbed his hands together as if he were trying to warm them. A short person emerged from the same door as the archbishop and came to stand beside the dauphin. At first, I thought it was his squire, but the peasants burst into applause for Jeanne and began a frenzied chanting of her name. It was the Maid, I realized, as she turned her head toward the altar. She didn't acknowledge the cheers as she stared at the crucifix, her lips moving in silent prayer. Her hair burnished in the candlelight, and she wore armor instead of flowing robes. She carried herself proudly, but the armor looked as if it weighed upon her small frame. She who fought to set our land free should feel as free in her clothes as everyone else did in flowing robes.

Her clothes didn't matter. Whether she dressed as a man or a woman, she had a presence that made her more powerful than any of the robed men around her, especially the dauphin.

The day Ameline had stood her ground with the moneylenders flashed into my mind. She had wielded power over them in spite of their brute force and threats. She had been like Jeanne, and she had shared Jeanne's courage and strength. I clasped my hands and stared at Jeanne's pale face, and I knew where my journey would take me now. To Jeanne.

She would help me just as Ameline would have done if she were still alive. I no longer needed help to survive; I had proven that I could do that on my own. But I did need Jeanne's help to be reunited with Father. Without Fleabane, I could no longer risk hiding behind the lepers. I would seek shelter from Jeanne until Father and his men returned with the weapons that she had enlisted them to buy. I would seek to be her friend.

As the Mass was over, the Archbishop of Reims lifted his arms heavenward, and a hush fell upon the crowd. The archbishop anointed Charles with the holy oil and placed a gold crown on his head, and a radiant smile lit Jeanne's face as tears streamed down her cheeks. My eyes too filled with tears of joy at her victory.

"Long live the king!" the people chanted at a deafening pitch. He and Jeanne turned and proceeded down the center aisle as the organ burst into joyous music. They left the cathedral, followed by the cheering crowd.

Too soon, the ceremony was over. I fought an urge to fold Charlotte in my arms, knowing that it would only make my leave-taking harder for us both. I savored my last glimpse of her kneeling beside Juliane, watching the priests as they waved the censers. She didn't even turn her head when I slipped through the door to the cell. It took every bit of strength for me to keep walking away toward the Grande Rose, the colors muted in the morning light.

Nine

Dance of Death

July 21, 1429

Jeanne and the man who guarded her entered the magistrate's house. The door slammed behind them. A groan of disappointment rose from the crowd gathered outside the house, but the clamors for Jeanne soon resumed.

"Pray with us, oh Holy Maid!" they shouted in unison. I joined them, hoping that our loud pleas would make her appear, just as she had once appeared among the lepers. After all, tonight was the fourth night after the king's crowning, and eight was Father's lucky number when he gambled. I closed my eyes as Father always did when he kissed his dice and invoked the lady of fortune. "Please, Lady Luck," I whispered, "give me a chance to speak with Jeanne at last."

The chant for Jeanne grew louder as more people crowded around the door. I pushed my way to the front and sniffed the aroma of roasting meat that rose from the magistrate's chimney. I clutched the last of Gaston's money, savoring the weight of the single franc, knowing that it would be gone after tonight.

The longer I smelled the meat, the more my hope waned. At the end of every day, my feet ached, and my stomach growled as I tried to reach Jeanne at the center of a vast crowd. But it was always an impossible barrier, and then she disappeared into an important person's house. She would sup on roasted meat tonight while I would gnaw on stale bread and sip water.

A week ago I had wondered what it was like for a girl from a small village to become famous and have constant attention. I had been certain that in a night or two, I would be able to ask her that question myself. I believed I would talk with her alone about matters of the heart, as I once did with Ameline.

I kicked a rock with my foot, berating myself for thinking it would be an easy matter to gain her ear. Why hadn't I stayed with the anchoress a while longer? This very evening, I could have eaten supper with Charlotte instead of being tormented by the smell of meat as I stood alone on a dusty street. My tears welled up again as they did every time I thought of her. She had filled a hollow place deep inside me that I did not know existed until she was gone. And now the hollow place was for me alone to bear.

The door to the magistrate's house opened, and a red-faced servant ordered us to disperse. "The Maid is supping with the magistrate and his family," he added. "He bids me to tell you that she won't appear tonight. Disturb us no more."

I had to speak with her. Something came over me born of desperation. "I have a message for her," I shouted, squirming my way toward the thin space between the open door and the frame. I thrust a foot inside the door, but the servant grabbed my tunic and shouted for a guard.

He emerged from the house at once, holding a lance. He thrust it at my chest, knocking my breath away. Gasping for air, I was pushed into the crowd, and someone grabbed me around the middle. "Foolish boy!" the man shouted. "The Maid would have come to the door if it weren't for you."

As I struggled to get out of his hold, he struck my face with his fist. I screamed and jerked my head away. He threw me to the ground and people kicked me all over my body. Writhing in pain, I clutched the satchel against my chest to shield myself from their blows. Somehow I managed to roll myself toward the wheels of the carts that lined the street at the edge of the crowd.

A woman pulled me to my feet and dragged me behind her cart, which blocked me from the crowd. "Go quickly," she urged.

Blood dripped into my mouth as I stumbled away and slipped into an alley. I made many turns as I climbed to the top of a hill where the street opened onto a deserted square. Panting, I drew a rag from the satchel and wiped the blood from my face. The flesh around my eye burned, and I longed to press a cool wet rag against it, but my flask was empty.

As I searched for a fountain, something brightly colored caught my eye. I wiped more blood from my face to see it better. I stood before a painting on a tavern wall, horrified and yet unable to wrench my eyes from it. The mural showed skeletons with worms crawling through their eye sockets. They held hands and danced across a field where the grim reaper clad in a bright red cape threshed grain. Father had told me about the *Danse Macabre*, the Dance of Death that he had seen painted on murals throughout the countryside.

I turned my gaze, but the image wouldn't vanish from my mind. It was an omen of what would happen to me. I would wander from village to village, following Jeanne until I died a beggar's death in a dark alley, with rats crawling over me and worms gorging themselves on my flesh. I would die alone, and Father would never know what had become of me. That night I spent the last of Gaston's money for a room as far as possible from the Dance of Death. Inside a cabinet there, I found a cracked looking glass and gasped at my reflection in it. My hair was matted, my face crusted with blood and dirt, and the flesh around my right eye swollen and bruised. A wild changeling had taken possession of my body. She, not I, had chosen to set out on this journey. She had made me leave Charlotte at the cathedral to dance in the moonlit nave, and she had engraved the tanner's image on my mind to torment me forever.

A Tale of Two Maidens

Through the rain, I could hear horses whinnying from a poplar grove, a piercing lonely sound. In a sudden gust, rain lashed against me. I pressed my hands to my face. "Jeanne, heal me," I whispered. "Make me whole again."

I had joined a caravan of mad people, too dispirited to care about catching their disease. The monks and nuns had gathered them from the forests where they had been exiled and were taking them to Jeanne to be healed by her touch. As a middle-aged nun gave me food and water, she gazed at me with pity. She must have taken me for mad. Maybe it was true.

Thunder rumbled through the forest, and the mad people on the cart in front of me screamed and waved their arms. One of them was a half-wit with dark hair, a short round woman like Charlotte. Charlotte was far away, while this woman who meant nothing to me stood close enough to embrace.

Shielding my eyes from the rain, I forced myself to keep trudging behind her. At the forest's edge, the monks hung blankets from low branches as a crude shelter. The mad people huddled together beneath it, their wails and screams rising up over the rain and thunder. With a blanket draped over my head, I stood apart from them and peered out at a meadow filled with dark shapes. Slowly I realized that it was a vast supply of cannons and war machines, maybe the same ones that Father and his crew had brought to the army. I consoled myself with the thought that I had made the right choice to journey here. I would be all the closer to Father and my dream for my future.

My spirits restored, I watched the rain taper off and the clouds scuttle away to reveal patches of blue sky and the sun's rays. Steam rose from the sodden earth. The sun's rays beat down just as they had before the storm, and I cast the soggy blanket aside. A trumpet signaled for the army to reassemble. Men in soaking wet clothes emerged from the forest to dry their horses and saddles and wring out blankets.

"Look!" someone shouted, pointing at something that I couldn't see from my vantage point. "A rainbow!"

Everyone around them stopped what they were doing to glance at the sky.

"A double one!" a man exclaimed.

I wanted to see the rainbow too, but I didn't dare go any closer to the soldiers. Even without Charlotte, they might see through my disguise. The news of the rainbow spread to men nearby, many of whom fell to their knees and made the sign of the cross. "An omen for victory!" they shouted.

The monks who tended the mad proclaimed that Jeanne had wrought this miracle. They turned toward the covered coaches where the king and his entourage had taken shelter during the storm. "Holy Maid, perform another miracle!" they cried. "Heal these mad people!"

"And me," I whispered.

"Look, she is coming!" a monk cried, pointing to a figure who strode toward us.

It was Jeanne. I stood there staring at her in amazement as the old man hobbled to catch up with her. How had she heard me when I hadn't even uttered my request aloud?

She headed toward the mad people, but the old man glared at us. "Holy Maid, you don't have time for these wretches," he scolded. "You must prepare to lead the march."

Jeanne stopped her forward motion and turned to face him. "Good squire," she said, "I will be only a moment."

"As you wish. I will see that your horse is ready." He sighed and took his leave. She strode faster toward the mad.

"Heal them, oh Holy Maid," one of the monks called again.

"Good Brother, I cannot," she replied in her clear voice. "Only God can. Let us pray for them. It is all that we can do."

She repeated almost word for word what she had said to the caravan of sick people a few weeks ago. She had led the king to be crowned, and yet she hadn't let that make her too proud. Just as before, she led us in prayer, but I was too excited to feel the reverence she inspired. I waited until she was done and pushed my way toward her. As she raised her bowed head, a mad man spit on her, hitting her broad cheek. She laughed heartily as she wiped it away with the sleeve of her tunic.

"You were right, Holy Maid," the monk shouted. "It is not God's will for them to be healed. But your healing touch will bring them peace in the days to come."

"Peace to all of us," she said quietly and turned to leave.

"Wait," I called, running after her, still not believing my good fortune. She turned toward me, smiling with the same compassion she had shown the rest of the mad people. "Good Brothers," she called to the monks. "Come and fetch this boy."

"Please help me," I whispered in my girl's voice.

Her dark brows lifted. "Wait," she told the monks, "I want to pray for this boy. I will send him back to you shortly."

"As you wish, Holy Maid," one of them replied.

Jeanne's gaze returned to me, her eyes narrowed in suspicion. "Who are you?" she asked. "One of those girls who pretends to be me?"

"No," I stammered, "I didn't even know there were such girls. Do you remember helping a girl who smelled like rose oil?"

"You are that girl?" she asked, her voice rising in surprise.

"Yes."

Her dark eyes bored into mine and I looked down, her scrutiny unsettling me. "It was night when I taught you to ride, but I do believe you are thinner," she observed. "How did you get that black eye and where are your aunt and Fleabane?"

Before I could tell her, drums beat, and a trumpet blared. "Soldiers of the king, return to the road!" a herald shouted.

"How can I help you?" Jeanne asked as we set out.

Before I could answer, her squire approached her, glancing disdainfully at me. "Your horse is ready," he told her. "Don't you remember what I told you about those seeking favors?"

"Yes, d'Amboise," she said. "I will meet you by the horses as soon as I make my rounds."

"As you wish."

I walked with her through the ranks of the army, and she rallied war captains and foot soldiers with the same good cheer. "The sun will soon dry your things," Jeanne proclaimed for all to hear. "If not, there are plenty of dry clothes and blankets in the supply wagons. Make haste. By sundown, we will be quartered in Vailly, and you will have a fine supper set before you."

The men applauded her as they assembled along the road. It still seemed like a dream that I was walking with Jeanne de Domrémy. A dark-haired noble called to her. I recognized him as the leader of the three nobles who had come to pay Father's men for the supplies. His fine wool tunic was drenched with rain, and he hobbled on one foot as he dumped water out of the other boot. "I see that you had the good fortune to stay dry," he said in his lilting accent.

"Well, at least one of us had the good sense to take shelter," she teased.

"Good Maid, I was calming your horse," he said, taking mock offense. "He was terrified of the thunder."

She bowed to him. "Thank you then, gentle Duke, for getting soaked on my behalf."

He bade her goodbye, and we took our leave. "Who was that?" I asked.

She smiled. "My friend, the Duke of Alençon. He taught me to ride my steed."

Last winter when rumors about her had circulated around Troyes, I'd wondered how she had learned to ride a war horse so quickly. I never guessed that I would know anything else other than rumors about the answer.

A Tale of Two Maidens

We skirted around branches that must have fallen during the storm. I was about to tell her about Father when the trumpet blared again. "What sort of work can you do?" she asked quickly, her eyes on the army before us.

"I am learning to be a scribe."

"The king already has a scribe," she told me. "He writes letters for me."

A feeling of pride swelled up within me. Not only was I taller than she was, but also I could write. "I could teach you how to form your letters," I told her.

Her lips pursed together. "I have far more important things to do." Her words shamed me into silence.

She stopped suddenly, her eyes fixed on a cluster of carts across the meadow. "Hersende the Barberess has need of a scribe. She is the only woman healer traveling with the king, and she will protect you from the men."

I shuddered, thinking of the leeches that barbers used to suck blood from their patients' arms. Just as we reached the barbers' caravan, a woman was wringing water from wet blankets off the side of a cart.

"Hersende the Barberess!" Jeanne shouted. "I must speak with you." Hersende looked up with a frown. She was short and round with silver-gray hair braided down her back. Her thick lips were pursed as her hands quickly squeezed out water. She wore a bloody apron over a gray work dress, with many small pouches dangling from a rope tied around her waist.

"Be quick," she muttered. "I have much work to do."

My mouth opened in surprise. I had expected her to be in awe of the holy Maid coming to see her, but Jeanne didn't seem to notice her rudeness as she went to confer with her. After speaking for a few moments, they approached me together. Hersende gently touched the swollen flesh around my eye. "No more getting into trouble now that you are with me," she warned. "You'll need a poultice for that."

Dance of Death

The trumpet sounded again, and Jeanne bade us farewell. She strode away while I stood there in a daze, trying to grasp what had just taken place.

I had succeeded in speaking with the Maid and getting shelter with the army, protecting myself from my pursuers. True, I hadn't expected to become a healer's servant and had no desire to tend to wounded men, but that didn't matter. Father would return soon. In my mind, I lifted my arms skyward and danced to the sun like Charlotte.

Ten

Gathering

July 24, 1429

Jeanne disappeared behind a group of mounted soldiers. "Get up on this cart now," Hersende barked, bringing me back to earth.

I obeyed at once. Rows of pallets lined the floor of the cart. Men with bandages over every part of their bodies lay upon them. Blood seeped through the white cloth. I turned away, sickened at the thought of the horrible wounds they hid.

Hersende strode over to me, reeking of garlic. "Don't be so faint of heart," she whispered harshly. "The Maid tells me you are a girl, and she wants me to protect you from the men. You must be like her and act with courage—like a man. Now, we must give you a boy's name."

"My name is Felise," I said, searching for a man's name that sounded like it. "I know—I could be called Philippe."

"Philippe," she repeated as she handed me a huge stack of wet blankets. "Wring these dry."

A captain shouted the order to depart, and soon our cart headed out along the rutted road. I had to hold onto the barrels to steady myself. Hersende leaned over one of the men to inspect his bandaged arm.

"The Maid says you are learning to be a scribe," she mused. "I have many remedies stored in my mind that are not yet on paper. Until the army of the king does battle again, you will be my servant and scribe. You will help me make a book of my remedies."

I bowed my head, suppressing a secret smile of delight. By my beautiful script, I would prove to Jeanne that writing was important.

Though early in the morning, the day was already sultry without so much as a breeze to stir the thick air. Underneath my hood, sweat dripped down my neck. With a mortar and a pestle, I mashed cloves of garlic to feed the cauldron of broth that simmered constantly over the fire. Hersende insisted that the wounded men drink a cup of it every day to ward off diseases. My hands reeked of garlic even after a vigorous scrubbing. Yet I didn't mind the garlic or the hard work from dawn to dusk or even the gaping wounds so much anymore. My work for Hersende helped me stop thinking about Charlotte and Father . . . and the tanner.

A shadow fell over me as Etienne the Barber, Hersende's husband, scowled at the mound of garlic. He looked like a bear with his thick black beard and black eyes.

"That is more than we will need in a week," he snarled.

"But, monsieur, your goodwife told me to prepare this whole basket." I looked for Hersende to support me, but she was tending to wounded men on the meadow.

He dumped the basket of garlic onto the table. "You will obey me, not her," he commanded. "Go to the meadow and pick enough of the yellow flowers—the dandelions—to fill this basket. Pick the flowers, stems, and leaves. Bring them to me at once."

"Yes, monsieur."

On the meadow, I set to work picking dandelions. When the basket was filled, I returned to the healers' trestle. Etienne had his arms folded across his barrel-shaped chest and stared angrily in the direction of Hersende. She had her back to him and was stirring the contents of the cauldron. "Enough of this garlic everywhere, woman," he bellowed. "You are wasting money and our servant's time. We need to prepare for battle."

I shifted my position, unsettled by the mention of fighting.

"I am not wasting anything. I too am preparing for battle," Hersende insisted. "Some of the men are coughing and sneezing. In Cerbuey near here, villagers are dying from a summer fever. The garlic will stave off sickness and strengthen the men for battle."

"I forbid it," her husband ordered.

Hersende clenched her jaw in defiance. "I will not obey you unless you have a better remedy."

She glanced at my basket of dandelions and her gaze darkened. "Husband, did you tell my servant to stop chopping garlic?"

"Yes."

"Philippe is my servant, not yours."

Their angry words snarled together, like the Burgundians and Dauphinists on our streets. I set the basket down and strode out of earshot of their argument. It stirred memories of Mama and Father arguing long ago about his debts. One of the reasons that Ameline wanted to remain a femme sole was that she believed most married people argued from dawn to dusk. Maybe it was true even if a man and a woman weren't married. The tanner and I had only talked one day, and we had set to sparring almost at once.

A loud cheer startled me. It rose from soldiers who greeted Jeanne as she walked across the meadow and made her morning rounds. She looked much the same as last time, only this time she wore a tunic made of pale blue wool. Soldiers thronged around her, talking and laughing as if she were their friend.

She had been eager to help me, but could she ever become my friend, sharing secrets with me as Ameline once did? I waved at her, but she didn't see me as she bade the men farewell and strode along the road. The barbers, who were still hurling angry words at one another, wouldn't miss me for a few more moments if I went to tell Jeanne about Father. I ran to catch up with her, calling her name.

She turned around and waited for me to reach her. I was too far away to see her face clearly, but I could tell that she wasn't smiling. Someone else called for her from farther down the road—the Duke of Alençon. She waved back at him, and I noticed something on her hand gleaming in the sun. It was a ring, a plain silver band that looked like a wedding ring. And yet everyone said she had chosen to remain a virgin as long as it pleased God.

"Who gave you that ring?" I blurted as soon as I reached her.

"My mother," she replied, quickening her pace toward the pen where the warhorses were corralled. Inside it the duke and another man were saddling a huge black stallion.

I walked faster to keep up with her, thinking of the amethyst ring that Mama had given me. It was far more valuable than the ring Jeanne's mother had given her, but of course I didn't mention this.

"Why have you come to see me?" she asked.

I bristled when I heard the impatience in her voice. "I think you know my father," I replied. "He is one of your arms merchants, Henri of Troyes."

Jeanne halted, turning to look at me in surprise. "You are Henri's daughter?"

"Yes."

"Do you know where he is?" she asked.

I shook my head and told her about seeing the rest of his merchant crew that day on the meadow.

"You must tell me if he sends you a letter," she said, her voice low with urgency. "Do you know where he secures his supplies of weaponry?"

"No. I wanted to go to him but his second in command said that it was too dangerous."

When we reached the pen, the duke and the other man were trying to calm the stallion. "Good morrow, Jeanne!" he called from a stone's throw away. "Are you ready for your lesson?"

"Yes, my good Duke!" she shouted.

"You still need lessons?" I asked.

"Yes. We could go into battle any day, and it is important to keep Midnight trained to my voice."

Again my stomach churned at the mention of battle, but her voice was steady, displaying no trace of fear. I wondered if she ever felt afraid during the hours before a battle.

"Where is your aunt?" she asked abruptly. "And Fleabane?"

I quickly explained what had come to pass, hoping she would not be angry at me for losing her horse. "I miss Charlotte very much," I concluded, my voice breaking as I spoke her name.

"Her song is with me still," Jeanne murmured, her eyes misted with tears as she looked toward the sun rising higher in the sky. When her gaze returned to mine, I saw that she had cloaked her sadness behind a look of resolve. "Remember," she said, "let me know as soon as you receive word from your father."

When the midday meal was done, Etienne carried the wounded men into their tents to rest. He and Hersende worked together quietly, and I couldn't tell whether they were still angry at each other. I didn't understand married people at all.

Hersende and I set to work at the trestle, which was shaded by an awning. Even in the heat of the day, she never grew sluggish as I did. She bustled about, pouring brightly colored liquids into glass vials and filling clay crocks with nasty-smelling pastes. She told me the name of each concoction and dictated the recipe. I copied them down and wrote labels that would later be glued to their containers. It was so hot that I had to keep wiping sweat from my hands to stop the ink from smearing. On a scrap of parchment, I struggled to figure out the spelling of a remedy called *sal ammoniac*.

"Don't trouble yourself so," Hersende chided, wiping her sweaty brow. "Just make your letters large and easy to read."

"What is this sal ammoniac used for?" I asked.

"It keeps pus-filled wounds open and draining," she replied, reaching for another crock containing a bright yellow paste. "When you are done with that label, make this one next. It's called *onguent des apôtres.*"

"I've noticed that men stop moaning when you put that ointment on their burns."

She gave me a rare smile. "It got its name because it has one ingredient for each of the Apostles. I am pleased that you are learning some things about barbering."

"Who taught you your craft, madame?" I asked.

"I will tell you the story, if you keep working," she replied, handing me a clump of fresh herbs. "Remember, laziness is the worst of the vices. Cut this mint."

I took out my knife, but she yanked it out of my hand. "By God's ear, don't ever let that rusty blade touch my medicines. Here, use mine."

She handed me a small knife with a sharp clean blade, and I started to chop the mint. "Too big," she instructed.

I cut it more finely. She grunted her approval before going on to her next task, spooning out goose fat into a small crock.

"My mother was a potter who died soon after my birth," she began, mixing in a bitter-smelling herb, "and my father was famous for his barbering skill. He wanted me to become a potter like her, but I had no desire to do so."

She paused to add chopped mint to the crock of goose fat. "When he wasn't looking, I would steal scraps of bandages so I could pretend to heal my dolls. As I grew older, I practiced real cures on cats and dogs and beggars in the market."

I tried to imagine Hersende as a child healer, but it was impossible.

"One Sunday in the spring, the mayor's servant knocked at our door. His master had terrible stomach cramps, and Father hastened to his bedside. Not an hour later, a rich man came to our house carrying a boy wrapped in a blanket. The child's eyes were closed, and he moaned in pain.

"We laid the child down on the bed in my father's shop. His leg was swollen to twice its size. The flesh was so taut that it looked as if bones and muscle and blood would burst forth from inside his body. I knew that some creature had bitten him, and I grabbed my father's thinnest knife. I found two puncture wounds that rose from a mound on the boy's calf, a sign of a snakebite. Just as I had seen my father do, I made a cross-shaped cut directly over the fang marks. With all my strength, I squeezed the poisoned blood out of his leg until the bedclothes were soaked."

Hersende paused, her gaze somber and far away. "I'll never forget the panic I felt at that moment. The boy's face had grown so pale that I thought I had killed him. I had never prayed as intently as I did then. I hoped the boy's father wouldn't notice my hand trembling as I poured a cupful of potion that Father used for snakebites.

"By nightfall when my father returned, the swelling had diminished, and the boy had fallen asleep. My father quickly inspected my work and turned to me, his face full of pride. He told me that he would have treated the snakebite just as I did.

"God forgive me," Hersende continued, her face aglow, "but I was so proud of my feat that I hardly slept that night."

Hersende's tale moved me so much I couldn't speak. Her calling to heal was like my calling to write. She must have a watermark too.

"Around that time, my father took Etienne as an apprentice, and we learned the healer's craft side by side. When I was sixteen, we were wed. A year later, my father died, and Etienne inherited his shop."

She paused to look at Etienne, who was carrying water to the wounded. "I know that my husband and I often spar with one another," she admitted, her sharp eyes upon me. "I see full well how uncomfortable you become when we do so. But you must realize that things are not always as they seem. Usually, Etienne and I have time to discuss our opinions, but a battle could take place any day now, and we have much to do. Our tempers are short. Even so, we are better healers working together than we would ever be on our own. My husband notices things that help me serve the sick and wounded better, and I do the same for him."

A partnership between a man and a woman was something I had never considered. I wanted to talk more of it, but Hersende stood up and wiped her hands on her apron. "We have been idle too long," she said briskly as she mixed up a concoction of mint and goose fat. Then she hurried over to get another crock and bade me to write a label for *verdigris*.

I shuddered at this medicine named for its power to turn green pus to gray. "How did you come to attend the king?" I asked, both to distract myself and to know more of her story.

Pride illuminated her wrinkled face. "One day, heralds came to the street of healers. On the dauphin's behalf, they were seeking healers to tend soldiers wounded in battle. My husband and I decided to serve, for we knew we would learn much about wounds."

She bowed her head and made the sign of the cross. "Heavenly Father, we have served our king at many battles in this long war," she prayed. "I have seen enough bloodshed. I beg you, let this maid end the suffering, once and for all."

Carts rumbled behind us—a mule train laden with many sacks. "Ah, the rest of the remedies that my husband and I purchased," Hersende announced. "Hopefully we have all that we need now to treat the wounded."

Hersende instructed the driver to lay the bundles in a pile next to the trestle.

"So many remedies," I murmured, thinking of how immense a battle must be.

"It is better to have too many than not enough," she said, surveying the packets. "We never know what course a battle will take. All we can do is prepare as many medicines as possible and provide the wounded with our best care. God forgive me for boasting, but we are among the best healers in this army. Do not tell anyone, child, but my husband and I are more skillful than the king's own physician."

"Then why do you not attend him?"

She snorted. "Kings falsely believe that physicians must be the best doctors because they attended university. We barbers do not attend. Not that it matters. Women cannot attend university anyway."

I nodded, remembering Father's tales of Italian women who were educated in secret, dressed as men.

"In truth, I am glad I did not attend," she declared. "The university would have served me no purpose at all. Learning Latin charms would hardly help me on the battlefield. Besides, physicians are priests and are therefore forbidden to shed blood. What good could they do when a leg must be cut off? Now, find that rusty knife of yours and help me untie these packages."

The next afternoon, I sat at the barbers' trestle cutting strips of cloth for bandages. Would they all be used in the same battle, and when would it take place? Hersende didn't know, but it seemed the captains drilled the soldiers longer each day.

Hersende rewarded me for my quick work by allowing me to practice writing whatever I wanted instead of just making labels for her remedies. She even gave me a blank gathering of parchment, eight leaves stitched together in the middle. I dipped my quill into the inkpot and set to work on writing a magnificent capital "G." How I loved the word *gathering*, for it made me think of gathering unruly thoughts into just the right words. As I practiced all my favorite capital letters, I thought about how much I was learning from Hersende. Not just about healing, but about her life. One day I would set her story down in writing. I would write a book that was a collection of stories about women, much like the Lady Christine's *Book of the City of Ladies* . . . about Ameline, Charlotte, Juliane the Anchoress, Hersende, and Jeanne. My excitement grew as I pictured my book covered in green vellum. It would be called *A Gathering of Women.*

Hearing footsteps, I noticed Jeanne striding toward the barbers' tents. I set my quill down, hoping that she had news of Father. I had expected him by now, and worry was starting to gnaw at me.

But instead of coming to me, she went to Hersende, who was simmering a foul-smelling concoction in a cauldron. "May I borrow your servant to write something for me?" she asked.

Hersende looked puzzled. "Why can't the king's scribe do so?"

"My king has need of him this afternoon, and I can't wait until the morrow."

"If the writing is done quickly. As soon as this purgative is ready, I will need Philippe's help."

As Jeanne walked over to the trestle, I took a deep breath to calm myself. I opened and closed my right hand and rubbed my thumb over my quill mark. Other than Hersende's labels and André's texts, I had never copied down a person's spoken words before.

Pulling out a sheet of Hersende's finest paper, I smoothed it on the trestle while Jeanne paced back and forth, a worried look upon her face.

"You haven't heard from Father, have you?" I asked.

"No." She directed me to address the letter to the people of Reims. At first, I was so intent on making my writing beautiful that I understood the message only in bits and pieces. For her part, she seemed used to speaking to a scribe who copied down her words. She spoke slowly and paused when she saw me struggling to spell.

From what I could gather, her letter was an account of what had come to pass since she was in Reims several weeks ago. She wrote of her work for the king and her mistrust of a truce that the Burgundians had offered him. Even worse, she believed that they were trying to trick the king out of his just due. Thus, she was preparing the men for battle in order to claim lands that were rightfully his.

Jeanne concluded her letter by asking the people of Reims to protect their city for the king and to be wary of traitors who wished to harm them. She promised to remove these traitors as soon as possible. What did she mean—did she intend to kill them?

She signed her name at the bottom of the letter. It took her a very long time to produce the *J* in the same childish script that I had when I first learned to copy the *F* in my name. Her clumsy word lay in sharp contrast to my flowing script, but I understood that her calling was different from mine, just as Hersende's was different from both of ours.

Watching her strike flint, I tried to imagine what it was like for her to lead the king's army. I wanted to ask her how she had been called to become a warrior. But her mood was somber, and I decided against it. Instead, I watched her use the flame to soften a tray of sealing wax before dipping her seal into it and affixing the capital "J" onto the scroll. My gaze drifted to a stack of blank paper. I picked up a page and held it up to the sunlight. "Do you know about watermarks?" I asked.

She shook her head. "No, what are they?"

"Here, I will show you."

The sunlight shone through the paper, illuminating a crown. "It seems the stuff of magic," she said. "How was it made?"

As I explained what Michel my teacher had told me about watermarks, I wondered what hers would be. Maybe it was a unicorn. In stained-glass windows, they represented virgins.

As Jeanne stood to go, a man's voice called out, "Wait, Jeannette."

Looking up, I saw a peasant soldier walking toward the trestle. It was Pierre, the man who had camped with her that night in the vineyard.

"It is good to see you, Brother," she greeted him, beaming with affection as she started toward him.

He looked much like her, despite his girth and light hair, truly like her brother.

"Why are you visiting the barbers?" he asked. "I pray you're not ill."

"No, Pierre. Hersende's servant just wrote a letter for me," she answered, not revealing that I had been the young man in the vineyard.

It didn't matter, for Pierre showed no sign of recognizing me. "Do you have any news from home?" she asked eagerly.

"Father has probably returned to Domrémy by now," her brother replied. "He wanted to speak with you when he came to Reims for the crowning, but the king's men wouldn't let him."

Her mouth drooped in sadness. "I didn't even know he was there."

"He wanted me to give you a message," Pierre added gently. "He has forgiven you for breaking your betrothal and running away."

Ameline and I had heard rumors that she had been engaged, and now I knew it to be true. When her saints called her to become a virgin warrior, she had disobeyed her father to fulfill her sacred duty to save our land. But had she loved the man?

"Mama and Catherine didn't come for the crowning?" she asked wistfully.

"No."

"Is Catherine well?"

"Yes, but she misses you, as does Mama."

"I miss them too," she said, twisting the ring on her finger before handing him the letter. "Take this to a courier, Pierre. And please, come to church with me tonight."

"I doubt the captains will let me," Pierre whispered angrily. "Remember how we used to ride away from the army and camp by ourselves? Now they do their best to keep us apart. Why do they mistrust your own brother?"

"It is not you they mistrust. It's me." Her voice was low, but by straining my ears I could catch most of her words. "They know that I don't agree with the truce that they want to sign with the enemy. They also know how loyal the villagers are to me, and they don't want me to rally them to fight harder."

Her eyes closed briefly. "There's something even worse than that. Now that I have led the king to be crowned, many of his ministers are trying to convince him that my work is done." She raised one hand in a tight fist. "It is far from done."

Pierre clasped his hands around hers, his eyes shining with love. "I'll do everything I can to help you. Until we meet again, Jeannette."

"You always lift my spirits, Pierre," she said with a smile. "Dispatch my letter as soon as you can and may God be with you."

She had Pierre, and Hersende had Etienne, but I had no one. Fighting back tears, I picked up a blank gathering of paper and ran my fingers along the edge.

Eleven

The King's Tent

July 26, 1429

Across the river cannons boomed and horses screamed, the din scattering flocks of birds from the forest. The skirmish that I'd dreaded for so long had finally come to pass.

Thankfully, tall trees blocked it from view, but I couldn't block the noise or the smoke that made my eyes burn as I filled buckets of water. Something caught my eye, and I looked up to see a young man dressed in the king's red, green, and white, running away from the fighting. His face was white with terror, and he held his hands over his ears as he sprinted toward the forest.

"Be strong, men!" A powerful voice arched over the skirmish. "Do God's will!"

"God's will be done!" the soldiers clamored in reply.

It was Jeanne rallying her men. I imagined her riding Midnight in the thick of battle. Her voice sounded nothing like the girl who had dictated the letter to me. This voice was much louder but also more musical, a host of drums and trumpets and recorders all together.

After what felt like many hours, the cannons finally stopped firing. I looked away as our wounded men were carried on litters to the meadow, their howls of pain as terrible to my ears as the sounds of battle. A herald announced that the king's army had gained no advantage. That the men had suffered their wounds in vain appalled me.

A smoky sweet smell mixed with the smoke from the cannons. Etienne told me that the wounded were to inhale the fumes from dried poppy flowers. This remedy put the men into a deep slumber in which they no longer shrieked in pain.

All the healers who served the king worked together to care for the wounded men. Hersende and Etienne tended to the men who had suffered burns during the skirmish, starting with a gunner. Cannon fire had burned him so badly that the barbers used up most of the onguent des apôtres. He hardly looked like a man any more underneath his charred flesh. As they swaddled his face in bandages, he whimpered like a baby. I stood there watching Hersende soothe him to sleep. Inspired by Jeanne's voice, he had fought to do her bidding. She hadn't meant to harm him, only to obey God and his messengers the saints. Hersende had told me that Jeanne carried no weapon and killed no one. Whenever a soldier fell from a mortal wound, she wept as she prayed over him that the angels would carry him to heaven.

What a cruel God to want men to suffer horribly and torment Jeanne so. I didn't understand his purpose.

The morning after the skirmish, a new scent filled the air, one of earth and rain and the lingering bitterness of gun smoke. The birds were strangely quiet. I glanced at Hersende, who hovered over the gunner to change his bandage. I turned away from the sight of his raw flesh and looked at the meadow. There, soldiers sprawled in the sunshine and passed the time playing dice and chess. Although they bantered and joked, I suspected that their terror rivaled mine.

Sometime before noon, a royal page came to speak with Hersende. A dark-haired boy of about twelve with fat cheeks, he wrinkled his nose at the stench of the barbers' concoctions.

The King's Tent

To my surprise, she motioned for me. "The king needs your services," she explained. "His scribe was a young man who had never witnessed a battle before. He was too cowardly to endure it and record the events, so he has fled. Until the king can send for a scribe from his castle at Chinon, another one is needed. Jeanne told him about you. Come with me." I hurried after Hersende, filled with pride. I had never witnessed a battle before either, and I was a girl, yet I had not fled like the king's scribe.

In the privacy of her tent, Hersende scrubbed my face and hands until they felt rubbed raw. She opened a chest where she kept clean clothes for the men and found a deep-green tunic almost my size. She helped me put it on and tied a good leather belt around the middle. With a deft hand, she trimmed my hair, for it had grown halfway down my neck since I first cut it.

"Act sure of yourself," she advised as she handed me a clean hood. My hand trembled as I took it. I was about to go inside the king's tent, to take part in an important matter for our country.

I put the hood on, imagining myself writing on fine parchment set out on a writing table. I remembered my teacher Michel's advice: inspect the parchment before you take a quill to it and find the uneven places.

Picturing the alphabet in my mind, I followed the boy up the hill to a round tent trimmed in the red-and-green colors of the king. The front flap was open as well as the back. Hopefully, there would be enough light to see my script as I wrote.

The sounds of an argument grew louder, the words all snarled together, making it impossible for me to understand them. When the page and I entered the tent, I saw half a dozen noblemen shouting and pointing their fingers at each other across a trestle. I discerned a few words here and there—*foolish, untrustworthy, money*—but I still didn't know the reason for their dispute.

The king sat at the end of the trestle, looking small without his crown and armor. His eyes blinked uncontrollably as the quarrel accosted him from both sides. The page led me past the trestle just as Jeanne and the Duke of Alençon entered through the rear flap. They went to stand by the king, and the argument stopped. The nobles turned to them, some glaring.

I was shocked to see how pale Jeanne's face had become—like that of a wounded soldier who had lost much blood. The dark shadows under her eyes bespoke a sickness or restless nights or both. She kept twisting the ring her mother had given her. I had to write well: it was the only way I knew to help her.

The page and I reached a table set with the finest writing supplies I had ever seen. This was really happening—I was to write a document that would be sealed with the fleur-de-lis of the king. My legs trembled as a dark-haired man dressed in a scarlet tunic rose from the table and came over to me. His cold blue eyes unsettled me. I had to write well to please him. I wiped my sweaty palms against my tunic.

"The Maid swears that you are a scribe," he whispered, "but you look like you have spent more time holding a hoe than a quill. Show me your hands."

I lifted them up, hoping he wouldn't notice how small they were. "Sit down and write my name: Claude de Tourelles," the nobleman bade me.

Swallowing hard, I lifted the quill and dipped it in the ink-pot. His name echoed in my mind, but I had no idea how to spell it. To bide for time, I wrote the C bigger than the other letters, as I once did to embellish the beginning letter of each chapter. Feigning confidence, I wrote the first letters that appeared in my mind for the rest of his name.

He grunted his approval. "By God's thumb, another of the Maid's miracles. The barber's servant can write after all."

His hand clenched my shoulder so tightly that it hurt. "I will stand here and tell you what to write," he whispered. "Don't dare write anything else."

I bowed and took my seat, wondering why he didn't just write it himself. It must be an important document that had to be written in a fine hand. As I practiced making loops and lines on a scrap of paper, King Charles told the page to ring a silver bell. Everyone grew quiet.

A nobleman rose to his feet. Never had I seen a man of such girth and height, a mountain of swarthy flesh that ended in a pinnacle of curly gray hair. "Good friends," he began, patting his huge belly. "Today we are gathered to discuss the terms of a treaty with the enemy."

"Write down what Georges de la Trémoille said and record his name," Claude de Tourelles whispered behind me.

"Never will I agree to such a truce!" Jeanne cried in a shrill voice.

As I followed the instruction to write this too, I was ashamed for her sake. She sounded like a petulant child. Most of the men scowled at her, and shouts rose up again, so loud that I feared the men would come to blows. The king bowed his head and pressed his hands against his ears. A red-faced nobleman pounded his fist on the table. "Silence," he bellowed. "We have offended His Majesty."

Everyone grew quiet at once. The king took his hands away from his ears. "Ah, that is better," he murmured in a deep voice. "Now, my dear friend la Trémoille, if you will calmly explain why we must cease our attack, I'm certain everyone will understand."

La Trémoille cleared his throat, frowning at Jeanne and the Duke of Alençon beside her. "The English and our cousins the Burgundians are just as weary of fighting as we are. They have drafted a peace treaty that is quite acceptable. It will soon be autumn, then winter. There is not enough time to take Paris. Come, doesn't everyone agree that the late summer would be far more pleasant spent in our castles than on this godforsaken road to Paris?"

The ministers on one side of the table murmured their assent as I followed the instructions to write what he said. The quill began to slip in my sweaty hand, and I gripped it more tightly, trying to write every word that was said as neatly as I could. To do so, I had to write slowly and feared that I wouldn't be able to keep pace with de Tourelles' instructions. "It is not our comfort that matters," Jeanne argued. "We fight to do God's will and regain the king's rightful lands. Never will I honor this truce!"

De Tourelles bade me to write her words, along with a note that she had insulted la Trémoille. "Why don't you speak the truth for all to hear, Georges?" the Duke of Alençon challenged. "It's not that you want peace. You only want the king to honor the truce because you have already promised the enemy that you will convince him to do so. In exchange, they will cross your palms with many gold coins."

Finished with my writing, I glanced up and saw la Trémoille glaring at the duke. The other ministers squirmed uncomfortably but said nothing as their eyes darted back and forth from the duke to the fat lord. King Charles, looking sad and helpless, offered everyone wine and fruit. Only Jeanne and the duke refused this token of peace.

The silence continued as the men nibbled on fruit and sipped wine from silver goblets. Jeanne went to the king, her eyes silently beseeching him to heed her, but he lowered his gaze to his plate. She knelt on the ground beside him and bowed her head. "My gentle King," she begged him softly, "we must do as God bids us. My saints have come to me many times in the past few days. They urge me to tell you that you must march on Paris at once."

Her words moved me; surely they would move the king. I dipped my quill in the ink pot, but Claude de Tourelles grabbed my wrist, blocking me from writing what she had said. I didn't understand. He let go, but I felt his cold eyes upon me still.

His purpose suddenly came to me. The words that he bade me write were not intended to be a true record of this meeting. On the contrary, they were intended to give a false idea of Jeanne, to malign her. Why had I agreed to do this? I was suddenly seized by an urge to flee the tent.

La Trémoille waved his hand at her as if he were swatting a fly. "Don't you see that you have served your purpose by helping the king to be crowned? Go back to your village. We will listen to you and your saints no more."

Jeanne jerked her head upright and rose to her feet. She stared at la Trémoille in disbelief and swallowed hard. "No, milord, you are wrong," she said, her voice filling the tent. "My mission is not over. It is God's will for me to fulfill it."

A nobleman with shaggy brows jumped to his feet. "She speaks the truth. The Bishop of Poitiers himself declared that God sent her to save our land."

A trio of gray-haired nobles bowed their heads in silent assent; others made the sign of the cross. The Duke of Alençon stepped forward. "How dare you insult the Maid!" he shouted at la Trémoille. "Ask her forgiveness."

La Trémoille snorted. "Ask a peasant girl to forgive me because a mere boy orders me to do so? As for God sending her, I never believed it. I only thought we could make use of her in order to win battles. I will ask her forgiveness only if my king commands me to do so."

Many of the other nobles mumbled their agreement with him while the king bowed his head, his lips moving in silent prayer. Then his gaze shifted back and forth from la Trémoille to Jeanne. "No, milord," he decided at last. "You need not ask her to pardon you."

The king cleared his throat. "Now I will settle this debate once and for all. We cannot march on Paris. We lack the money and supplies to do so. The good la Trémoille has been kind enough to loan us the money that we needed to win back the Loire Valley. We thank him for that, but we cannot abuse his generous spirit. He advises me to honor this truce, which he himself helped to draft. We have no choice but to take his advice."

De Tourelles bade me write these words. As I dipped my quill into the inkpot, I saw Jeanne fighting back tears and the

Duke of Alençon trying to comfort her. My own tears rose up at their courage and support of one another even in defeat.

"And I have no other choice but to obey God," she said, looking around the table at the king and his ministers. "I pray that one day soon you will all find the courage to do his bidding."

"I stand with the Maid!" the duke cried out. "If we have to march on Paris with my men alone, we will do so!"

Taking Jeanne by the arm, he led her out of the tent. A few of the nobles went with them, but most of the rest stayed, talking loudly in praise of the truce and of la Trémoille's effort to forge it. The king motioned for the page to pour more wine.

"Read over what you wrote and check it," de Tourelles bade me. "Then you may leave."

"Should I add flourishes to the beginning letters?" I asked as an idea formed in my mind.

"Yes, of course," he replied.

The moment he went to the king's table, I set to work amending the document and changing the letters in the parts that went against Jeanne. The writing still looked flowing, yet when I read it back, it made no sense at all.

What had I done? De Tourelles might not be able to read well enough to notice, but other nobles might realize that a scribe had deliberately altered the document. They had every right to punish me for supporting Jeanne, whose fortune was surely falling. I could lose everything: my refuge with Hersende and my chance to be reunited with Father.

I picked up an inkpot and held it over the parchment, poised to spill it. If I did, de Tourelles would force me to rewrite the original document denouncing Jeanne. *You have to help her,* the voice inside me urged. My hand trembled as I set the inkpot down.

Long after the camp had grown quiet, I lay awake on my pallet near the barbers' tent. The stars above granted me no respite. I kept thinking of what had happened that morning in the tent. In a way, la Trémoille had been right; a truce would bring peace after all. No more would men's faces be burned beyond recognition like the gunner's. Yet Jeanne believed that God himself wanted her to continue this war.

The chill air crept through the thin weave of my blanket, and I rolled onto my side, clutching it closer. Unable to get warm, I rose to get another blanket. Other than the stars, the only light came from the soldiers' smoldering campfire a stone's throw away. It guided me toward the barbers' cart where I found a blanket. A noise startled me, a scraping sound near the fire, followed by the hissing sound of a torch being lit. A pool of light glowed there, and in its midst stood Jeanne. Her shoulders were hunched, and she clutched her arms to her chest.

She looked so small and forlorn that a wave of pity swept through me. I would go to her and offer her what solace I could. I walked quietly toward her hoping that I wouldn't wake the barbers or the wounded men.

She nodded when she saw me coming and gave me a wan smile. "Help me build up this fire," she whispered.

We arranged the kindling into a tent shape, and then she struck two pieces of flint together. It caught fire quickly, soon spreading to the larger sticks. We sat on the ground and warmed our hands over the blaze.

"Have you heard from your father?" she asked. I detected the urgency in her question and understood why she needed the weapons so badly.

I shook my head. "I'm worried about him."

"You say he does much of his business in Flanders?" she asked, hardly listening.

She didn't care about Father's safety. Her focus on the weapons and the plan to capture Paris had also blinded her to her declining fortune. "Yes." I bristled. "I must—"

"Which town?" she interrupted.

I turned toward her abruptly. "I don't know, but please listen. I have something important to tell you."

"About your father?"

"No, about you. Today in the king's tent, Claude de Tourelles commanded me to record only a part of what was said and to add certain notes. The record thus portrays you as stubborn, rude, and quarrelsome."

"What?" she gasped, her eyes wide. "I thought scribes wrote an honest record."

"When I tried to do so, the lord de Tourelles blocked the paper with his hand. But at the end I did change some of the words that were against you by adding flourishes to the letters. Unless someone reads the parchment very carefully, no one will find out."

She turned to me, her gaze soft in the firelight. "Thank you for taking such a risk for me."

"You took one for me when we traded horses."

She shook her head. "Your risk was far more dangerous than mine. I will pray that no one discovers it." She paused. "It is true what you said about writing being important."

She remembered? I looked at the fire, not knowing what to say.

"I don't understand all these secret dealings that nobles have with one another," Jeanne continued in a dispirited voice. "Their lies and plots." But the way she had spoken this morning was too honest—blunt even.

"The king's men don't want your honesty. It will turn them away. La Trémoille told you to go back to your village. You should protect yourself from what he and the others might do to you."

She turned to me, her face somber in the firelight, her gaze as intent as it had been that night in the vineyard. It made me feel just as uncomfortable as it did then. I picked up a stick from the ground and fed it to the fire. "I already know that my path is a dangerous one," she said quietly, "as is yours."

"Not anymore. You have found me a haven with Hersende for the time being. I could repay your kindness by helping you find a way to return to your family."

"My family," she murmured, smiling at the fire. "What respite it would be to go home again. To sit around the hearth after supper talking of ordinary matters."

Her jaw tightened, and she shook her head. "No. I have promised God and my saints to be strong for the men and to do his will."

Over the crackling fire, I heard her crying. I took her cold hand in mine and held it tightly to my heart.

A few days later, I was still trying to think of what I could do to help her. I had come to understand that she had two voices within her: what God and her saints wanted from her and what she wanted most of all—to go home. Fortunately, I had but one voice that had grown stronger over the course of my journey. I trusted it would speak to me whenever I needed it most.

Today the king's army set out toward Compiègne, a town on the road to Paris. For some reason, the army hadn't disbanded as la Trémoille had wanted it to do. Maybe it was because the enemy troops were very close to us, and we heard rumors that more soldiers had joined their ranks. Why then did we not defend ourselves and engage them in battle? The more I observed of war, the more confusing it became.

My seat, a vinegar barrel on the barbers' cart, was uncomfortable, but at least the sun warmed my back, and the fragrant smell of wildflowers filled the air.

"Don't just stare out at the countryside," Hersende shouted. "Cut more bandages."

At noon, we stopped at a village to eat and to rest the horses and mules. Outside the wall, the townspeople, who had pledged loyalty to the king, had set out baskets of plums for the army. The soldiers rushed toward the baskets while I helped Hersende feed the wounded.

After our meal, Hersende handed me a small wooden chest and bade me to collect spider webs. She pressed them on wounds so they would heal more quickly. When the chest was filled with all the spider webs I could find, I turned back to the barbers' cart. It startled me to see Jeanne hurrying along the road toward me, her squire by her side. Her frown stirred a feeling of dread within me.

A stone's throw away, she stopped and turned to d'Amboise. He folded his arms across his chest and clucked his teeth in disapproval as she strode toward me.

"Walk with me," she said.

We headed down the road, our backs to the army. "Are your tidings about Father?" I asked in a wavering voice.

"Yes. We sent spies to Flanders to find him," she replied, her voice somber.

"Has something happened to him?" I asked, my dread growing.

"The moneylenders have thrown him into debtors' prison. He is alive but gravely ill. The spies tell us that he may be dying."

"No," I moaned, covering my face with my hands. Would I ever see him alive again?

Jeanne clutched my arm. "Felise, your father needs you. You must go to him. I will ask Hersende to go with you."

Her grasp on my arm tightened. "I need you too. The duke and I are marching to take Paris, and we must have more weapons. We do not know if your father had already secured them when he was seized, or if he was on his way to do so. Whichever it was, we must have the weapons. If he recovers, you are to help him bring them to us. Will you do this for your father and me? For France?"

I lifted my head from my hands. "You don't care about Father; you just want the weapons he brings to you. It's not for France or the king that I will go to him. I'll go to save his life. That's all I can promise."

She released my arm, and her gaze upon me softened. "I do care about your father, but it is my duty to care for everyone in our land. If God takes him from us, the Duke of Alençon's squires, who will escort you to the city of Bruges, will be charged with securing the weapons. You must travel with them and help them as best you can."

She set a quick pace toward Hersende, and I followed behind her, clutching the chest full of spider webs as tears streamed down my face.

Twelve

Mist

August 1, 1429

Across the canal, the debtors' prison loomed, its gray stone darkened by the rain. Not a single window, statue, or gargoyle softened the front facade. It looked so forbidding and impenetrable that it made me shudder. As soon as the coach stopped at the prison's front door, I leaped onto the road. *May Father still be alive!* I prayed. My mind closed to everything except the battle we might soon have to fight for his life.

Hersende descended after me and called the Duke of Alençon's two squires to join her. They were young noblemen in his vassalage, not much older than me. After only an hour of the journey, I knew full well how much they despised being sent off with an urchin and a barberess to Flanders.

I was grateful that Hersende had no ear for their whining along the way. In fact, it seemed to render her even more commanding. Because of her, we made our way to Father as quickly as possible.

"Jacques, stay here with the horses," she barked. "Louis, you knock on the door. When they answer, I'll ask them to lead us to Henri the Merchant of Troyes. If they refuse, I'll offer them some of the money Jeanne gave us."

I led the way as the three of us strode to the prison door. Louis rapped on it, trying to look important. "Let us in!" he shouted.

A long time passed before a tall man covered in armor and

carrying a spear opened the door. Another armored guard with a spear hovered close to him as if ready to defend the prison.

"What is your business?" the first man demanded in a thick Flemish accent. The helmet hid his face, but his voice sounded cold. I squeezed my hands behind my back, knowing that he wouldn't make things easy for us.

"We have come to secure the release of Henri the Merchant of Troyes," Hersende replied in a steady voice. "We had word that he is gravely ill. Is he still alive?"

"How would I know?" growled the first guard. He spoke in rapid Flemish to the other guard. The man nodded and turned to do his bidding.

I prayed for Father until the guard returned. My heart raced as he spoke in rapid Flemish to the other man.

The guard who opened the door turned to us. "He is still alive, but barely."

"Thank God," I whimpered.

"Take us to him immediately!" Hersende commanded.

"We have strict orders," the guard muttered. "He can't be released until you go to Pietr Wervecke the Moneylender and pay his debts."

He turned and started to close the door. "Wait!" I shouted, and the guard spun around.

"Have mercy on my father and pity on me, his only son," I pleaded, my voice breaking. "Let me go to him while the others pay the moneylender."

"No. The moneylender has left strict orders."

"We will pay you well for your kindness," Hersende said, showing him the purse in its wooden chest.

The guard thrust his spear toward the bag, and she jerked it away. "No!" he shouted. "Others may stoop to bribes, but never will I. To my dying days, I will abide by the laws of God and man. Heaven will be my reward. Begone, and don't return until you have a letter bearing Wervecke's seal."

He slammed the door shut before I could dart inside. There was no choice but to get back on the coach and go to the moneylenders.

The squires rode down the main street of Bruges and, at the cathedral square, asked for directions to the street of the moneylenders. After we turned onto a busy side street, the coach stopped in front of a half-timbered building that loomed over the others. Richly clad merchants strode in and out of the building as if they had important business. As we descended, one of them drew back, wrinkling his brow at the sight of my shabby clothes.

After summoning Louis to join us, Hersende waited until the merchants were out of earshot to speak. "We will follow the same plan here. Louis will do the talking. First, ask someone to point out Wervecke to us. Now, for the most important thing," she added, handing Louis the wooden chest, which contained a purse full of the Duke of Alençon's money.

"It's as heavy as a sack of bricks," he groaned.

"Remember, Louis," she whispered, "don't get close enough that he can grab the chest."

"Woman, do you take me for a fool?" the squire seethed.

"Yes. Prove me wrong today," she replied, grabbing his arm. "Let's go."

No guards blocked us from entering the front door. Inside, a foyer led into a large open room that reeked of mud, sweat, and leather. Merchants babbling in many languages crowded around tables cluttered with ledger books, parchment, and quills. Curses erupted, and parchment was ripped and swept to the floor. How would we ever find Wervecke among all these men? Would he take the money and write the letter we needed without arguing?

Halfway across the long room, Louis asked a French merchant to point out Wervecke.

"By God's mouth, why do you want to do business with him?" he asked.

"We were told he has large sums of money," Louis lied.

"True." The merchant shrugged as he pointed to a table in front of the hearth. "But make certain that you pay him back by his deadline. He isn't forgiving of late payments."

I groaned. Father was two months late on his. We headed toward the table, jostling through the crowd, and with each step I prayed for God's help in softening Wervecke. His name rose up in snippets of conversation around us. A man with a high-pitched voice claimed that he knew someone who had repaid Wervecke in full, yet the moneylender still held his son in debtors' prison. I clenched my jaws, hoping this wasn't true.

We passed a table just as a moneylender unlocked a large silver chest. Suddenly a guard darted over to stand beside him, clutching a sword and watching carefully as the chest was opened. Everyone at the table grew quiet. If one of the merchants so much as moved toward it, his hand would be chopped off right here at this very table.

Hersende halted. A man with red hair sat at the biggest table in the room and the one closest to the hearth. This must be Wervecke. He scowled at a blond-haired man who held up two jewel-studded books for his inspection.

Wervecke stood abruptly and grabbed the books. "Go to the devil, you idiot!" he shouted. "I will take these two, but you need ten more to pay your debt. Don't darken my door until you have secured them."

The day his agents had barged into our house came back to me. Ameline's jaw had been clenched and her voice steady as she dealt with them. May Louis be just as strong today, and may I be just as strong too. Amid the quills and parchments scattered across the table lay Wervecke's seal. I imagined grabbing it and forging a letter from him to release Father from prison. But the moneylender's guards would seize me, and he would never write the letter.

We took our place in a line of five men waiting to borrow money from Wervecke. The first completed his business and the second, but then the moneylender spent a long time working out a loan with the third man. When they were finished, the next man stepped up to the table, but Wervecke waved him away. He rose and patted his ample belly. "Time for dinner. Come back in an hour."

As he turned to leave, Louis caught Hersende's eye, silently asking what to do.

"Go to him and show him the chest," she whispered fiercely. "Wervecke," he called, striding to catch up with him. Hersende and I followed a few steps behind.

"We have a debt to settle with you," Louis said.

Wervecke wheeled around. His small eyes seemed to disappear in the broad flesh of his face as he stared at the money chest that Louis held just beyond his reach. "Show me what's inside," he commanded.

Louis opened the chest and loosened the drawstring of the purse. He scooped gold écus into his palm. Wervecke's eyes were riveted on the coins gleaming in the firelight. "Give me the purse."

"First, allow me to explain. I am the agent of Henri the Merchant of Troyes," Louis said, exuding bravado. "The guards at the prison told us they must have a letter with your seal showing that the debt has been paid in full. Only then will they release him."

The moneylender shifted his gaze to Hersende and me. "Who are they?" he asked Louis.

Louis paused. I clenched my sweaty fists behind my back, hoping he remembered what we had rehearsed.

"His sister and nephew who live in Bourges," he replied at last. "The boy is like the son Henri never had."

My fists relaxed. A cruel smile twisted the moneylender's lips. "We caught Henri the Merchant on the road to Troyes a moon ago. We had already sold his family into servitude to help defray his debt. These two would have been sold too if we had known about them."

His lie gave me strength. I squared my shoulders.

Wervecke's beady eyes returned to Louis. "Give me the money or my guards will whip you out of here."

The entire room grew quiet as curious merchants crowded around us.

"But the letter," Louis pleaded. *Tell him about the extra money,* I silently urged him.

"Damn the letter," Wervecke growled. "Begone."

Hersende stepped forward to stand beside Louis. "Good sir," she began, "this purse contains the sum that my brother owes you, as well as an extra three hundred gold écus. But first you must give us the letter."

Wervecke snorted. "You expect me to trust you without seeing the money? Dump it on the table at once."

"Yes, Monsieur," Hersende complied. She took the purse and loose coins from Louis as Wervecke strode back to his place at the table. Hersende set the loose gold écus down, before carefully emptying the purse. Everyone's eyes shifted to the table. They murmured in awe at the enormous pile of gold coins. Wervecke smiled as his hands made quick work of stacking the coins and counting them.

When he was done, he inspected one of the coins before fondling it in his palm. He turned to Hersende. "Thirteen hundred gold écus as you promised," he said, his eyes narrowing. "But for all his trouble over the years, your brother doesn't deserve to be released. I have suffered far more than this money for his constant cheating and false promises."

He bellowed for the guards. They came running at once, waving their whips. The merchants hurried to make a path for them, and the guards headed straight toward us. Panic surged through me, rooting me to the floor as Louis fled. Hersende grabbed my arm and wheeled me around to face Wervecke's table. She lunged for the seal with the other. Just as she was about to grab it, a whip lashed my back, searing me through my clothes. Hersende and

I both screamed, and the whip struck again, the pain jolting me into action. I had to get Father released.

Pushing myself between Wervecke and the money, I turned to face the guards, holding up my arms to protect my face. "Let me speak!" I shouted as the whip lashed against my arms. I wedged myself between two of the guards, too close for them to strike me again, and faced the merchants whose eyes were riveted on me. The merchant who told us about Wervecke's vengeance stood at the front.

"Get the boy out of here," Wervecke commanded.

Dropping their whips, the two guards seized my arms. They lifted me off my feet as I kicked at their legs, fighting to free myself.

"Listen to me, merchants!" I shouted. "You see those coins. We have more than repaid my uncle's debt. He is dying, but Wervecke refuses to give us a letter to release him from prison. Will you borrow money from this man?"

The gathered merchants shifted their weight uncomfortably, but no one answered. The guards wheeled me around toward the door, but I turned my head toward the merchants.

"Spread the word to all the merchants in Bruges this day and all that you meet henceforth on your journeys," I shouted. "Borrow no more from Wervecke—"

One of the guards clapped his hand to my mouth and I kicked harder as they carried me through the crowd. The rumble of complaints about Wervecke grew louder and angrier. "The boy is right!" someone yelled.

"We won't stand for Wervecke's cruelty anymore!" another man shouted.

A cheer rose up, and men surged forward, blocking the path to the door. Men grabbed the guards, pinning their free arms behind their backs. The merchants lifted me down and led me back to Wervecke's table. "Borrow no more from Wervecke!" they shouted. I joined in, while inside I thought only of Father.

The merchants hoisted me up on his table, knocking papers and coins to the floor. I looked down at Hersende and she nodded at me, her jaw clenched. Wervecke's face had taken on a purplish hue like an angry bruise. "Silence!" he bellowed and called for more guards. A hush fell over the crowd as they surged into the room, their swords flashing in the firelight. They swarmed around the table, forming a ring that separated Wervecke and his money from the merchants.

"Get the boy down at once," Wervecke barked.

Two of them grabbed me by the middle and dropped me to the floor next to Hersende. The guards gripped our arms behind our backs and jerked our bodies around so that we faced Wervecke. He leaned so close to us that I smelled the sour wine on his breath. "I hope Henri dies," he whispered. "I know his secrets, and if he lives, I will make him suffer on account of them."

A moan escaped my lips.

"Not so cocky now, are you, boy?" The moneylender sneered and rose to his full height. He turned to his scribe. "Write the letter on your coarsest scrap of paper," he commanded, his voice choked with rage. "I hereby release Henri the Merchant of Troyes."

Silence filled the room except for the scratching of the quill on the paper and the clinking of écus as Wervecke scooped up the coins from the floor and thrust them back in the purse. He ordered his men to keep their eyes on it while he signed and sealed the letter.

He thrust it at Hersende before the wax had time to harden. "Begone and never return. The same for Henri."

The three of us strode toward the door, almost colliding with a group of fur-clad merchants. They yelled at us in another language, but we pushed past them into the street. A light rain soothed my hot face as we hurried to the coach.

Clutching the sealed letter, Hersende threw her arms around me. "You did well!"

"I was afraid my voice would give me away," I said, suddenly aware of the searing pain across my back.

"You sounded just like a boy," she said as we climbed onto the coach. My sense of triumph soon vanished as the squires steered the horses along the crowded street. *Wait for me, Father,* I prayed. *We are almost there.*

Hersende clutched my hand in hers. "I need to prepare you for something. Your father will look very different from the way you remember him."

"But he is hardly ever sick," I murmured. "And he's a trickster. Maybe he's only feigning illness, so they'll take pity on him and release him."

"I doubt that," she said.

At last we reached the prison. Jacques stayed with the horses while Louis, Hersende, and I hurried to the front door. The squire rapped loudly, and when the head guard opened the door, his mouth gaped in surprise at seeing us again. Hersende handed him the letter, and he inspected the seal closely before opening it. After reading it, he crumpled it into a ball and turned to open the door.

"Follow me," he bade us.

The prison was so dark that it took my eyes a moment to adjust after we entered it. The stench of stale cabbage and rotting fish permeated the hall. Was this the air that Father had been forced to breathe for nearly two months? At the far end, we descended a stone staircase that led to a lower hallway lit with torches hanging in sconces along the walls. The stench—of mold and sweat, piss, vomit, and dung—hung in the damp air. We passed a row of cells with iron bars tightly interwoven. I peered into each of them looking for Father.

One of the cells contained a group of men playing dice as if they were in a tavern, except that they were sitting on the floor. Father wasn't among them. The next cell contained dozens of men wearing ragged clothes, some of whom clutched the iron bars and stared at us blankly. In the back of the cell, two bare-chested men were chained to the floor, jagged lines of whip marks across their backs. I shuddered to think this might have happened to Father.

We reached a cell at the far end crowded with men. They lay on thin pallets on the floor, some coughing and others moaning in agony. While the guard unlocked the door, I scanned them, desperate to find Father. But there wasn't a torch nearby and it was impossible to discern their features.

"This is how you tend to the sick?" Hersende choked.

The guard shrugged. "These men are all debtors. God sees fit to punish them for their sins."

The door rattled open, and the guard stepped aside. "He's in here somewhere," he said. "Take him at once so I can return to my post."

"Father," I called, pushing past the guard and into the cell, almost stumbling over a man's outstretched arm. Most of the men's faces were hidden under their mantles, which also served as blankets. They were all too dirty and muted to distinguish a deep brown one. Instead I looked for the cloak's hem embroidered with orange thread—his favorite color, which Ameline had sewn for him. There, in the back corner, was such a mantle covering a man who lay on his side facing the wall.

"Father," I called again. Still he gave no reply.

I crouched down beside the man. In the dim light I could barely see Father's bearded face, so thin that his cheekbones protruded. I touched his brow, and it was still warm. He was alive! Tears sprang to my eyes as I bent over him. "Father! It's me, Felise."

"Move back," Hersende bade me. "Louis, carry him out."

Louis obeyed with a groan, not from Father's weight but because he stank so badly. He had been forced to lie in his own excrement for weeks. I took his clammy hand in mine. As we turned to leave the cell, Hersende spotted something left behind on his pallet and pointed it out to me. It was his beloved recorder, and I ran to retrieve it. "May you play this again soon," I whispered, while inside I wondered if he would ever have the strength to do so.

We climbed the stairs and hurried along the upper hallway. Outside, the fog had thickened, obscuring the coach. Hersende mounted the coach first and threw blankets across one of the benches to make a pallet for Father while Louis lifted him up and laid him on the bench. I knelt on the floor near Father's head.

"Ask that man walking on the other side of the street for directions to a beguinage," Hersende bade the squires. As they did so, she turned to me. "If this first house of holy women doesn't have a bed for your father, we'll search for another. I have heard that many communities of Beguines serve the sick people of Bruges."

As the coach lurched forward through the fog, Hersende sat on the bench beside Father. She pressed her hand to his forehead and put two fingers to his wrist.

"Will his health return if we feed him?" I murmured.

She shook her head. "It isn't that easy. He looks as if he stopped eating a while ago, and now the damp of the prison has settled in his lungs."

A sudden downpour of rain pelted the top of the coach and blew in sideways. Fearing it would drench Father, I grabbed a blanket and pressed it against either side of the doorway to block the rain.

The coach stopped at a wooden house with crossed beams on the upper story. Cursing the rain, Jacques and Louis made quick work of tethering the horses. Hersende jumped to the ground and went to beat on the door. A tall woman holding a torch opened it and a cat darted inside to get out of the rain. Drawing a black shawl over her head, the woman hurried to the coach with Hersende.

"Bring him inside at once," the woman said, her eyes full of concern after she saw Father.

She lit the way for Louis to carry him into a large room illuminated by torches held in sconces. Twelve or more patients rested in beds along the wall where two other Beguines tended to them. The woman led us to an empty bed. "My name is Madame Catherine, and I own this house," she said quickly, speaking French with a Flemish accent. "What can I bring for you?"

"Saint John's wort, warm lavender water, soap, chamomile, and chicken broth," Hersende replied, rolling up her sleeves.

"What should I do?" I asked, frantic to help.

"Sit here with your father and help me bring him back."

As dusk fell, I sat in a chair beside my father's bed and massaged his hand, yearning for him to awaken. But he remained in a far-away place, deeper than sleep. His heartbeat was faint and his body quite still. His breathing was so shallow that I found myself breathing deeply for him. I held a cup of broth to his lips, but he didn't drink.

Hersende took the cup from my hand. "We will try again later," she said. "For now, let us bathe him."

Together we removed his filthy shirt. I gasped at the sight of his protruding ribs and sunken belly that once was rounded from enjoyment of many a hearty meal. My throat tightened as I dipped a cloth in the lavender water, remembering how Father always liked the scent. We bathed him and dressed him in a soft linen nightshirt that Madame Catherine had given us. As twilight fell, she and another Beguine gave sleeping draughts to their patients.

"May God watch over him," she murmured when she approached Father's bedside. "Knock at the first door in the hallway if you need me during the night."

Is God truly watching over him? I wondered as Hersende went to put another log on the fire. At her suggestion, we were going to take turns keeping vigil. We did so through that night and the next day. Madame Catherine brought us meals and warm broth for Father, praying with us each time she came. Nothing changed in his condition even though we managed to get him to drink a little.

On the second night it seemed that I had slept for only a few moments when Hersende awakened me for my turn. I sat up and rubbed my eyes.

The fire had died down to embers and the only light in the room came from a candle on the bedside table.

"How is he?" I asked.

"Alive by a thread. His breathing is more labored now. It is an hour or so from dawn. Often this is the time for the sick to take a turn for better or worse. Awaken me the moment anything changes about him."

Stumbling to my feet, I went to sit near his head and tried to get him to take some broth, but he didn't stir. His raspy breathing frightened me. I clasped his cold hand and rubbed it briskly. Everything I had felt on Ameline's last night came back to me in full measure, the urgency to do everything I could to keep him alive.

I ran my fingers through his straggly hair, remembering a night long ago when Mama cut it while Charlotte and I played with our dolls. My parents had been happy with one another that night, with Father telling jokes and Mama laughing.

An idea suddenly came to me. "Do you have a comb and scissors?" I asked Hersende as she lay down on the pallet.

"In the black wool satchel," she mumbled sleepily. "What are you going to do?"

"Cut Father's hair."

"Do you not need more light?"

"If I do, I can build up the fire again."

By the time I found the scissors and comb, Hersende's snores echoed about the great room. Just as Mama had done that night long ago, I combed the tangles out of his hair as best I could.

Then I held a lock of his beard taut between two fingers and cut away a goodly length. When I finished cutting his beard, I gently rolled his body to one side. My heart lurched when I felt how light he was; as thin as Ameline on her deathbed. No, I wouldn't give him up for dead.

I held back my tears as I cut his hair, humming a song he had once played on the recorder, a merry one that used to make me laugh even after I fell and hurt myself. I hummed the song more loudly, but it didn't make me laugh. I needed Father's hearty laughter to join mine. I snipped his hair as evenly as I could and turned him onto his back again while I gathered the shorn locks together with trembling hands.

I stopped humming. His breathing had grown so quiet that I could no longer hear it.

I hurried over to Hersende and shook her arm. "Come quickly."

She sat up at once. "What has changed?"

"His breathing."

She jumped up, and we hastened back to his bed. Bending down, she listened for his breath.

She raised her body and smiled. "I have seen this happen before. His sickness is lifting. His breathing sounds different because he is laboring less to take each breath."

"Are you certain? I can't hear him breathing at all."

"Yes. I will show you," she replied. She went to get something from her satchel and returned with a small looking glass. Then she sat on the other side of the bed and held it close to his mouth. Except for the wind blowing against the windowpanes, silence filled the room. Tears gathered in my eyes as I leaned closer to look at the mirror and saw a tiny ring of mist there.

Thirteen
Star Stories

August 6, 1429

Sitting by Father's side, I held the mirror to his nostrils again. The ring of mist had grown wider as the sickness left his lungs, but his sunken cheeks and ashen color remained. Hersende joined me at his bedside, carrying a cup of her healing draught. It was made of mint to ease the stomach into digesting solid food again, as well as ginger to heat Father's cold hands. She smiled when she saw the mirror.

"I have more good news," she whispered. "Madame Catherine has arranged for her servants to hide the carriage and horses at her brother's house in the countryside. They draped it in black to make it look like a funeral carriage, as if your father had died. In exchange, her brother has given us one of his carts and three workhorses to pull it."

"Good," I said. Catherine knew about Wervecke's threat, and she had helped us take precautions. None of us walked the streets of Bruges, not even the squires, and Madame Catherine kept an eye out for strangers when she went to market. She had done so much for us and hadn't charged us anything. Hersende found out that she was a rich widow who had devoted her fortune to helping others in need. Every day Hersende and I thanked God for sending Catherine to us.

When the noon bells rang, Father stirred. For the first time since we rescued him, he squinted his eyes open and turned his head to look at me. "Felise?" he murmured.

"Yes, Father," I replied as tears of joy brimmed in my eyes.

"Why are you dressed like a boy?"

"I'll explain later. Drink this broth."

He drank a few more sips before collapsing back on the pillow. "Felise," he whispered. "The moneylenders told me that my family had been sold into slavery to pay off my debts. I wanted to die. I would have died if you hadn't come."

Bowing my head, I clasped his hand. His hold was so feeble that he couldn't grasp mine back. "Wervecke lied," I whispered, struggling to contain my fury at him. "I'm not a slave."

"How about Ameline?" he asked, his voice thin with worry.

I glanced at Hersende and she shook her head. We couldn't tell him the truth yet as it might set him back in his illness. I swallowed despite the lump in my throat. "She's at home with Charlotte."

Father grew a little stronger each day. He continued to ask about Ameline, and each time I told him I didn't know how she fared. Today he finished an entire cup of broth before sinking back onto the pillow.

"Tell me how you escaped becoming a slave," he said, reaching out to touch my cropped hair. "You do look very much like a boy in my old clothes."

I told him about the night I ran away and about the rest of my journey, except the parts about Jeanne and the weapons and Wervecke's threats and the tanner.

He scratched his head, looking puzzled. "How is it that Ameline and Charlotte stayed at home?"

Breathing deeply, I started to tell him the lie I had crafted: how Ameline had gone into hiding with Charlotte at Anes's house after helping me disguise myself as a boy. But the lie stuck in my throat.

"Father," I began, my eyes filling with tears, "when I told you that Ameline was at home, I meant that she was in her heavenly home."

He turned to me, suddenly alert. "She is dead?"

I gulped. "She had terrible headaches, and I tried all kinds of remedies from many healers, but nothing could save her. She died last May."

He gripped my hand. "She was well when I left. If only I had known—"

"I wanted to write you when she took ill, but I didn't know where you were."

"Oh, God," he moaned.

He struggled to hold back tears. I had seen him shed them only once before, and that was when Mama died. I wrapped my arms around his shoulders, and we wept together.

We sat in chairs near a window, the shutters thrown open to allow sunlight to pour into the sickroom. Hersende and Catherine agreed that the light would help Father to heal and to grieve for Ameline. Indeed, in the past two weeks, Father's body had grown stronger as he took solid food. He even got out of bed, at first leaning on me for support and then walking a little more each day by himself. He asked more questions about Ameline—if her hour of death had been peaceful and where she was buried. A weight lifted inside me now that I could share the sorrow, which I had borne alone for so long.

He closed his eyes, basking in the warmth. "In prison I believed that I would never see the light of day again," he murmured.

"Don't think of that horrible place," I pleaded.

He asked about Charlotte, and I told him that she was living with the anchoress at Reims Cathedral, and that through some miracle, she knew Ameline was at peace. He closed his eyes and grew quiet.

"I wish I had heard this anchoress speak those words about

Ameline," he murmured. "To be with such a holy prophetess is a good place for Charlotte. She sees the Grande Rose every day."

"I saw the Grande Rose once in all its glory," I told him, remembering Georges's face as he stood transfixed in its radiance. The cathedral had bestowed so many blessings—refuge for Charlotte and victory for Jeanne and the king. For me, the cathedral had bestowed the clarity to see a way of finding Father.

Now that I had found him and he was healing, everything began afresh. I clutched his hand. "Let us go to Charlotte. We can live peacefully in Reims while you heal. I can start my apprenticeship again, at a book shop there."

What about Georges? the voice asked, but I ignored it while waiting for Father to speak.

He stared out the window. Whenever he set out on a merchant journey, he had this very look on his face, and it always made me sad. He would put his satchels by the door as Mama comforted me. She explained that he was with us in body, but his mind was already far away, somewhere down a road that we had never traversed.

This time he wasn't on his journey alone, as I too was steering our course. "Please, can't we go to Charlotte?" I asked again.

He shook his head, still not looking at me.

"Why not?" I demanded, my anger at him stirring for the first time since we rescued him.

He turned to me, squaring his arms against his chest, his lips pressed tightly together. "It's not safe for us there."

"Because of your secret trade?"

His face grew pale as his eyes locked with mine. "How did you know about it?"

Everything spilled out of me then—the sulfur smell in his warehouse, Gaston and his crew that day on the meadow, Jeanne giving me shelter and her instructions to secure the weapons. He interrupted me midway through my story of what had happened at Wervecke's place of business. "After you paid my debt, how much of Alençon's money was left?"

"Seventeen hundred gold écus."

"By God's fist, that is the most money I have had in many moons," he said, smiling for the first time since we found him. "Jeanne *is* my Lady Luck."

"How can you say that? Wervecke intends to harm you. He knows about your secret trade too."

His smile vanished as he leaned forward to close the shutters, glancing at the patients nearest us to make sure they were sleeping. "Tell me everything," he whispered. "But speak softly."

Father listened intently to my tale of the moneylender's threat and the measures that Hersende and I had taken to thwart him. "You and Hersende have saved me twice," he breathed, clapping me on the shoulder. "But our troubles aren't over. Wervecke may have already told the Burgundian spies here about me."

"But how could they have discovered us? We haven't gone out in public."

"Spies for the king and for the enemy are everywhere, Felise, like invisible spider webs," he replied. His back straightening and his face alert, he went on. "It isn't safe for us in Bruges. We must go at once, in disguise, to Troyes. Jeanne's weapons are hidden there."

"Troyes?" The cup of broth almost dropped from my hand. Georges . . . had he returned home by now? But I didn't dare go to Troyes with André and Thibaut searching for me. And Barthélemy. I shuddered at the memory of his naked body.

Father and I hadn't had a chance to talk about my future yet. If I told him about André's plans for me, would he force me to marry the dyer? Or would he seal his contract with Georges? I didn't know but decided not to risk telling Father yet.

"I can't return home," I told him. "I stole a horse when I ran away."

"My daughter a horse thief?" Father shook his head in disbelief, but his eyes shone with pride. "I knew you were daring, but I never guessed you would take such a risk to escape slavery."

He clasped my shoulders, his gaze becoming somber. "In prison I thought that I had lost you on account of my debts; I won't risk losing you again, to the spies or to the magistrates of Troyes for horse thievery. No one will know that you have returned. You won't walk the streets in the daylight. At night, with your ragged boy's clothes and haircut, no one will recognize you."

I stared at his face, still pale and thin. "But, Father, you've barely recovered and you're still not strong enough to undertake this journey."

Father shook his head. "I promised Jeanne that I would bring her supplies."

"Couldn't someone else set out on this mission instead of you?"

"No. I have the best chance of coming out alive. I know every street in Troyes and every hiding place. I alone know how to outsmart the Burgundian spies there."

"Father, let's find another merchant who knows Troyes too," I pleaded, wishing Hersende were here.

"We're wasting time arguing." His hands dropped from my shoulders, and he looked away, swallowing hard. "Felise, I am ashamed of what I am about to tell you, but I must do so before we leave. Troyes isn't our home anymore. The moneylenders took possession of our house. They have surely sold it by now."

Tears sprang to my eyes. The urgency of rescuing him had blinded me, but now everything became clear. Because of his debts, another girl slept in my room and another woman worked in Ameline's shop.

I rose to my feet and turned to the door. "I'm sorry, Felise. Forgive me," he pleaded.

I shook my head.

"Please. I need your help."

"You want me to forgive you because you need my help?" My voice trembled.

"Listen to me," he snarled. "You've been involved in this too, whether you like it or not, ever since you set out for Bruges. No, even before then, since you told Jeanne I was your father. If you don't help me, you're only putting us in more danger."

"What?" I asked. I wheeled around to face him. For the first time ever, he glared at me, his anger a mirror of mine. "You're the one putting us in danger. Is your service to Jeanne more important than our lives?"

"Of course not! But every moment that you argue endangers us. Go. Bring me a quill and paper."

Never had he ordered me to do something in such a forceful manner, and never had I opposed him so squarely. I stood glaring at him, my lip quivering. His anger at me lingered, but something had changed. His lips were pursed and his eyes wide. For the first time ever, I saw his fear unmasked. He truly did need my help . . . to keep us all alive.

I strode across the room to my satchel and searched for his writing supplies, which were buried at the bottom. When I returned, he held my gaze as he took them from me. "Your journey has proven to me that you have the mettle of a man. Don't think of yourself as my daughter, but as a member of my crew. Trust me and simply do what I tell you."

I said nothing, clasping my hands behind my back and vowing to rely on my own judgment. He set the paper and ink on a small table and began to write a list of what he needed to do, step by step, detail upon detail. Making such lists consumed him for many hours before he left on his journeys. His work always took him far away from us, just as it did now. He wasn't truly here anymore either. He was somewhere in Troyes, securing Jeanne's weapons for her.

"We have no choice," Hersende said when she heard of Father's plan. In the kitchen we were packing provisions and chopping nettle and barley wort for his tonic. "He knows more about these spies than we do. Madame Catherine told me that a stranger was asking about her patients today at the market. It's time we leave Bruges. We must do everything we can to help him remain alert and strong."

Father and I didn't speak to each other all afternoon and evening as he directed our preparations. The squires' mood darkened at the news of another unexpected journey. When Father insisted that they dress in peasants' clothes like the rest of us, they spluttered in rage.

"My God, merchant, we have noble blood!" Jacques cried out in his nasal voice. "This is an insult."

"Do you want the Burgundians to behead you and put your heads on poles to warn other men not to buy weapons for the king?" Father asked, thrusting the shabby tunics at them.

The two squires exchanged terrified looks as Hersende and I did the same. In all that had happened, I had forgotten that Father's crew had talked about such punishment that day on the meadow. Fear mingled with my anger at Father that he had forced us into such a dangerous situation.

All day he followed Hersende's orders and rested in bed. After midnight we loaded everything onto the cart. Once again, Madame Catherine stood in the doorway holding a torch. "With God's grace, we will meet again," she said, embracing Hersende and me. "May he watch over you."

And protect us from spies, I added silently, wishing we could stay with her but knowing that it would endanger her and the other Beguines.

We traveled southward, hiding in the forests when the sun was up and riding the horses hard as soon as darkness cloaked us. I slept in bits and pieces, just as I had when I'd traveled alone. Whenever I was awake, I kept watch with Father, but we still didn't speak. When we passed Reims, I imagined Charlotte asleep in Juliane's cell.

On the third night, Hersende began to snore almost as soon as she lay down for a nap. The cart swayed back and forth as

Father and I faced the road behind us, watching for pursuers while Louis and Jacques drove the cart. Every noise in the darkness— the hooting of an owl or howling of a wolf—made me jump.

The cart's wheel rolled into a rut, shoving me against Father's arm.

He started to put his arm around me, but I drew back.

"Felise, I can't bear this silence any longer," he sighed. "It's never been our way before."

"What good would it do to speak of small matters?" I muttered. "In our hearts we would still be angry with one another."

"Maybe not, if we didn't talk about Jeanne's weapons. There are so many other subjects to discuss."

We used to talk late into the night, of the wondrous sights and stories of his journeys, of things that happened long ago, and our thoughts about what happened after death. Father believed that after death, our souls took a journey to places that living people could not imagine. I believed that heaven was a beautiful castle with endless rooms for each family. I asked Father questions and told him stories from the books I was copying and my own stories of people I had invented. I always slept soundly those nights, filled with stories and ideas that I had never before considered.

"Watch the road," he said. I heard him uncorking his flask and smelled Hersende's tonic. "Nasty," he said, shivering in disgust. "Beef stew and wine—that's what I need to rid my mouth of this nettle taste." His love of fine meals had once revealed itself in his portly body and round face. He loved cooking too. Once he had taught Ameline and me his recipe for egg pies and made up a song to help us remember it.

"How about some bread or cheese?" I asked. "Hersende wants you to eat little meals throughout the day to build your strength."

"I know. She's already fattened me up a little. But you need to take more food too. You're thinner than you were when I last saw you. And taller too, almost as tall as I."

I smiled in the darkness, pulling off two hunks of bread and spreading them with cheese.

"I still haven't gotten used to seeing you dressed as a boy," Father said as we ate.

"It's strange for me to look down and see that I'm not wearing a skirt, but your tunic."

"I always wished for a son to be my apprentice and share my adventures. Now that you're here and dressed as a boy, part of my wish has come true. Yours too, since you always wanted to journey with me and didn't understand why a girl couldn't."

"I understand now," I said, thinking of my narrow escapes from men and wolves.

"Thank God no one discovered you," he breathed. "You've always been clever, but I never guessed that your wiles would help you survive."

"Your stories of how you survived helped me, as well as your advice about using the North Star as a guide." As I said this, my anger at him diminished. If it hadn't been for him, I might have died. Didn't I owe him complete loyalty and support on the mission to secure the weapons for Jeanne?

"Have you thought about dressing as a girl again?" he asked.

His question took me by surprise. I didn't understand his reason for asking it. Was he making plans for my future, such as a marriage contract with the tanner or someone else? But Georges was a Burgundian—surely Father would no longer want to pursue the original contract with him. Yet if Father did decide to seal that agreement, how would I feel about it? I was glad for the darkness that hid my confusion about these possibilities.

"Ever since I ran away," I faltered, "everything has been happening so quickly that I didn't have much time to consider my future."

"That's what every day on a journey is like," he agreed. "And even if you had time to make plans, they often change. Your mother and sister never understood this."

He took my hand in his and this time I didn't snatch it away. "At home you were my only ally, Felise." His voice was earnest in the darkness. "And now we have only each other. Let's not argue."

"I can't promise you that."

"Why not?"

Many thoughts churned within me about things I had never spoken aloud. "I'm not a child anymore, who obeys without thinking," I said, staring at the road. "Since Ameline died, and after I ran away, I became used to thinking for myself."

"I see that full well," he said quietly. "You are much changed from the child I saw in February."

He put his arm around me. This time I rested my head against his shoulder, still alert for spies. A flash of light shot over the trees, a shooting star. "Look," Father exclaimed, pointing at it as it trailed into nothingness.

"I saw it too," I whispered. A thin band of clouds drifted here and there, like a lady's gossamer veil strewn across the sky, bejeweled with stars.

"I have learned something from my travels," Father mused. "You may have learned it too. All manner of things happen on the road, some pleasant and others not. When the mood is merry or the weather fair, it's best to savor that time, knowing that it could be snatched away in the blink of an eye."

"That is so true," I sighed, recalling that the glory of the coronation had long vanished like the fading light of the shooting star.

"For the moment, we are safe from the spies and the night is ours to enjoy," he said. "Do you remember our star game?"

"How could I forget it?"

"Let's play. You watch the road while I find a shape." He spoke in that hushed voice that I knew so well as he readied himself for the telling of a tale.

If only I were a child again. There would be no spies and no mission for Jeanne, and Ameline would still be alive. In our courtyard at home, the three of us would take turns finding shapes in the stars and making up stories about them as we had long ago. At that time, I hadn't suspected that I would soon lose Ameline and my home. Tears welled up in my eyes.

Not even a miracle could make that time return. Everything was changed, and even my love for Father, once as steady as the beating of our hearts, now ebbed and flowed like the ocean that I only knew from his tales. I had to accept that. I swallowed and held back my tears.

"I'll watch the road while you look straight up and find three bright stars in a row," he bade me, not noticing anything amiss. "That's Orion the Hunter and the three stars that form his belt."

I arched my neck to find them. Father had once told me Orion's story: how he was a famous hunter who had fallen in love with Diana, the goddess of the hunt. Yet I knew Father would tell me a different story tonight because he never told the same one twice.

He played a trill on his recorder, barely audible over the sounds of the horses. I lifted my head from his shoulder to hear the call to the story better. A familiar anticipation came over me.

"Tell no one what I am about to tell you, Felise," he began in his storytelling voice. "I'm going to tell you a tale that truly took place. There's a river in my story, just as there is in Orion's, but other than that, my story has nothing to do with his. My tale is about Jeanne and the first time I met her. It takes place at an inn near the River Vienne, on Saint Valentine's Day of last year."

I peered at the dark road ahead, eager to hear his story.

"Lady Fortune abandoned me at the gambling table that night," he continued. "Before long, I'd lost all my money and even some clothes. I was down to my woolen hose and white silk shirt, the one that Ameline sewed for me. I played my recorder and danced on the table, too drunk to care what anyone thought."

He softly played a merry dance tune, probably the same one he had played that night, but I blushed in the darkness. Why was he telling me this tale that only made me ashamed of him?

"The door burst open, and travelers hurried in, rain-soaked and muddy," Father continued. "They flung off their drenched outer garments and hastened to warm themselves by the fire. Suddenly chilled, I stumbled over to join them. I stood next to a young man called Jean de Domrémy and asked him why they were traveling so late on such a God-forsaken night.

"'My Lord sends me to the dauphin with a message. He is the rightful king, and I am to help him win back his crown. Who are you?'

"When I told him, he asked what troubled me. His clear eyes pierced through me to a part that was untouched by the wine. Never before had anyone looked at me that way."

I shivered, remembering how Jeanne had looked at me the same way that night in the vineyard and several times since then.

"When I told him of my debt," Father continued, "he made the sign of the cross and told me to give up gambling. Many priests preach the same message, but I always scoffed at them. That night I listened to a ragged peasant boy giving me the same advice."

My eyes grew wide with wonder. "You have given up gambling?" When we rescued him at the debtors' prison, I thought that the guards had taken away his lucky dice against his will. My heart lifted with hope that giving them up had been his choice and that my dream of living together as a family could come true.

"Just as impatient as ever," Father clucked his teeth and laughed as he always did when I tried to hurry his story along. "But you'll have to wait for the answer. A month later, I knew that Jean was actually a girl, the one that Marie d'Avignon had prophesied would win back France from the enemy. I journeyed to the dauphin's castle in Chinon in hopes of persuading her to buy weapons from me.

"I waited at the castle gate all morning, and at midday she rode through the gate with two companions. A nobleman on horseback approached her and asked if she was the maid who claimed she would save France. When she said yes, the nobleman brought his horse closer and spat on her face.

"'Are you denying God's intent for me?' she asked in a low voice that nonetheless pierced the cold air. 'And you, so close to death?'"

I shifted my position, frightened by the course Father's story had taken as he picked up his recorder again and played a soft, haunting melody.

"The man's sneer vanished, and his face grew pale," Father continued, his voice so soft that I had to strain to hear it. "He rode away. That afternoon, I walked along the River Vienne, which was swollen with rain and reflected the sunset. Gathered along the bank ahead, men pulled something from the water. I walked closer and saw a dark mantle, disheveled hair and, underneath it, the bluish skin of someone's neck. A man had drowned that day.

"Even before they turned the corpse over, I knew who it was; the man who had insulted Jeanne."

"Did she have him murdered?" I asked tremulously.

Father took my hand. "No, she just knew that he would die that very day."

"But how?"

"Some would call it a miracle," he responded in a voice that didn't sound like his. He had never believed in miracles before and used to call people who believed in them sheep.

"That day I threw my dice into the River Vienne," he continued, "and gave up gambling forever. Since then I have devoted myself to Jeanne's cause. I believe she will bring peace to our land, but I have baser motives as well. She has brought me good fortune, Felise, more than I have ever had before." He played a joyous ending song on his recorder. "Do you understand now why I serve her?"

Despite the night's warmth, his words sent a chill down my spine. "No, Father, I don't. Nor do I understand why I serve her and why we both take such risks for her." I reached for Ameline's shawl and wrapped it around my shoulders.

"Your sister's," he whispered, touching its fringe. "I wonder what she would say about Jeanne if she were here."

"She helped me to understand that Jeanne is a girl like me and her. Father, sometimes Jeanne's power seems like a curse, not on France, of course, but on her. She can never be an ordinary girl again."

"What's wrong with that?" Father demanded. "Our land has no need for her as an ordinary girl. France needs a virgin warrior to help us end this war once and for all."

"But I am thinking of her now. She has changed greatly since I met her a month ago, and some of the king's ministers are turning against her. She is suffering a great deal."

"Her saints always take care of her. With their help, she'll win back the captains and lead us through to victory." Father patted my shoulder. "Now it's your turn to tell a story. I'll watch the road."

I wrinkled my brow in disbelief. Hadn't he heard me? Jeanne was his Lady Luck, and he needed her to be invincible, as did the people of France. I shook my head and arched my neck to feast my eyes on the field of stars above. So many possibilities for stories lay there, maybe even one that could chart a new course, if not for Jeanne or Father, at least for me. Four brilliant stars caught my eye—the chest of a massive horse.

Other stars suggested its neck and head, and a small star became the point of a horn.

I watched the road while Father found my unicorn in the

stars. "It lived in a forest far away from any town," I began. "By day it grazed in woodland meadows with its own kind, galloping freely without rider or saddle. Every night the unicorn sprouted wings and flew to the sky, its white mane shining in the starlight.

"One day a man found the unicorn and asked it to help his people, who had been sickened by a deadly poison. The unicorn agreed and followed the man to a land of farms and cities.

"The poison caused men to kill one another in battles, burn villages, and steal animals and food from starving peasants. The unicorn led this man into battles to draw out the poison from the people and release them from war.

"Alas, the poison entered the unicorn's body and weakened it more each day. One night as the unicorn tried to reach the stars, it collapsed on the roof of a cathedral. A hawk flying toward its nest saw the injured beast and flew to its side. The hawk plucked one of its own feathers to make a quill. Holding it in its mouth, it dipped the quill into the unicorn's blood to write a charm upon the roof. The charm stanched the flow of blood but was not strong enough to draw the poison from the unicorn.

"'Stay here with me,' the hawk pleaded, 'and the poison will leave your body.'"

"'I must go.'"

"'You will die,' the hawk protested. 'I beg you to save yourself. Send for another unicorn.'

"The unicorn tossed its mane and rose unsteadily to its hooves. 'No, I am the unicorn called to help release everyone from the poison. Thank you for your help. In return for your kindness, I will grant you your heart's desire.'

"'Grant me a nest, far away from the poisoned land," the hawk said. "Big enough for all those I love.'"

I paused to imagine a beautiful house where Father, Charlotte, and I lived. "The hawk continued, 'And ink aplenty, fine parchment and leather to bind it into a book, that I may write your story for all to hear. And other stories too, that my father taught me long ago. . . .'"

Father hugged me tightly as my story echoed in the night. "Your tale surpasses mine," he whispered. "Thank you for telling me your heart's desire. I can make no promises, but I will try."

Fourteen

Troyes

August 28, 1429

Father suddenly clasped his hand against my mouth and pointed to the road. The unmistakable sound of horses came from a league or so behind us.

He scrambled toward the squires and alerted them. The horses broke into a gallop and the cart lurched, awakening Hersende. "What is happening?" she demanded.

"Men are following us," I moaned, crawling toward her.

The poor horses. I winced when the whip struck their backs, but its sting caused them to carry us faster. Father gripped the edge of the cart to steady himself as he kept watch. In accepting Jeanne's mission, I had saved his life, but I had also set everything in motion to trap us in this black night, with mysterious riders closing in from behind.

The fields gave way to forests. Father ordered the squires to veer right onto a hidden side path and then to halt. Our pursuers, two men on horseback, galloped by without noticing the path. There we waited, with weapons at the ready, for the rest of the night and the following day. Thank God our pursuers never returned to look for us.

When we reached Troyes, Father commanded the squires to stop far away so that the gatekeeper wouldn't notice us.

"Listen well," he told them. "The men who pursued us have

probably warned the Burgundian spies about us. They already know that I am an arms dealer for the king. You must walk the streets and do my business for me."

No one spoke. There was no turning back for any of us. We were Father's captives. Without a trace of fear, his eyes glittered with excitement.

"Trust me," he said, adjusting his hood so that it covered most of his face.

Trust him, trust him, the words echoed within me as we entered through the north gate. I lay down on the cart, pretending to be asleep and hoping the gatekeeper wouldn't notice my body shaking all over.

"Pass through to the marketplace," the gatekeeper slurred. To him, we were just a peasant family, arriving before dawn to sell beans in the market. Hersende, playing the part of Father's wife and mother to the rest of us, even offered the gatekeeper some of the beans that Father had us pick each night as a prop for this ruse.

Relief washed over me as the cart finally rumbled through the gate. After secreting it in a warehouse and stabling the horses, we walked a long way to confuse the spies and finally arrived at a decrepit inn. We waited outside while Louis went in and secured two adjacent rooms.

We soon discovered that the beds were infested with fleas and the blankets threadbare. Hersende and I sprinkled fleabane on the beds. She insisted that Father take the bed in our room while we slept on the floor. I tumbled onto my pallet as she snipped herbs to make another batch of the healing draught. I wished she could make one for me too, one that would take away my fear.

The sound of people in the street awakened me. They were probably on their way to work, just as I once set out to the scriptorium every morning. Would I ever return to such an ordinary life? And what of the tanner—had he given up searching for me? I started to go to the window and look for him but stopped when I remembered the spies. In my mind, they wore black hoods that covered jagged scars like the moneylender's. They pressed their ears to closed doors, hungry for secrets.

Hersende and I passed the day cutting herbs and making medicines while Father made a list of the tasks to be done. The most important of these was to send the squires for more horses and carts, also more barrels and sacks of flour in which to hide the war goods.

As soon as the squires returned safely from this mission, Hersende insisted that Father nap. Aided by her sleeping potion, he fell asleep at once and didn't awaken until after dark.

He rose, gripping the bedpost to steady himself. "I must attend to a few urgent matters and try to assemble Gaston and the rest of my crew," he announced to Hersende and me, his voice filled with resolve.

I hurried to his side. The gray cast to his face was more pronounced despite the healing draught. "You're not going alone, are you?" I asked.

"Yes."

"But you should have someone with you. If you falter on the streets, and they find you, we may all die."

His eyes grew wide. "God forbid that I do anything to endanger you."

Hersende stepped in, touching his forehead. "You have a slight fever. You're not well enough to go anywhere tonight, much less alone. Take one of the squires."

"Trust me, I am well," he breathed, his eyes still on mine, "but as a precaution I will take Jacques with me tonight. And as another precaution, I want the two of you to take shelter with someone in Troyes, a person who can also help you journey to Jeanne and the army."

"Why aren't we going with you and your caravan?" I asked, clutching his hands.

He squeezed mine back. "It's too risky. Above all else, I want you to be safe."

"But if we involved other people in your secret trade, we would endanger their lives too," I argued. "Why couldn't we secure a horse and ride to meet you?"

He shook his head. "You and Hersende need a man to travel with you and protect you."

I jerked my hands away from his. "Have you forgotten that I survived for over a month on my own and took care of Charlotte?"

He gripped my shoulders so fiercely that it hurt. "Those pursuers didn't hunt you down for the sole purpose of torturing and killing you."

His words echoed in the silence between us. He wrapped his arms around me, hugging me tightly. "Don't go," I moaned. "I didn't rescue you from prison only to lose you again."

"Trust me. I will return home safe and sound, well before first light. Promise me that you'll find someone in Troyes who could offer you a safe haven and help you leave."

I nodded against his chest. He kissed the top of my head and then he was gone.

I stood there staring at the door and clutching Ameline's shawl. Hersende came over and led me to the hearth. "Nothing you said would have stopped him. All we can do is to pray."

All through the "Ave Maria," I imagined Father and Jacques creeping down alleys and hiding in doorways whenever the night watchmen approached. Afterward, we sat in the barrel-shaped chairs and snipped more herbs. "Do you know of someone who could help us?" Hersende asked.

Georges the Tanner sprang to mind. "There is someone. . . ."

"And you can be certain of this person?"

"He's a Burgundian." I purposely didn't mention that he was also a leader of his guild in the fight against the king.

"Surely there's someone else."

Anes would be relieved to see me alive and would take good care of Hersende and me, but she wanted me to marry Thibaut.

My teacher Michel? André might find out. And I didn't know any of the women in the cloth workers' guild well enough to trust them. I shook my head. "No one else comes to mind."

When I told her about Father's intention to wed me to Georges, her eyes widened. "Your father was planning your marriage to a Burgundian?"

"I don't understand it, but yes. Please, promise me that you won't tell Father that I know about the contract."

Hersende shook her head. "But does this Burgundian know that you favor the king?"

"Yes. And there's more. I stole his horse when I ran away."

"So you chose to run away rather than marrying him?"

I nodded, sifting my hands through the basket of spearmint in my lap. "Before I ran away, this Burgundian spoke tenderly to me. And after I left, I think he went to search for me."

Hersende pursed her lips. "He could have been searching for his horse and not you. Going to him is very risky."

I set the basket of spearmint down and rose to put another log on the fire. His tortured face at the cathedral came back to me, as well as his urgency to receive penance. What had happened to him?

I took the poker and repositioned the logs. "I know it's a risk, Hersende, and yet I trust him. Last June he wanted to help me. Maybe he would help me again, especially if I pretended to be a Burgundian."

"And if I made it look like you were injured," she added. "So you would be willing to go to his house?"

"Yes, but we can't tell Father. We'll tell him that we're seeking help from Anes and her husband, Mathieu, instead."

The bells rang the midnight hour as I paced back and forth by the hearth. I heard a faint knock at the door. Racing to it, I listened intently. "It's me," Father whispered into the crack.

I flung the door open and there he stood. He entered the room, quickly barring the door. Sweat dripped down his face and there was blood on his sleeve. Hersende yanked it up and inspected his arm. "You aren't wounded. What happened?"

"A spy was following us," Father whispered. "I did what I had to do or else we would have been caught."

I drew back from him. *Father had killed a man.* I collapsed on my pallet, wishing this night had never happened.

My horror at what he had done disturbed my slumber and my thoughts the next day. How could he gaze at the stars and tell stories with me one night and murder a man on the next? And then just clean the blood from the knife that he used as the weapon and carry on? I turned away from the sight of it, staring at the fire and unable to lift a finger to help Hersende.

Soon after the noon bells rang, someone knocked on the door three times and slid a scrap of paper into the room. Motioning for us to be quiet, Father went to the door and bent down to pick the paper up. "'Barley,'" he read. "That's my sentry's password to leave this inn—it may not be safe anymore. As soon as it's dark, the squires and I will go to a new hiding place."

I joined him at the hearth and watched him throw the scrap of paper in the fire. Before it burned completely, I read the rest of the message that Father kept to himself: *hide in the secret room of the Red Rooster.* That was Father's favorite tavern. But it was on a busy street, and someone might see him entering it.

"Let us go with you, Father," I pleaded, fearing that he was still weak and not thinking clearly. Perhaps his love of risks was blinding him.

He shook his head. "Did you think of someone who could give you shelter and help you travel to the army?"

"Mama's friend Anes," I lied, glancing at Hersende. "Her husband Mathieu could help us rejoin you."

Father sighed in relief. "An excellent choice. As soon as dusk falls, you must go to their house."

"And until then you must rest, Henri," Hersende said, bringing him a cup of tonic. "This will put you to sleep for several hours, and then you will awaken refreshed and strengthened."

As soon as he fell asleep, Hersende and I set to work concocting ways to enhance my disguise. "The tanner has never seen me dressed as a boy," I told her. "Father says I'm thinner and taller than I was last spring."

"Good," Hersende said, reaching for a satchel of bandages and a pair of scissors. She cropped parts of my hair very close to my scalp, causing it to stick out in little clumps here and there. Father once told me that he had witnessed the hanging of an accused witch, and her hair had been cut in the same manner. But since I was dressed as a boy, I hoped that no one would think I was a witch.

Hersende dipped a long strip of bandages into a jar of reddish liquid. "It won't hurt. It will make it seem that your face has been bleeding." She wrapped the bandages tightly around my head and forehead, then stood back and surveyed her handiwork. "Your eyes are your strongest feature. This tanner will probably remember them."

Opening another drawstring bag, she pulled out an eye patch. After tying it around my head, she added another layer of bandages and smeared soot from the fireplace around my other eye. She nodded at her handiwork. "What story will you tell him?"

"I could say that I'm a messenger for the Burgundians and that I was injured by the king's men. What will we tell him about you?"

"I'm not going with you," she said quietly.

I clutched her hand, unprepared for this news. "But you must come with me! What if he finds out who I am? What if I'm wrong about his feelings for me? Or if they've changed and he captures me and hands me over to the Duke of Burgundy?"

"Run to me in the cathedral square. I will be disguised as a beggar woman there. It's best for us to be in two places—in case one of us needs to escape quickly. I think that two people knocking on his door would make him more suspicious than if just one of us came to his house. Besides, we don't want the spies to see us together if we can avoid it."

"You're going to sleep outside tonight in the midst of beggars and thieves?"

"Don't worry. I have a knife." She brushed strands of cut hair off my tunic. "If the tanner does agree to help us leave Troyes, tell him about your 'aunt' who needs to go with you. If he doesn't, come to me. Be strong of heart. It's our only way to leave Troyes safely."

At dusk, I awakened Father. He bolted upright and touched the bandage on my forehead. "My God, Felise, you look horrible. Poor Anes will faint away the moment she sees you."

He quickly donned his traveling cloak and boots. He looked bigger and more powerful than he had since we rescued him. As he hugged me tightly, I could feel his courage like a real thing that could be touched. "God willing, I will see you safe and sound in a fortnight."

"And you too," I said, wishing we could both be spirited away to a safe haven.

Hersende, dressed as a beggar woman, slipped out of the inn first. By the time I reached the street, she had already disappeared. I resisted an urge to follow her to the cathedral square.

The church bells rang the evening hour in the street where the silk thread makers plied their craft. One of these shops, festooned with brightly colored threads, had been Georges's mother's where we had played hide and seek. His street was a short walk farther on. I kept my head down, not daring to look into the eyes of anyone I passed. André and Thibaut wouldn't likely enter this part of town, but I didn't want to take any chances.

With each step, my hands, which were hidden in Father's old

gloves, grew slick with sweat. *God be with you.* Hersende's last words echoed in my mind. With my satchel slung over my shoulder, I hugged the shadows along the sides of the streets, looking all around to make sure no one was following me.

Since the day was warm and sunny, many of the tanners had thrown open the shutters of their shops and set their hides to dry in the sun. Not a single tanner was working, even though the it was past time for the midday meal, but the sun had not set. I scanned the trademarks at each shop looking for the tanner's cedar tree, the trademark I had seen on his satchel at Reims.

The shutters to the shop under the cedar tree sign were closed. Leaning my ear against the door, I heard nothing inside. Like the rest of the tanners, he probably wasn't home. Perhaps there was a guild meeting.

Shaking, my hand slipped down his door. I had to force myself to knock and seek his help in providing safe passage to Jeanne. *There's another reason too,* my voice gently reminded me.

I leaned my head against the door and put myself back at the cathedral, recalling how he had turned and set his satchel on the floor. Even in the shadowy nave, anguish had filled his face. When his eyes caught sight of the Grande Rose, the anguish had given way to wonder: wonder that I had seen before on the face of the dark-haired boy. I had turned to the Grande Rose too, and all my resistance had fallen away. I was ready to step from the shadow of the Virgin's altar and face him.

Lifting my head, I knocked on his door. A boy with dark hair opened it. I drew back at this apparition from a silk shop long ago. The boy's eyes widened as he took in my bloody bandages. Who was he?

"Is Georges at home?" I asked, forgetting to disguise my voice.

He took no notice; he shook his head and started to close the door. I clutched the handle. "Wait, I need help. Get your mother."

She quickly appeared at the door, a young woman with dark hair like her son's and freckles sprinkled across the bridge of her nose. She looked at my bandaged face with a mixture of curiosity and pity.

"I was sent to speak with Georges the Tanner," I told her, making my voice as deep as possible. "When will he return?"

"Who sent you?" she asked, her eyes narrowing in suspicion.

"I don't know his name, but he was a leader of the Burgundians."

Her gaze softened. "Georges will be home by suppertime. You can wait inside."

Thank God, he had returned safely to Troyes. The darkness of the foyer folded itself around me, concealing me in shadows. The acrid smell of leather mixed with that of wood smoke. In the great room beyond, the boy sat at a game table playing chess with a round-faced man who had brown curly hair. He glanced up at me as the woman explained why I was here.

"What do you need to tell Georges?" the man asked.

"The man who hired me said the message was for his ears only."

The man scowled, folding his arms against his chest. "At least you can tell me how you got hurt."

"In a fight," I muttered, wishing he would stop asking questions.

"With those who support the king?"

"Yes, they threw rocks at me." I leaned against the wall and lowered my head, pretending I was about to faint.

The woman took me by the arm. "You need to rest."

She led me to an alcove off the great room. "Stay here until you feel better," she said as she left.

A hoop and a pigskin ball on the floor caught my eye, as well as the wooden figure of an archer poking out from beneath a stool: the child's toys. Seeing a chamber pot in the corner, I used it quickly and listened to the conversation by the hearth. The woman spoke of a sick friend whom she had visited that day. "Her fever broke," she said. "She even took a little soup."

"Good," her husband replied. "Don't move there, Jacques. My queen will take your knight. Here's a better move."

Someone added wood to the fire. The woman hummed a song that Charlotte liked.

"I won, Papa," Jacques exclaimed suddenly.

"You played well," his father praised him.

I smiled, remembering how Father used to let me win. May he be safe at the Red Rooster and Hersende amid the beggars and cutthroats.

I turned to a shelf and picked up a dried silkworm's cocoon that felt like a fuzzy egg. Beside it a crockery bowl contained metal pieces with raised surfaces that were bigger than coins: pilgrims collected these badges from shrines they visited. One badge bore the stamp of the Cathedral of Chartres near Paris, and another depicted the statue of a Black Virgin that Father had seen at the shrine of Rocamadour. I drew out an object bigger than the badges—a seal like the one Mama had given me when I first learned to write. Holding it up to the sunlight streaming through the window, I looked at the flat part and clutched it tightly in my hand. It was my seal of the letter *F*. In my hurry to leave home, I had left it wrapped in a piece of cloth on Father's desk. Sometime before the house was sold, Georges must have gone there and taken it. To keep it safe until I returned? I kissed the seal and forced myself to put it back.

As I listened again for Georges, the smell of onions wafted toward me. He would be home soon. My belly fluttered at the thought of seeing him. Better to face him when I was with the family, who might distract his attention from me.

I stood in the shadows of the alcove noticing the details of the tanner's great room. It looked bigger than ours and was also filled with more furniture. Cooking vessels of every size hung from hooks in the ceiling, and crockery bowls and pitchers were stored in a side cupboard. How could his family afford all these possessions?

Emerging from the alcove, I walked toward the woman, who was scaling a trout at a side table, while the boy and his father whittled poplar sticks at the main table.

The mother glanced at me. "Your color looks better, boy," she said and went back to work.

"Could I help you?" I asked, feeling awkward just standing there.

"Chop the carrots," she said.

Standing where I could see the front door, I scraped them and cut a few neat carrot coins like Ameline had taught me. A beggar boy wouldn't make them so neat. I shifted to making uneven slices instead, hoping that the woman wouldn't realize I was a girl in disguise. Thankfully, she kept her eyes on the scaling knife. When she was done, she picked up the trout. "Follow me with those carrots," she said, turning toward the hearth.

I glanced at the front alcove. Any moment, Georges could walk through it. Jeanne's advice echoed in my mind: *Act like a peasant boy.* I tried to calm myself by noticing everything set before me. A pot hung over the fire, and in it, a sauce simmered, glistening with butter and onions and smelling of ginger.

Jacques came over to watch. I made room for him between his mother and me, positioning myself so I could see the door.

"Jacques, you're too close to the fire," his mother warned, and he quickly moved back.

She bade me put the carrots into the pot before placing the trout on top of them. Whenever Ameline and I made this dish at home, it was always my job to lather sauce over the trout's silvery gray flesh and tuck the carrots underneath it. It was so familiar that I forgot to be clumsy. But the woman hummed a song and didn't seem to notice.

Jacques helped me set the table while the father cleaned up the wood shavings scattered on it. I chose a seat where I could watch the front door while the woman served the trout on a platter. She had sprinkled chopped parsley on top and held a loaf of bread under her arm. The man licked his lips, eyeing the fish with anticipation. "Georges said to start supper without him. It's going to be hard to save him his share."

My eyes darted toward the door, and my heart thumped against my chest. How much longer would I have to endure this? When I glanced back at the couple, the wife was grinning at her husband, her face flushed from standing close to the fire.

He kissed her on the forehead. "I suppose I'll forgive you for beating me in chess, Hauviette," he joked.

"Blame Georges, not me, Antonin," she replied, laughing and waving a fork at him. "He taught me too well."

After cutting off the trout's head, Hauviette sliced it in half and deftly removed the bones. My face started to sweat as she served the fish. Antonin poured us each a cup of wine, adding water to Jacques's and mine.

I was glad that the family was too busy talking and eating to notice that I hardly ate a bite. Jacques kept interrupting his parents to prattle about his day, helping in the tannery. From their conversation, I gleaned that Antonin was a journeyman in Georges's shop and Hauviette the servant.

At the end of the meal, Jacques yawned and went to sit on his mother's lap. The talk turned to the tasks for the morrow. Hauviette would wash clothes in the river, and Antonin would sell hides at the market. How lovely these ordinary and predictable tasks seemed. I myself had no idea what tomorrow would hold. Or tonight.

I heard the sound of feet stomping outside the front door, as if someone were removing mud from his boots. My body tensed as I watched the front door open. Georges entered the foyer, his face hidden in the shadows. I lowered my head and tried to rehearse what I would say to him, but I couldn't. Even worse, I saw him in my mind as he looked the day he led the tanners in the riot. His face was bright red in his hatred for the king and Jeanne. Why had I come here?

Jacques ran to the foyer carrying a stick. "Georges, I whittled this for you."

"Thank you," he said. I heard the sound of his boots striking the floor as he strode toward the table. "Who is this boy and how was he hurt?"

"He wants to speak with you," Antonin answered for me. "The king's supporters threw rocks at him after he delivered a message to a Burgundian."

I heard Georges coming to stand beside me, his leathery smell overpowering the fish and ginger. Surely in the silence, everyone could hear my heart pounding against my chest. "What do you want from me, boy?" he asked. His voice sounded different than I remembered it, lower pitched and listless.

"The enemy threatened to kill me," I replied, keeping my head down but unable to control my unsteady voice. "I barely escaped from them. I had been told to seek sanctuary with the leader of the tanners if I were ever in danger."

"Who gave you that advice?" he asked suspiciously.

"Masons," I replied. It was the first guild I could think of that supported Burgundy.

"What was this message and to whom you were delivering it?" Georges persisted.

"They gave me a scrap of paper, but I can't read, and they didn't tell me the man's name; they just told me what he looked like. I gave it to the man and when I ran away, the king's supporters chased me."

"What did the man look like?"

"Tall and thin with gray hair."

"What was his guild?"

"I don't know."

Though my gaze was still on my lap, I could tell he was looking at me. "Someone bandaged your face quite well. Who was it?"

"My aunt."

"Where is she?"

"In the cathedral square."

"Why didn't you hide at her house?"

"We are beggars. We have no home."

He fell silent. I heard him sit down on the bench across from me. Hauviette served him a plate. He thanked her and set to eating quickly as if he were very hungry.

All I could do was sit on the bench and wait, listening to Antonin take Jacques to bed and Hauviette clean the dishes.

"Good night," Georges bade her. I heard her footsteps on the stairs. When he got up from the table and walked away, I lifted my head and saw him at the hearth. I was terrified to be alone with him, not knowing what would come to pass between us. I yawned loudly, hoping he would let me sleep.

"Boy, bring me another log from the foyer," he called to me.

Crossing the room quickly, I noticed the thick log at the top of the pile. It looked too heavy for me, but if I tried to take one from below, the logs might roll onto the floor. I strained to lift it and bring it to him, panting with the effort.

A groan escaped my lips as I dropped the log into his outstretched arms. As he positioned it in the fire, I clasped my hands behind my back, praying that he didn't suspect anything. He reached for the poker, and I noticed that the blister on his hand from earlier this summer had healed. As he adjusted the wood to coax more flames, shadows played about his back and arms, which were just as strong as I remembered. But his face: even the shadows couldn't hide the strain etched there.

He rose to his full height, standing so close that my arm touched his. On purpose or by accident? But whatever his intent, his closeness made my cheeks redden. Fanning my face in pretense of being too hot, I stepped back from the fire, away from his arm.

He stepped back too. "What's your name?"

"Philippe."

"Ah, so your parents named you after the Duke of Burgundy. Are they still alive?"

"No, just my aunt."

"You have a hard life, boy," he said. "You may take sanctuary at my house. It is the least I can offer you for your bravery on behalf of the Duke of Burgundy."

But he had just met me. How could he be certain that he could trust me in his house? "Thank you," I murmured.

He turned away from the hearth and I glanced back at him, hoping that he was going to get me blankets for a pallet, but he went to the game table instead. "Come, play a game of chess with me before you settle down to sleep."

"I don't know how," I replied. My pretense was exhausting me. I worried that I would make a mistake and he would find out who I really was. I needed a night's sleep to refresh and help me persist with the ruse. Tomorrow I would try to convince him to help my "aunt" and me leave Troyes.

"Do you want to learn to play?" he asked, setting up the board.

"It looks too hard."

"I can teach you. Take the white pieces."

I joined him at the table, listening as he explained how to move the pieces. His hands were raw and callused. Heat rose to my face again as I imagined rubbing Hersende's salve on them.

He bade me to practice the moves he had shown me. Since my gloves were too big for my hands, I almost knocked some pieces over.

"Why don't you take off those gloves," Georges advised. "I have built up the fire. Your hands should be plenty warm."

I slipped them off in my lap without a word. My hands wouldn't stop trembling, but it was impossible to keep them hidden because I had to show him that I remembered how to move the bishop, rook, and knight. Then he set up the pieces midway through a practice game and asked me to move my knight to the best place. I purposely moved him to a square that put him in danger. Before I could put my hand back on my lap, Georges grasped it in his. His hand, rough and warm, sent an invisible current through mine and I did not pull it away. "Your hand is cold," he said in a concerned tone. "I understand why you kept your gloves on so long. Do you want to warm your hands by the fire?"

I shook my head. "They're always cold," I muttered.

"There's a better move," he said as he lifted my hand that held the knight and moved him to a different spot. It made me feel like a child again, learning to form my letters with Ameline moving my hand that held the quill.

We each played a half a dozen moves or more in silence, broken only by the crackling of the fire and the pieces tapping into their new squares. I kept my eyes on the board and on his hand as he deftly moved his chosen piece. I clumsily moved mine, hardly able to focus on a plan of attack. But I had not forgotten all those years of practice with Ameline, and without my bidding I chose a good move.

"You learn quickly," he observed. My heart beat faster at the hint of suspicion in his voice, and I didn't respond.

He set up an imaginary end game, with only a few pieces left on the board. "Queens are very important pieces to save for the end game," he said, setting my queen on a square near the center of the board. "Where can she move from here, Philippe? And what would the best and safest place be?" His voice had grown softer.

My hand grew sweaty as I pretended to consider several spots for my queen. I was trapped—unless I ran for the door, but that would give everything away. I swallowed and chose one of the worst squares.

Without any warning, he clasped my hand again with his, more tightly this time. I kept my head down and tried to pull my hand away.

"You can quit your pretense, Felise," he said, pressing my hand to his heart, which beat as rapidly as mine. "Thank God, you're safe."

His words echoed within me. He rejoiced that I was safe! I met his gaze and saw that his eyes were misted as they sparkled in the firelight. With his other hand he reached over to touch my bandaged forehead. "Are you really hurt?"

"No. How did you know it was me?"

"Your voice. It sounded very much like your true voice, only deeper. And then when you said that you had no home, I heard the same sadness in your voice that I heard at your sister's funeral."

He remembered my voice from three months ago? Not once had I considered that it would give me away. "I fooled so many others, I thought I could fool you too," I murmured.

Drawing his hand back from the bandage, he shook his head and smiled into my eyes. "Not me. Why did you think you would need a disguise in my house?"

"I stole your horse. I didn't know what—"

"You were afraid I would turn you over to the magistrates?"

"At first yes, but . . ." My voice trailed off.

His thumb caressed the indentation on my writing finger where I held my quill. "I was angry at you, true." He paused. "But how could you believe that I would want to have you hanged?"

I bowed my head while he continued to clasp my hand. "No one hurt you?" he asked.

"Some tried, but through the grace of God, I escaped."

"I went to search for you," he whispered. "I feared you were dead."

On my journey to Bruges, a fear of losing Father had gripped me day and night. I had not intended to do so, and yet I had caused Georges to endure it too. He let go of my hand while I struggled to hold back my tears.

"Do you want me to help you take the bandages off?" he asked. I nodded.

When he had finished unwrapping them, my face felt cool and light. His gaze rested on my hair. Was he remembering me as I was, the day he'd told me about Father's contract, and I had flung off my coif and let my hair tumble free?

"It must have been very hard to cut it," he said.

"It was." I kept Jeanne's inspiration to myself, not wanting to argue about her as we had earlier in the summer. "But once I cut it, there was no time to regret what I had done."

He brought me a cloth and a bowl of water, which turned red as I wiped away Hersende's medicine. "You look like you've been out in the sun all day," he said with a smile. "You didn't need to go to so much trouble with a disguise on my account."

I remembered him leading the riot. "I didn't know if you had changed," I said. "If you would still want to have words with your enemy."

He shook his head. "My feelings toward you haven't changed at all. They never will." He turned to look out the window, his mouth set in a somber line. "But in other ways I have changed. For one thing, I'm weary of this war."

He went to the fire and stared at it for a long time before turning to me. The anguish that suffused his face at Reims had returned in full measure. He covered his face with his hands. I rose from the table and went to stand beside him, wanting to help but not knowing what to do.

He withdrew his hands and looked at me. "It shames me to speak of a terrible deed I did. But I told myself if God ever answered my prayers and let me see you again, I wouldn't keep it a secret. Nor would I expect you to forgive me."

He swallowed as if to gather strength. "Ever since I was a boy, the tanners have been like brothers to me," he began. "Many of us were apprentices together. My mother died when I was a child, and my father and sister around the time that I became a journeyman. The tanners became my new family. Above all else, I wanted their acceptance. They pledged their allegiance to the Duke of Burgundy, and so did I, without questioning. I fought the Dauphinists by their sides, and even became one of their leaders. As one of them, I had a place and a purpose. I finished my masterpiece, and the guild deemed my work worthy of a master tanner. All I needed was a wife, one who sided with the Duke of Burgundy.

"One day, I saw you in the market with your sister, helping her sell her garments. I remembered playing with you as a child. At the market you seemed to be full of curiosity as you watched the people passing by. I was drawn to you. Though I knew you were an enemy, and I tried to resist my feelings for you, I could not. As you know, I found out that your father sought to sell you in marriage. We were about to seal a contract, but he left on an urgent journey before that occurred."

I stared at the fire, remembering my anger the day Georges told me about Father's intentions. Everything had changed.

"That day in the cemetery," Georges continued, "I wanted to ask you to marry me secretly, in order to help you escape the marriage that André was planning for you."

I turned to him abruptly. I hadn't suspected this at all. If he had proposed, would I have changed my mind about running away?

"You spurned me," he went on, "and I decided not to ask you. It was clear that you, with your fine blood, wanted nothing to do with a lowly tanner. I became bitter. I avoided the streets where I knew that you walked and threw myself into the guild's work of defeating the Dauphinists.

"When you ran away, I searched for you whenever I could. But I was still loyal to my guild. I was prepared to fight to defend Troyes from the Maid and the dauphin the day before the duke surrendered to them."

He paused, his face pale in the firelight. "Soon after that, I went with a group of tanners to a village east of Troyes. We had reports that spies for the king were hiding there." His voice had become so low that I strained to hear him.

"We found them in a peasant's hovel," he continued, looking down at his hands. "I watched while my brothers murdered the spies and the unarmed women and children who had offered them a hiding place. I did nothing to stop the tanners."

He bowed his head as mine filled with outrage. How could he have done this? It was even worse than what Father had done when he killed a man to protect his own life.

I moaned, sinking to my knees, imagining Georges as he watched the slayings. He must have stood in the shadows, his face like a stone. But I knew that wasn't all. I knew that inside of him, a voice had screamed for him to stop the tanners, just as my voice would have done.

He sank to the floor beside me, and I looked at him knowing at last what had caused his anguish: the choice of not heeding his voice.

"Never again will I put my loyalty to my brothers over my heart," he said. "I have told them that I won't be a part of the killing and fighting any more. I'm going on a pilgrimage. It was my mother's dying wish that I would go to many shrines and pray for her soul. Now I must go on pilgrimage for my soul too. To do penance for my wrongdoing."

He bowed his head, and I reached out to touch his arm. My hand hovered in the air, but touching a man was something I had never done before. I withdrew my hand and bowed my head, praying that he would find release.

Fifteen

The Labyrinth

August 30, 1429

Georges and I sat on the floor, staring at the fire.

He was the first to break the silence. "Why did you come here?"

"To see if you would help me leave Troyes safely." I hesitated, not knowing how much to tell him. But he had been forthright with me, and I owed him the same honesty. "I'm here with my father. He has a supply of weapons for the king and Jeanne—"

His jaw dropped. "Is your father the arms dealer who almost killed one of the tanners?"

"Thank God, the man still lives," I said. "But how do you know this?"

His eyes narrowed, intent on mine. "Before I say any more, you have to tell me if you're helping your father."

I looked at the fire, thinking of the day Jeanne had asked me to rescue Father. I hadn't promised her that I would help secure the weapons, but against my will I was helping her. I turned back to Georges. "I'm only involved in this to keep Father safe. Please trust me."

His face grew pale. "Even though the tanner that your father wounded will live, my guild still seeks revenge. One of the members of your father's crew came to our guild meeting. In exchange for money, he betrayed his leader's plan without revealing his name. He told us that this unnamed weapons procurer would leave at first light tomorrow by the south gate."

I jumped to my feet. "They're going to ambush Father at dawn? I must warn him!"

Georges rose too and seized me by my shoulders. "You're part of your father's crew. They'll kill you if they find you."

My legs buckled. I would have collapsed to the floor if he hadn't held me so tightly. "I have to try," I said.

His gray eyes bored into mine. "I'll do everything I can to keep you safe, but I won't be a part of any more killings." He paused, and I could see that his mind was casting about in search of a solution. "The only way I know to do both of those things is to stop the ambush."

"But how?"

We paced back and forth on separate paths. "Do you know your father's men by name?" he asked.

"Most of them. Which one came to your guild?"

"His name is Gaston."

"Gaston?" My heart sank when I heard it. That day on the meadow when he gave me money and food, I never suspected that he might be a traitor.

"We can't let him slip away before we warn your father," Georges said.

"And you have to stay hidden—he might recognize you from the guild meeting."

Guilt coursed through me that I had involved Georges in this danger. I set to pacing again, desperate to devise a safe plan.

Father could hit Gaston hard enough that he would fall to the ground unconscious, but I would have to persuade Father that Gaston had betrayed him first. That could take a long time unless—I wheeled around toward Georges. "A barberess travels with us too; her name is Hersende, and she's the one I pretended was my aunt. She's disguised as a beggar in the cathedral square. This Hersende is very skilled at making medicines. She could make a potion that would put Gaston into a deep sleep. We'll bind and gag him, and then we'll flee. He wouldn't be able to tell the tanners that my father knows about the ambush until it's too late."

"It's a bold plan, but it might just work," he said with a look of surprise in his eyes. "If we tell your father that the poison is deadly, he won't kill Gaston with his own hands."

I closed my eyes. Georges had pledged to kill no more, but he knew full well that Father had made no such vow.

"We'll go as soon as we pack a few things." I ran to get my satchel.

"Your bandages," he said. "You'll be safer if you put them back on."

"Father is the only one who knows about them. When he sees that I've taken them off, he'll know that I found help. I should tell you that Father thinks that my mother's friend Anes and her husband helped me. He doesn't know about you. We'll have to explain it to Father later."

Georges nodded, handing me a flask. "Fill this with water while I gather my things."

As I lifted the pitcher of water, I heard footsteps on the stairs. Antonin burst into the great room, rubbing his eyes. "By God's eyelids, Georges, why are you still awake at this hour?"

"I must leave early on pilgrimage," Georges replied, throwing flint and candles into his satchel. "You will take my place in the shop starting tomorrow."

Antonin glanced at me, his eyes wide. "What happened to the boy's bandages?"

"Don't say a word about him to anyone," Georges warned him. "Our lives depend on that. Tell Hauviette too."

"But, Georges, it's the middle of the night. There are thieves on the road—"

"I know. Tell the tanners that I left at first light. And pack us some food if you will." He bolted upstairs.

"I can help you," I said to Antonin, carrying my satchel to the door. With shaking hands, I helped Antonin shove food into one of Georges's bags. When he finally joined me in the foyer, we threw the satchels over our backs and stepped outside into the cool night air that smelled of rain. Creeping in the shadows, Georges led the way toward the cathedral square. I clutched my satchel and followed him as quietly as I could. Whenever a night watchman approached, we slipped into an alley. Every creaking shutter and every swaying shadow of a branch caused my heart to lurch. The rats pattered at my feet, but I bore it without making a sound. A fat one darted across my hand as I gripped the wall for balance. I yanked my hand away, barely stifling a scream.

We emerged from the alley at the back of the cathedral. Oil lamps swung on poles around it, but only a few were lit. Georges and I hurried around the cathedral, and I peered into the shadows under the eaves. There the beggars slept with their backs resting on the stone plaza. Only one beggar sat with her back against the wall—Hersende.

"Stay here," I told Georges before I tiptoed toward her. She dozed with her knife drawn. Keeping my distance from it, I whispered her name.

As usual, she slept so lightly that her eyes opened at once, wide with fear until she recognized me. I motioned for her to follow me, and the three of us slipped back into the maze of alleys and passageways until we reached the stable. Inside, Hersende and I hid in an empty stall while Georges went to wake the stable boy, the same one who had saddled his horse the night I ran away. I told Hersende what had come to pass.

"A strong poppy brew—that will make Gaston fall into a deep sleep," she whispered, stroking her chin. "But it tastes nasty—"

She opened her satchel and drew out a small vial and a leather flask. While I held the flask, she poured the contents of the vial into it. She shook the flask. "This honeyed wine and poppy will make him sleep until noon tomorrow. But tell me, how will you arrange it so that he alone drinks it?"

We had devised a plan by the time Georges returned to the stall. "I think it's best for you to hide in this stall," he whispered to Hersende. "The stable boy will be too busy saddling the horses to know that you're here."

She squeezed my hand. "May God be with you," she whispered for the second time that night.

Georges and I threaded our way along the alleys again, toward the Red Rooster where Father and his men were hiding in a secret room. Footsteps sounded on the road behind us. Grabbing me by the arm, Georges pulled me toward a wall. When he climbed over it, I followed. It was low enough that my feet soon found the earth. We crouched in the wall's shadows as the footsteps grew louder.

Even without a lantern, the man knew the course of the road and didn't stumble. He stopped so close that the smell of his sweat wafted over the wall. A hair tickled my face, but I dared not lift a hand to move it. Just outside the wall, the person slipped past us, continuing in the direction Georges and I were heading. For a long time we remained crouched behind the wall. Gradually my eyes adjusted to the faint light cast by oil lamps flickering here and there. The dark shapes of trees swayed in the wind, but other shapes, low and rectangular, remained still. They were headstones, and I realized we were in the cemetery of the Church of Saint Madeleine where we had buried Ameline. *Watch over me tonight, Ameline,* I prayed silently. *Help me act as you did the night the moneylenders came.*

Georges and I entered an alley as the church bells tolled. The sound jolted me. It was an hour after midnight. So little time remained to warn Father! The alley spilled onto a street, but we waited in the shadows and listened. The Red Rooster was on the opposite side of the street, with torches still burning inside. Drunken laughter and shouting blared through the open window.

Georges clutched my hand. "I'll wait here," he whispered. "If you don't return soon, I'll come to help."

Holding onto the flask, I crept in the darkness on the edge of the torchlights, my footsteps muted by water dripping from the tavern's gutter. I ducked into the back doorway as the front door of the tavern opened and the sounds of a fistfight poured out.

The back door was unlocked, and I entered an anteroom where barrels of wine were stored. Father had said there was a cellar there. By the firelight in the great room beyond, I searched the floor looking for a trapdoor, but found none.

Setting the flask down, I tried to shift the wine barrels to see if there was a trapdoor beneath, but they were all too heavy for me to lift. Where could the cellar be? I reached the last barrel in the darkest corner, and when I tried to move it, I found it empty. Beneath it was the outline of a trapdoor. Grabbing the flask, I opened it as quickly and as quietly as possible, peering into the candlelit darkness below. Should I call Father from up here? No, Gaston could realize that things had gone awry and escape from a door below.

Taking a deep breath, I jumped onto the straw floor. Shadowy figures all around me unsheathed their knives. "Father, I have news!" I cried, searching for him among the men surrounding me.

"Put your knives away," Father commanded as he hurried to me. He reached up to close the trapdoor, and I threw my arms around him. "Don't drink," I whispered in his ear. "Trust me."

I turned back to the crew and found Gaston. "Come here. The good news is for you too."

As he came to join Father and me, he looked puzzled at my unexpected arrival. I uncorked the flask. "Anes's husband Mathieu sends both of you this honeyed wine—to thank you for the dangerous work that you do on behalf of the king and France. He also has carts and horses and money to give you."

Father and Gaston exchanged a look of surprise. "But why is

he helping us now?" Father asked in a terse whisper. "He never has before."

"Anes was so relieved to see me alive that she begged him to do so." I turned to Gaston, holding the flask out to him. "Gaston, I would have starved to death if you hadn't given me food and money that day on the meadow. Here is a small token of my thanks."

Father clapped him on the back. "I didn't know about that, my friend. Drink heartily—it's a small flask. Our heads will still be clear enough to leave Troyes."

Gaston shook his head slightly. "This is a stroke of good fortune. We can buy more weapons." He took a long swig. Then he dropped the flask, coughing. "This wine is poisoned."

"Seize him, Father," I urged. "He told the Burgundians about your plans to leave at daybreak."

"That's a lie," Gaston spouted, writhing and spitting out as much of the potion as he could.

Father's eyes darted from Gaston to me. "Are you certain of this? Who told you?"

"Trust me. Gaston's a traitor."

Gaston rushed toward the back corner of the cellar. "Seize him," Father ordered his men.

Gaston struggled as three of the men grabbed hold of him. I snatched the flask from the floor. Some of it had trickled out. *Dear God, may the remainder be enough.*

"My daughter wouldn't lie to me," Father seethed before he spat on Gaston's face. "You rat. You deserve to die."

He pried open Gaston's jaw while I poured the remainder of the potion down his throat. He gurgled and tried to spit it out but most of it stayed down.

"Hersende said the poison may be slow to kill him," I whispered in Father's ear. I didn't want to lie but knew full well that I would have caused Gaston's death if I didn't.

Father ordered his men to bind and gag Gaston. He told the

biggest and strongest man to press his hands against Gaston's ears. As he fell into a deep sleep, Father gathered the rest of his crew around him. "There's not a moment to lose," he whispered tersely. "All the carts will now meet near the north gate, and we'll leave by the next bells. Make haste to your warehouses to load up the weapons. We discovered one traitor but beware of others."

The men left in groups of two. Only Father, Louis, and Jacques remained.

"Philippe is your daughter?" Louis asked, scratching his head.

Father clapped me on the back, grinning. "Yes, but she's got the courage of a man. Thank God you're safe, Felise. And Hersende is too?"

"Yes."

"Tell Mathieu to leave through the east gate as soon as possible."

I glanced at Gaston, who was still struggling. I couldn't risk telling Father about Georges until we were alone.

Father embraced me tightly. "By God's grace, we will meet again soon."

Georges's cart swayed from side to side as it moved through the dark streets of Troyes, sometimes bumping me against Hersende, who lay hidden beneath the straw next to me.

He steered the cart to the right, shoving me against the wooden chest that held his possessions. The straw piled on top of me muffled the sound of the horses' hooves clomping on the road.

Drawing in a deep breath, I pushed the straw away from my cheek. Hersende squeezed my hand, but that did nothing to dispel the fear in the pit of my stomach. *May Father be safe*, I prayed.

We stopped at the gate, and I heard Georges telling the gatekeeper that he was going on pilgrimage.

"In the middle of the night?"

"Yes. Part of my penance is to deprive myself of sleep."

"You should have my post then," the gatekeeper said, yawning.

The cart rocked back and forth along the road as Georges set the horses to a fast pace. Light filtered through the straw, and birds started to chirp, many more birds than could be heard within Troyes' walls. I scarcely breathed whenever carts and riders approached us. Once, Georges urged the horses into a gallop, and Hersende and I clutched each other's hand underneath the straw.

Much later, the cart slowed and then halted. "The horses need water," Georges called back to us. "There's no one on the road, so we should be safe for the moment. One of you must keep watch."

Hersende and I emerged from the straw, brushing it off our faces. We were surrounded by the same vast countryside of rolling hills that I had traversed alone earlier in the summer. But now the air smelled of ripening grapes, and in the distance, peasants with large woven baskets stood among the rows as they picked them.

"You get water first," Hersende said, turning to watch the road toward Troyes. I followed Georges to the stream where the horses were already drinking. I squatted down on the bank and splashed water on my face, trying to revive myself after the sleepless night. As I rose to my feet, I saw the dark shadows that ringed his eyes, yet his tenderness for me burned brightly too. I hung my head, riddled with guilt again for the danger in which I had thrust him.

"Let me hold the horses while you splash water on your face," I said. "It will refresh you."

"Thanks," he said, smiling as he handed me the tether ropes.

After the horses were watered, the three of us shared a loaf of bread and washed it down with water while facing the road behind us, watching for pursuers or for Father. I wouldn't be at ease until we saw him again.

"We must keep going until we reach Provins," Georges said. "The town is loyal to the king and we should be safe there."

"Felise should sit by you and help you stay alert," Hersende said. "I'll keep watch on the road behind us."

I reluctantly took the front seat beside Georges. I was also too fatigued to think clearly about what I should and shouldn't tell him. Just before Hersende turned, I saw her suppress a smile. She must have suggested this idea to allow Georges and me time to talk.

My cheeks burned in anger at her meddling as I tried to settle myself while he checked the hitch ropes. Last night he had clasped my hands in his, but today he could not. To those we passed, we had to appear as a young man and a boy.

He took the reins for the brown horse and handed me the reins for the white one. "Blanchette will follow the pace of my horse, Chestnut," he reassured me as we set out.

"Your other mare is with the king's army," I hesitated, not knowing how he would receive this news. "I didn't intend to steal her. I told myself I was borrowing your mare to keep Charlotte and me safe."

"It wasn't just my horse that kept you safe," he said. "Your wits must have helped you as well. Tell me about your journey. It will help us both stay alert."

As the horses trotted down the road, I began the story of the last two months. Ameline and Father were the only people who had ever listened to my tales before, and they usually asked questions throughout the telling. But Georges just listened.

"Do you want to hear the parts about Jeanne?" I asked with a glance at him.

"Yes," he replied, his jaw tightening. "It's part of your story too." And so I told him about her and the rest of my journey. The longer I took to tell my tale, the more dissatisfied I became with it. Although I embellished it with details and flourishes and changed my voice to sound like different people, something was missing from it. It wasn't until I ended with the part about Hersende bandaging my face that I realized what I had done.

I gripped the reins, staring at Blanchette's white mane. I hadn't told Georges the inner story of my journey: how I had changed and what I had almost done as he stood in thrall before the Grande Rose window. But I couldn't tell him that story. Ameline was the only person to whom I had ever revealed my heart. And yet, if she were still alive, could I have told her?

We had to slow the horses down when we reached a rocky part of the road. "Tell me, were there times when you forgot the dangers and enjoyed your journey?" he asked.

He had fathomed at least some of the truth. A blush spread across my face as I glanced at him. "How did you know?"

He smiled. "You remind me of my sister. She enjoyed riding and adventures. Mignon, the horse you stole, was hers before she died."

That day at the cemetery he had prayed for a long time at his family's graves, but I had been too absorbed in my own sorrow to consider his. We rode in silence for a while, passing more peasants whose carts were laden with chickens and vegetables.

When we were alone again, he turned to me. I might have deceived him with my storytelling, but I could not hide my turmoil from his gray eyes as they peered into mine. "Tell me," he said, "would you have sought me in Troyes if you hadn't needed my help?"

His question hovered in the silence. In my mind, I saw Ameline on her deathbed, urging me with her last breath to live our dream, to remain a femme sole. How could I speak out against her wishes? And yet to tell him no would have been a lie. *It's not just for Ameline's sake that you won't answer.* The voice inside me insisted. *You're afraid of opening your heart to him.*

I bowed my head and looked at his hands, which were laced with scars and calluses. "I owe you the same honesty that you've given me, but I need more time."

"I won't leave on my pilgrimage," he said at last, his voice low, "until your father rejoins you, and I know you will be safe."

Sixteen

Armor

September 6, 1429

"Garlic, white willow bark, dried poppies, spearmint, and lye soap," Georges recited as Hersende handed him money from her purse.

"You also need linen for bandages, mortars, pestles, and basins."

The dark shadows beneath his eyes had faded now that he had gotten some sleep, but I could tell that he was still tormented by what he had done. Last night the moonlight streaming into my room had awakened me. I found myself imagining Georges in the room next door, a moonbeam shining on his face as he slept.

My face grew hot, and I quickly resumed my task of snipping the blossoms from a dried chamomile plant. "How did you commit the entire list to memory?" I asked him. "I would need to write it down."

"I can't write much." He shrugged, pointing to the row of jars and piles that she set on the floor. "Instead I try to see this arrangement of things in my mind's eye."

Hersende handed him a burlap satchel to carry his purchases. "Go to the herbalist's shop on the church square," she told him. "And thank you for helping me to save men's lives."

I kept my head down, focusing on my work as Georges strode to the door. "I'll look for your father," I heard him say.

"Thanks," I mumbled, quashing my desire to go with him. I knew I couldn't since rumors about Jeanne's plan to attack Paris abounded in Provins, and Hersende needed my help to prepare for the battle. "I'm sure Etienne has been busy tending to the wounded men since I've been gone," she told me this morning as we set to work preparing medicines. "He may not have had enough time to stock our supplies."

After cutting a few more blossoms, I glanced out the window that overlooked the main gate of Provins. Where was Father? We had expected him to arrive by now.

A little later, I looked out at the gate again and saw a white fog: not the thick fog of a wintry day that obscured everything, but a fog so thin that the sun shone through it. It spread no farther than a row of carts.

Father had used sacks of flour to hide his weapons. Maybe it was the flour that caused the fog.

I sprang to my feet and told Hersende what I had seen. "May I go and look for him?" I asked.

"Of course," she replied with a smile. "I hope you're right."

I ran downstairs and pushed my way through the crowded streets toward the gate. A row of carts piled high with flour sacks rumbled down the street, surrounded by the white fog. Straining my eyes to see through it, I searched for Father. There he was, riding the horse that pulled the first cart. I ran toward him, calling his name. His face, gray with exhaustion, emerged from the fog.

After giving the command to halt, he dismounted and came to embrace me. "Thank God, you're safe."

"And you too, Father. But why did it take you so long? I feared the Burgundians had found you."

He leaned closer and whispered in my ear, "We took a short detour to buy more weaponry. Go and fetch Hersende and Mathieu and meet me here as soon as you can. We must leave at once for Saint Denis."

As he turned to leave, I grabbed his sleeve. "Wait, Father. I have to tell you something. It wasn't Mathieu who helped me flee from Troyes."

Father stared at me open-mouthed. "We don't have the extra horses and money from Mathieu? Who did help you, Felise?"

I hadn't intended to trick Father, but nonetheless I had. Not only that, but he had counted on Mathieu's money. I clutched my arms to my chest.

"Forgive me, Father," I faltered. "I sought help from Georges the Tanner, for I knew that you had almost sealed a marriage contract between us. I believed that we could trust him."

Father's face turned white. "Trust him? A Burgundian?"

"He has pledged his neutrality and no longer wants to be a part of the war or of the bloodshed it spawns. If it weren't for him, you and your crew would have been ambushed."

Father shook his head in disbelief as I told him the whole story. "You are certain that he is no longer a Burgundian?" he asked when I finished.

"Yes."

Father's shoulders slackened and he clasped my arm. "You've saved my life yet again, Felise. Tell Georges he can travel with us as long as he likes; it will be safer for him than traveling alone.

"Go and get Hersende; Georges too, if he's coming with us. Jeanne is already in Saint Denis. She and the Duke of Alençon have persuaded the king to break his truce with Burgundy. His army is marching to join her, and soon they will attack Paris. She needs my weaponry delivered at once."

I ran all the way to the church square and burst into the herbalist's shop. A plethora of odors—of cinnamon, rotten cabbage, and manure—filled the dark shop. I found Georges near the back, hoisting a full satchel over his shoulder. "Is something wrong?" he asked.

"No, Father is here safe and sound." I panted to catch my breath. "And he thanks you for saving his life."

"We did the job together," he said, his gaze off in the distance. "Now that your father is here, I will leave on my pilgrimage."

"But Father says you'll be safer traveling with us."

He turned to me as we stepped outside into the bright sunshine. His anguish was more pronounced than it had been in the morning. "You're going to Jeanne, and I don't want to lay eyes on her again," he whispered, looking around to make certain that no one was nearby. "The last time I saw her, she was ordering her men to put bundles of sticks around the walls of Troyes. She would have burned our houses and everyone else's to the ground if the duke hadn't surrendered."

I shuddered, "I know. I heard her voice that day—I was hiding in the woods outside Troyes—and I was afraid people I knew were trapped in the city and would be burned to death. Trust me, though. Jeanne has more heart than it seems. You don't understand her."

"What is there to understand?" His eyes narrowed. "She'll kill anyone—even women and children—to win back France for the king."

"Sometimes it seems that way," I replied, "but she doesn't carry a weapon."

"What difference does that make? She commands her soldiers to kill in her place."

"If you came with us to Saint Denis," I went on, "you would see that she has remorse for her part in the killing, just as you have remorse for your part."

I covered my mouth with my hands, my ill-chosen words echoing in the space between us. Pain filled his eyes, pain that my rash speech had wrought. "Forgive me," I said. "And please consider the protection my father offers you. Come with us."

"So that you can try to win me over to Jeanne? No. Besides, you don't need me. Your father is here to protect you."

It's not just your protection that I seek, I told him silently. He turned to leave. I clasped my hands to steady myself. "Wait—"

He stopped but didn't turn to face me. I bowed my head as a trio of housewives passed by, carrying laundry baskets and chattering about Jeanne's plan to attack Paris.

I stared at his strong back, his feet planted wide apart from one another. I couldn't let him go before I spoke the truth.

Something lifted within me as I walked around and stood before him. Pain was still etched on his face.

"I want you to stay with us so I can give an honest answer to the question you asked me yesterday, not to convince you about Jeanne," I whispered. "My answer is a story, very different from the one I told you as we rode here. It will take more than the few moments we have now. I'll have to tell it in bits and pieces."

I held his gaze without looking away, so close that I saw how his tunic rose and fell with each breath.

"I will stay to hear your story," he said, "and you will hear more of mine."

***

That afternoon, I rode with Hersende on one of the carts in Father's caravan. Georges's cart was somewhere behind us, and I could see neither Father nor him from where I sat cutting bandages for Hersende. The wooden chest that I used as a table contained weapons or munitions for Jeanne, but I tried not to think of the bloodshed they would cause. Nor did I dwell on Georges's dread of the battle, for my own dread of it grew with each bandage I cut.

To distract myself, I recalled our conversation. Neither of us had mentioned the marriage contract. In truth, it was only a sheaf of parchment, of little importance compared to the agreement we had made this morning. But how could we talk when soldiers surrounded us at every waking moment? And how much time was there until the battle began? I tried to compose what I would say to him in my mind, but it remained a blank slate. It was foolish of me to think I could write my own stories. I had no story, only a muddle of feelings that swirled within me. I slammed the scissors onto a wooden chest and clenched the side of the cart, staring at the yellowing poplar trees along the road.

"We're here!" Hersende cried. She jumped up from her seat, her gaze intent upon the road ahead. A green meadow was filled with tents and carts, and soldiers of the king practicing with their weapons. The gray wall of Saint Denis separated the meadow from a jumble of houses and churches. Towering over all the other buildings was the cathedral in which the relics of many kings and saints were stored.

Hersende pointed to the left, a smile illuminating her face. "There are the barbers' wagons, and there's Etienne." She leaned over the side of the cart and bellowed, "Henri the Merchant, stop the caravan!"

Father obeyed her at once, for he knew how eager she was to rejoin her husband. Hersende scrambled off the cart and ran to Etienne, faster than I had ever seen her run before. They threw their arms around each other while the wounded men and Father's crew cheered. I smiled at them, rejoicing that they were reunited at last. For all their bickering, they did love each other after many years of marriage.

I dismounted, looking for Georges. He was nearby, helping Father's crew tend to the horses. He looked over at me, and we smiled at each other. But when Father approached me, his eyes sparkling with anticipation, I had to turn toward him. "Jeanne is praying at the Cathedral of Saint Denis. Come with me, Philippe."

I stood there, torn about what to do. My work on her behalf could have caused Georges to die, and it would surely cause the deaths of many soldiers during the battle. Yet I wanted to know how she had fared in the month we had been apart, the month when she and the Duke of Alençon had broken with the king to launch their own attack on Paris. I told Father yes and looked back at the tanner. He was close enough to have heard Father's request, and his smile faded. I knew that he didn't want me to go to her.

I would try later to explain again, but now I hurried after Father. We strode across the meadow and over a drawbridge into town. Along the main street, townspeople were talking excitedly of Jeanne and her army camped outside their gates. Father and I soon reached the three gilded doors of the Cathedral of Saint Denis gleaming in the midday sun.

We entered the cool darkness of the nave just as the bells rang for the noon prayers. People thronged near a row of stone caskets even after the priest came to the altar to begin the service.

"Jeanne must be over there," Father whispered. We hurried to join the crowd gathered around the largest casket. Two statues of angels knelt atop it, holding an object in their hands that sparkled in the candlelight. "The relics of Saint Denis," he said, his eyes glittering. "Her prayers over his bones will set Paris free at last."

Father used to scoff at relics. He believed they were the bones of ordinary people, and that priests proclaimed that they were saints' bones for the sole purpose of extracting money from penitents who hoped to buy their way into heaven. I shook my head and shifted my gaze to the recorder hanging around his neck, the only remnant of my father of yore. As the bells tolled the hour, a hush fell over the crowd. Everyone knelt except Jeanne's guards posted around her. Her eyes were riveted on the bejeweled statue that the angels held. It was the head of Saint Denis, the bishop who continued to preach even after the pagans beheaded him, holding his own head in his arms until he collapsed in this very place. Jeanne's lips moved, and I didn't know if she was praying or speaking with her invisible saints. Her face was pale and gaunt. Only two months earlier in the vineyard, her face had been round in the moonlight, and her laughter had pealed like bells in my ears. She had been joyous and alive.

The prayers ended, but she remained entranced by whatever she alone could see. D'Amboise and the guards wielded their lances, herding her audience outside. "She doesn't have time for you wretches!" her squire shouted. "If you want her to set Paris free, leave her alone."

Father dared to approach him. "D'Amboise, do you remember me? I'm Henri the Merchant of Troyes. I've brought weapons and munitions that Jeanne and the Duke of Alençon ordered."

The old squire stared at Father for a moment before his scowl turned into a toothless grin. "Ah, Henri, the jokester merchant. Pray tell, how did you turn into an old man like me?"

"It's a long story—I'll tell you around a campfire one night," Father replied absently, his eyes upon Jeanne.

She rose from her knees and shook her head slightly as she emerged from her trance. "Jeanne the Maid," Father called as he hastened toward her. The closer we came, the more haggard she appeared, almost skeletal like the figures in the mural of the *Dance of Death*.

"Henri the Merchant," she called. There was an eerie cast to her eyes as she approached us. Had her saints contacted her with an apparition visible only to her?

"Jeanne," I whispered in my true voice. "I've returned safely."

But she didn't hear me or notice me as she strode by, her eyes fixed on Father.

"Do you have the weapons?" she asked him, her voice low and urgent.

"Yes," Father replied proudly. "Come and see."

We left the cathedral, with Father and Jeanne surrounded by d'Amboise and the guards as I walked a stone's throw behind them. Shutters were thrown open, filling the streets with the smells of roasted meat. Everyone cheered for Jeanne. "May you win Paris for our king, Holy Maid!" She waved to them briefly but didn't smile or speak.

After crossing the drawbridge, we passed the barbers' tents, and I spotted Hersende working at a trestle beside Etienne. She gazed at Etienne, smiling like a girl as she patted his hand. I looked around for Georges and found him collecting firewood. He nodded at me.

Past the barbers' camp, we came to Father's caravan. "Behold your weapons and munitions," he told Jeanne, brushing his hair back in a way I'd never seen before, as if he wanted Jeanne to see his face clearly.

We stood at the center of an arc of four and twenty carts. A white fog filled the air as Father's men finished removing sacks of flour. His shipment included dozens of cannons mounted on wheeled platforms. On other carts, wooden chests lay open to reveal cannonballs, bows and arrows, maces and swords. Captains and soldiers crowded around us, talking excitedly about the good fortune of receiving these supplies in time for the battle.

"I secured a surplus of supplies—an old trick—in case some were lost along the journey," he added, glancing from Jeanne to me. "Thanks to the quick thinking of my youngest crew member, we averted any such loss."

"I am pleased by your work, Henri the Merchant," Jeanne said as she surveyed the longbows. He bowed to her, his face suffused with awe and gratitude. I was shocked to see that he was fawning over her—for the first time I could ever remember. What had come over him? If she told him to ride into battle with her, unarmed as she is, would he do it?

A trumpet blared, and on the road ahead, soldiers broke out into a thunderous roar of applause. "The king has arrived!"

As the cathedral bells tolled in celebration, townspeople swarmed across the drawbridge. They raised their fists skyward and chanted the names of Jeanne and the king in unison. There he was, riding a black warhorse and surrounded by flag bearers waving pennants in the royal colors of red, green, and white. He waved to the crowd and from a distance was able to feign confidence. I jerked my head away from him, sickened by thoughts of the battle that would soon come to pass.

I watched Jeanne instead, her gaunt face contorted by an agony embedded so deeply that no remedy could ever heal her. This agony would surely lead to death . . . of the enemy . . . of her soldiers . . . and possibly of her. Guards encircled her, protecting her from the rush of townspeople, but they could not protect her from herself.

Is this how she had appeared to Georges as she bade her men to set Troyes afire? Was I seeing her with new eyes because of him?

That afternoon we set up camp with the barbers and a host of other healers who served the army. Father and his men tended to their horses and repaired the wagons.

Long trestles were erected where all the healers worked together to prepare huge quantities of remedies. It was my job to make labels for each crock or vat. Our trestles faced the soldiers' camp, and beyond it stood the king's billowing white tent, surrounded by smaller tents for his captains. Many of the soldiers on the meadow before me would probably be wounded or killed, yet they masked their fear by killing rabbits and frogs, which they pretended they were English and Burgundian soldiers.

I buried myself in my work, trying to forget the soldiers' vicious hunt. Georges strode over to us carrying his leather satchel. When we glanced at each other, I saw in his dark look how much the battle preparations unsettled him.

He turned to Hersende. "The soldiers have left us nothing to eat," he said. "I'll go to Saint Denis and buy meat to cook for supper."

"That will give me more time to prepare remedies for the wounded soldiers," Hersende said. She turned to me, smiling wistfully. "I would let Philippe accompany you, but we need his help here."

He gave me a disappointed look. I wanted to let him know that I was disappointed too, but I felt uncomfortable being so honest. Instead I looked down at my work while he set out toward the drawbridge.

The healers were still hard at work when he returned with the ingredients to make a liver and leek soup. He set to cooking it, and soon its aroma blended with others rising from cauldrons all along the meadow. Sitting on the ground around the fire, the five of us—Father, Georges, Etienne, Hersende, and I—along with Father's crew devoured the entire pot of soup. The sun was just beginning to drop behind the trees when Hersende rose from her seat. I expected her to tell me to return to the trestle and work even after the oil lanterns were lit. "Philippe, help Georges clean the dishes," she spoke louder than usual, her gaze upon Father's men gathered by the stream with the horses. "These two will help me with my woman's work tonight, but mark you, on the morrow, I will assign it to two of you. And I will brook no complaints."

The men groaned in mock protest, swigging a flask to drown their sorrow. Locking arms with Etienne, Hersende winked at me as they started toward the trestle.

I stacked bowls and brought them over to a cauldron of hot water where Georges stood rolling up his sleeves. I tried to calm myself by watching him slip a bowl into the water and scrub it until it came clean. Picking up a cloth, I took the bowl from him and dried it.

By the time I'd dried the third bowl, the sound of water splashing and the familiarity of the task had settled me a bit. "At home, Ameline always washed, and I always dried," I told him.

"I've never washed dishes before," he admitted.

"And cooking?"

"My mother taught my sister and me," he replied, his voice low. "I like to cook, but tonight I also needed a task to calm me."

I nodded. "Making the labels served that purpose for me."

We carried the clean dishes and spoons to Hersende's wooden chest. A brilliant sunset of swirling violet and amber lit the sky behind us as we put the bowls away. I wanted so much to speak honestly, but the words stuck in my throat.

A Tale of Two Maidens

A bowl slipped from my hand and would have cracked against the corner of the chest had he not caught it. Our eyes met. "I can see full well that your resistance to me is wearing down," he said, "but I know it must be hard to speak of it. It's enough that we have a chance to wash dishes together."

"Can you read my thoughts so well?" I smiled.

"No, but I can read your face."

As I can read yours, I wanted to tell him. But a band of soldiers walked by, and we had to finish putting the dishes away in silence.

"Where will you and your father go after the battle?" Georges asked as he closed the chest.

"I don't know—certainly not Troyes. Maybe Reims, since Charlotte is there, or with Hersende if she will have us. Wherever I go, I want to finish my apprenticeship. And you, will you return to Troyes after your pilgrimage?"

The fading light illuminated his clenched jaw. "No, at least not for now."

"How can you afford not to work in your tannery for such a long time?"

"My father hoarded a great sum of money, and when he died, I inherited it. He would be displeased that I'm spending part of it on a pilgrimage. But my mother loved pilgrimages. On her deathbed, she gave me the badges of all the shrines she had visited and asked me to go to them and pray for her soul."

I paused, gathering my courage. "I saw those badges at your house."

He smiled at me. "So the wounded Burgundian messenger was looking at my possessions?"

He opened his drawstring money bag. Reaching inside, he drew out the seal with the letter *F* and handed it to me. I clutched it tightly. "I saw it too, with your pilgrim badges," I confessed. "In my haste to leave on my journey, I forgot it."

"I knew that your house would be sold, and I wanted a token

of you . . ." His voice grew faint as he finished the thought, ". . . in case I never saw you again."

When we returned to the fire, Georges added more logs. The sun was sinking quickly, and the day's heat began to fade. Pressing my arms against my chest, I stood closer to the fire. Father's crew tethered the horses to a grove of poplars and joined us, talking and laughing.

"Here, man," said one of the men, offering the flask to Georges.

He shook his head.

"No matter, more for the rest of us." The man shrugged and took a good swallow.

Father patted his belly and grinned. He opened a small wooden chest on the ground and the men grew quiet as he sifted gold coins through his fingers. "We earned enough money to pay each and every one of you for your hard work and daring. Poor Gaston, his share won't do him any good in hell."

The men jeered at Gaston for his treachery until Father held up his hands for silence. "His share and mine will go toward our next venture on behalf of Jeanne the Maid. When you come forward to receive your just reward, tell me if you'll go with me on my next journey."

The men, all twenty-four of them, accepted their payments one at a time. The others cheered as each of them vowed to accompany Henri on his next trip to secure weapons. Father joked with his men as if they were his sons. He loved Ameline and me, but as I watched him with his compatriots in danger and revelry, I knew that they had become his true sons. I caught Georges looking at me and realized that I was twisting my tunic like I used to twist my apron.

When everyone had been paid, the men passed around a flask of wine. "We don't have to fight like the soldiers do," a young man crowed, guzzling his wine. "By God's arm, we have already claimed our victory."

"No wine for you, Henri the Merchant," Hersende called out from the trestle. "Your sickness has left you—aye, I even believe the danger helped you heal—but your body is still mending. Drink this instead. It will help restore you."

She brought Father a large cup of a steaming liquid and he grimaced as he took it. "God's throat, woman, this is the nastiest brew I've ever tasted."

He threw his head back and guzzled it down. Coughing and shuddering, he managed to grin at her. "You torture me with your remedies, but they did indeed help us get the supplies here safely. Hurray for Hersende!"

The crew cheered for her while Etienne, sitting next to her at the trestle, kissed her forehead. Never had I seen her smile so broadly.

The crew launched into some rowdy songs, and I blushed in the darkness, glad that it veiled me from Georges and pleased that Father didn't join in.

He rose to his feet. "The woodpile is low," he announced. "I can't drink tonight, so I might as well make myself useful. Philippe, get the barbers' wheelbarrow and come with me to gather wood."

As we set off down the forest path, the noise of the men receded in the distance. I wrapped my arms around my middle, trying to warm myself in the cool air. It was only a short time since Father and I had looked at the stars and shared stories. So much had happened in that time to distance me from him. Would we ever play our games again as before?

"You are quiet tonight, Felise. Are you dreading the battle?" he asked as we sat beside each other on a log.

"Yes," I said, remembering the pointed tips of the many hundreds of longbows that he had secured for Jeanne.

He bowed his head. "At the siege of Orléans, I helped restock the munitions. Never before had I witnessed such slaughter.

Knowing that the men who died were martyrs for our freedom helped me to endure the siege."

He paused, clasping my shoulders as he always did when a thunderstorm frightened me. "If you can't endure the battle, I'll deliver you from it. Hersende will accept that you must obey your father, and she'll never know why I took you away."

"But, Father, I don't want to disappoint her."

"She has become like a mother to you," he said, "as Ameline did when your mother died."

There was just enough light for me to see the sadness over-taking his face. His jaw tightened as he turned to me. "Hear me out, Felise. I left you and Ameline on your own far too much. I couldn't stop myself from gambling even when I lost all my money. I borrowed more and returned to the dice table. Because of my debts, you were almost betrothed to a Burgundian. I have never been so ashamed."

"How could you have betrayed me?" I murmured, honest with him at last.

"Believe me, it was a last resort. Wervecke and my other creditors were demanding immediate payment. Ameline was already earning money at her craft, but you were not. You were the most valuable possession I had." He buried his face in his hands, collecting himself before he continued. "Luckily for you, I discovered the secret trade before I gave you in marriage to this tanner. I was certain I could repay the moneylenders before you were forced to wed, or before they knocked on our door. But now because of my negligence, you've lost your home and apprentice-ship. Because of me, you were forced to flee from Troyes."

He sat upright and drew in a deep breath. "From now on, Felise, I'm going to make amends for all my wrongdoings and do my best to provide you with a secure future," he said. "I will earn enough money to provide for Charlotte and allow you to resume your apprenticeship."

I snapped a twig in half, knowing that I would have to find my own way to fulfill my desires.

"In the meantime," Father said, "I can't ask you to keep traveling with me disguised as a boy. You've proven your bravery and I would welcome you as a member of my crew, but it is far too dangerous. You need to return to your accustomed life."

I looked down at my tunic, trying to grasp his words.

"I know Ameline tried to persuade you to remain a femme sole, as I allowed her to live her life," he went on, "but you need a husband. This tanner has renounced his loyalty to Burgundy. I would give my approval if he asks for your hand in marriage again." Father paused. "But I promise you that it is your choice whether to marry him or not."

Staring into his blue eyes, mirrors of my own, I knew I could take him at his word. "Thank you," I whispered, resting my head against his shoulder.

In the distance his crew burst into another drunken song. They had forgotten all about Gaston's treachery and their brush with death at his hands. I lifted my head and clutched Father's arm. "I beg you, Father, promise me one more thing. Stop your secret trade. Become an ordinary merchant again, selling cloth and spices as you did before."

"I can't ever go back to that," he murmured. "There's no adventure in selling ordinary goods."

"But you could be killed! We didn't rescue you only to have you endanger your life again."

He clasped my hand. "It's all part of the risks. They may be high, but so are the profits. Besides, I am too clever to die."

I rose to my feet appalled at his pride. "How can you say that after what almost happened to you?"

"I've eluded death many times," Father boasted. "And now that I serve Jeanne and her saints, I'm even more certain of good fortune. Besides, my secret trade pays me other profit than money," he confessed. "I've come to understand that it is a penance for my sins. Through it, I'm helping to bring about peace in France."

"But Father, you've never believed in penance," I protested. "You always claimed that it was a means for priests to have power over us."

"I have changed, Felise, for the better."

"For the worse, you mean, and Jeanne too! I fear that you both will die."

"Hush," he warned, rising to stand beside me. "There may be soldiers nearby. She can win the battle only if she appears invincible in their eyes." I shook my head, too stunned to speak.

"Be assured of something else, Felise. Remember what I said about the king's soldiers who perish in battle? They die a martyr's death, and so would Jeanne, riding in the thick of the battle, as would I in procuring weapons for her. Our souls would fly straight away to heaven."

"Oh, Father, I want you on earth. I want you close by. I want you—" I could no longer contain my tears.

"If I could, I would promise you all that you ask," he whispered, his voice breaking, "but I can't. I can only promise you my love."

He threw his arms around me and embraced me more tightly than he ever had before, his tears commingling with mine in the gathering darkness.

Seventeen

The Gate
of Saint Honoré

September 6, 1429

I collapsed onto my pallet, crying like a baby. Even after the
camp grew quiet, I tossed and turned, unable to find sleep. By the
light of our smoldering fire, I rose and threaded my way around
the bodies of Father's men, scattered on the ground in drunken
sleep. Creeping through the darkness, I paused before Georges's
sleeping form. He was sprawled on his back, his arms spread to
form the letter *t*, as if he had fallen asleep watching the stars and
the waxing moon.

I returned to my pallet but still couldn't sleep. Turning on
my back, I stared at the stars, searching for a familiar object to
suggest a story, but nothing came. I continued to gaze at them
anyway, and a wondrous story welled up, not from them but from
within me, as if a vast sea of stars were contained there. Among
them I found a cluster shaped like a bridge.

Horses whinnied in the distance—Georges's horse, Mignon,
among them. I was filled with an urge to go to her and claim
her for Georges. I rose, slipped on my shoes, and draped a
blanket over my shoulders. The stars guided me down the hill
toward their pen. I heard footsteps approaching from behind and
stopped, hardly daring to breathe.

"Felise, is that you?" a voice whispered in the darkness. It was Georges.

I turned toward him, my heart beating fast. "Yes."

He came to stand by my side, but it was too dark to see his face. "Where are you going?" he asked.

"To find Mignon for you."

"I will go with you."

As Georges and I walked toward the pen, the first light of dawn glowed along the horizon. He glanced at my face, which was swollen with tears, and asked, "Did your father make you cry?"

I nodded without looking at him. "I tried to convince him not to go on another mission for Jeanne, but he wouldn't listen."

"What has he decided for your future?"

"He told me he will let me choose for myself," I said slowly.

The wind ruffled through his hair as we kept walking toward the pen.

"Do you know yet what you will decide?" he asked, averting his eyes from mine.

"I want to finish my apprenticeship," I said, keeping my gaze on the sunrise with its purple and red bands. I couldn't stop my mouth from quivering but went on, nonetheless. "And I want to see you when you return from your pilgrimage."

From the side, I could see his mouth open in surprise. He started to speak, but men carrying saddles and ropes were coming toward us. He turned away from me and faced the horses.

"There's Mignon," he murmured before he ducked his head to go through an opening in the ropes.

I followed him and we walked together across the field. We passed a white horse with a patch of bare flesh where a wound was healing. A shiver ran through me at this evidence of how the horses suffer in battles. Hersende told me that the healers couldn't take time away from tending to the wounded men to help the horses. They had to be left on the battlefield writhing in agony.

When we reached Mignon, she whinnied a greeting as we patted her nose.

"The night I stole her, she frightened me because she was so big," I smiled.

"Martine always called her a gentle giant. She was probably more afraid of you than you were of her."

Standing on either side of Mignon, we smiled at each other. Horses grazed around us, and the grass sparkled as sunshine glimmered on the dew. I sensed someone looking at us and shifted my gaze in that direction. Jeanne stood just outside the pen, a stone's throw away, her face as tormented as it had been yesterday. She wore a dark tunic and riding gloves, her mouth set in a purposeful line as she gazed at the pen where the ostlers were saddling her warhorse, Midnight.

I turned back to Georges who was watching her with anger suffusing his face. "I'll go to her and ask for Mignon," I told him.

He turned to me with a gaze so intense that it frightened me. "I know that's not the only reason you want to speak with her."

I glanced down at the wildflowers. "But you see, I've come to understand why I serve her, and I wanted to tell her that."

"Why do you?" He asked.

"Because her strength reminds me of Ameline's, and somehow I wanted Jeanne to take her place."

"Don't you see that she could never take your sister's place?" he scoffed. "Her mission consumes her. She's too single-minded to have a bond with you or anyone else. You wanted to be her friend, but she simply needed your help to secure the weapons from your father."

His honest words stung me because I knew he was right. I jerked my head up, my eyes filling with tears as I thought about the night I'd met her and the day Charlotte had sung the "Horse Girl" song to her. "She wasn't always as she is now."

"But you can't convince her to be what you want her to be.

There is nothing you can do for her, now or ever. She has chosen her path, just as you must choose yours."

"But I can't bear to lose her forever and Father too," I choked, hardly hearing his words. "The two people I have been seeking all summer."

He reached out a hand toward mine, but men were close by, and he had to draw it back. "That may be true, Felise, but while you were seeking them, I found you," he whispered. "Now go to her. I'll wait for you in the forest at the place where you gathered wood with your father."

He walked away in the opposite direction from Jeanne. I clasped my hands behind my back and walked toward her, stopping just across the fence from where she stood. I hadn't expected to speak with her again, yet here she was smiling at me, a shadow of her former self.

"Felise," she said, "I thought your father left you in Troyes."

"It wasn't safe there," I replied. "We had to flee for our lives."

"Thank you for your courage in helping your father secure the weapons for me. God willing, his supplies will help us win Paris."

I swallowed, thinking of the many deaths that they would cause. Never again would I be a part of securing weapons and munitions for anyone.

"This may be the last time I have a chance to speak with you," I said.

"You are not going to serve as Hersende's assistant any longer?" she asked.

"At the battle, yes, but then I want to return to my apprenticeship."

"I will pray that your desire comes to pass. Come with me," she said, turning to the warhorses in their separate pen ahead. "I must prepare Midnight for battle."

As we walked along either side of the rope fence, I remembered the first day I arrived at the camp and walked with her. Other than the sound of our footsteps, everything else had changed.

She glanced at Georges who had almost reached the edge of the forest. A wistful look came over her. "Who is that young man?"

"Remember the night you traded horses with me so I wouldn't be punished as a horse thief?" I asked.

"Yes—though it seems a long time ago."

"That is Georges the Tanner, the young man who owned that horse. If he hadn't helped us, the Burgundians in Troyes would have ambushed Father's caravan, and he could have been killed and your weapons destroyed. Please, could this tanner have his horse back now?"

"It is a small payment for all that he and your father have done for me . . . and for France. He may claim the horse today. I will tell the ostlers." The wistful look on her face deepened. "I believe this tanner cares for you and you for him."

"How do you know?"

She looked away to the east, toward her home. Was she remembering the man to whom she was once betrothed? She turned to me with tears in her eyes. "Don't think that I haven't known love," she said. "I'm just not free to choose it as you are."

"My sister didn't believe that love was possible," I stammered, "and I think of you as being just like her."

Her eyes grew misty again. "It doesn't matter what your sister or I believe about love. You must ask yourself if you believe in it and can give yourself to it."

I glanced at the forest where Georges awaited me and closed my eyes, feeling the sun's rays on my face. "May God be with you as you make your choice," Jeanne said.

I looked into her tortured brown eyes one last time, the dark shadows prominent beneath them. "And with you." I couldn't squeeze her hand in farewell because there were ostlers around us, saddling horses for battle drills and a mock battle. When the sound of trumpets rose up, Jeanne wiped the tears from her eyes and turned toward Midnight.

Heralds rode through the camp waving banners in the king's colors. "Prepare to fight at dawn tomorrow!" they cried. "God willing, Paris will be ours!"

The men roared their approval, and a clattering of swords and lances resounded across the meadow, a faint foreshadowing of the uproar that would come tomorrow. I hurried toward the forest filled with dread, both of the battle and of Georges's imminent departure on his pilgrimage. He stood a short way down the path. The taut lines of his jaw softened as I drew nearer. "Mignon is yours," I said.

"Thank you."

"You will start your journey today, then?"

He reached out his hands to clasp mine. "I don't want to leave you. Please, let me take you away from the battle."

I forced myself to reply, "I must stay and help Hersende."

"Why?" His question took me by surprise, and I stared at his face, which was shadowed by the trees. The noise of battle preparations grew louder on the meadow beyond us.

"She risked her life to travel with me to rescue Father and secure the weapons. And I promised her that I would help her in the battle. I can't break that pledge because of my respect and love for her."

He stepped closer, our eyes locking together. "And I will endure the battle with you because of my love for you."

As he spoke these words, his revulsion of bloodshed returned, and I could see sweat beading around his mouth. "No," I protested. "I couldn't bear to be the cause of any more suffering for you."

"And I couldn't bear for you to witness the battle without me by your side," he said. "You're not forcing me to do anything. It's my choice."

We heard soldiers approaching on the path behind us, and he let go of my hands, though our eyes were still fixed on one another's.

September 8

The gong of the bells jolted me awake, so many of them that I thought I was hearing all the bells of Paris. I pressed my hands to my ears. The bells weren't marking the hour; they were warning the Parisians that the battle was about to begin.

I lifted my head and saw that Georges's blanket covered his eyes. My belly churned at what would come to pass this day and how I had involved him in yet another horror. No, he had made this choice himself . . . because of his love for me.

Last night as we settled onto our pallets, Hersende had patted my shoulder. "Remember, Felise, each task that you do for me tomorrow will help keep men alive. Try to let that thought guide you and not your fear. We healers fight a battle to save lives, one small task at a time. Just do what you must do in each moment."

Her words echoed in my mind as I rose and put on my shoes. Harsh voices pierced the darkness, commanding the men to prepare for battle. Father's pallet was empty, and he wasn't with the healers preparing medicines at the trestle. Hersende and Etienne sat among them. Their tired faces told me that they had been awake for a long time.

"Do you know where Father is?" I asked her.

"He went to Jeanne's camp. You may go find him if you like but come back soon."

All around me, soldiers were donning armor and boasting of their prowess in battle, describing the brutal ways they would kill the enemy. I walked faster.

A torch illuminated a trestle table, Jeanne's tent, and a crucifix atop a pole. On the trestle was a parchment scroll; maybe it was a map of the battle plan, showing the Gate of Saint Honoré and Paris beyond it. I imagined Jeanne poring over the map and tracing her finger along the part that showed the army's formation.

She emerged from her tent just as d'Amboise arrived with a small wheelbarrow containing her armor. He helped her don a tunic made of linked metal coils. Father shouldered his way to the front of a group of foot soldiers who had gathered to watch her dress in her armor. He nodded at me, and I went to stand next to him.

"Hold still." The squire fretted like a parent trying to dress a squirming child. "I must be sure that these ties are fastened securely."

He finished with the tunic and handed her a plate of bread and cheese. She shook her head.

"You've hardly eaten anything in days," he protested. "You must, to keep up your strength during the battle."

Again she shook her head. "Put the rest of my armor on now."

He sighed, setting the food on a tree stump. When he bent down to pick up her breastplate, he was too feeble to lift it. Father and another soldier went to his aid, and the three of them carried the breastplate to Jeanne and placed it around her. Her body sank under its weight. Surely the king could have made her a suit from a lighter piece of metal? But maybe it was she who had chosen it—to make her appear more like a man in battle.

D'Amboise fastened the two ends of the leg plates together, then the circular piece around her waist. As he added each piece of armor—back plate, arm coverings, gloves, and gauntlets—she appeared bigger and stronger. Soon her body was encased in metal armor that glinted in the torchlight.

As d'Amboise went to get her helmet, a trumpet blared to summon the men. She picked up her banner and gripped it tightly, her gaze fixed on the crucifix, her mouth moving in silent prayer. Once I imagined that the banner was embroidered with the picture of wheat and sky and ocean. But now I knew that it showed an orb of blue held by her saints, just like the weight that she herself must bear for all of France. Her back straightened. For the past two moons, I had wondered about the source of her strength and now, as her hand clenched her banner pole, I understood at last. It rooted her to her saints and to God, just as my seal rooted me to my true voice.

A Tale of Two Maidens

When d'Amboise returned and placed her helmet on her head, Father dropped to his knees and made the sign of the cross. To him, Jeanne had become the woman warrior of Lady Christine's book in the flesh and his Lady Luck. To the men doing battle with her this day, she was the embodiment of God's will for our land to be set free from English rule. But I would always know the truth—that there was a girl beneath the armor, a girl who in sacrificing her own desires would become a saint.

"God willing, we will take Paris today!" she shouted. Her words echoed throughout the camp, and everyone joined in her battle cry.

"Follow me to the gate of Saint Honoré," she commanded her men, and they roared their assent. She mounted Midnight, decked in the king's livery, and the Duke of Alençon came to join her on his brown stallion. He exuded the confidence and strength that I wished I could summon.

Father and I joined the throng of men walking behind Jeanne and the duke. "Are you sure you don't want me to take you away from here?" Father asked over the uproar.

I almost said yes, wanting to flee with Georges from this madness. "I promised Hersende," I shouted to Father. "I must stay."

He clapped me on the back, his face shining with excitement. "That's the spirit. I'll be on the supply carts with my men, bringing more weapons to the rear guard. God go with you."

I joined the barbers and Georges on their cart. His face was pale as I sat next to him, and I wished I could take his hand in mine.

"Etienne wants me to work with him," he whispered. "Even though I won't be at your side, know that I am with you in spirit."

I nodded, trying to mask the terror settling in the pit of my belly. We rode to a field across from the gate but still a good way back from it. There the healers had already set up their tents and laid out most of their supplies—forceps, saws, bandages, and endless vials of many colors.

The Gate of Saint Honoré

As we dismounted, Hersende put Georges and me to work cutting more strips of linen for bandages. I couldn't help looking up from my work at the gate. How could Jeanne's army ever pass through such an impenetrable barrier? Even the thickest of battering rams could not shatter it. Beyond the gate's iron grillwork was a jumble of buildings that seemed to merge together into yet another barrier. On either side of the gate, the wall of Paris rose up, not crumbling like Troyes' wall, but strong and solid. Enemy soldiers clad in mail hoods and armor lined the parapet, barely an arm's length apart. Thin pieces of wood hung from their shoulders and draped across their chests.

Etienne, who was stocking a wheelbarrow with bandages and medicines, followed my gaze. "Those are English archers," he explained, "and very accurate with their longbows. That is how the English defeated us at Agincourt. Many of our soldiers will die or be wounded at their hands today."

I quickly looked toward Georges, and he moved closer to me. To the beating of drums, Jeanne and Alençon advanced to the gate followed by her chaplain, mounted soldiers, and thousands of foot soldiers. Behind them, huge war machines rolled toward the wall of Paris: battering rams, trebuchets, and catapults with their arsenal of deadly stones and oil pots that would soon be set aflame.

A stone's throw away from the gate, Jeanne lifted her banner high. "Let us pray for victory!" she shouted.

While her chaplain led us in the Lord's Prayer, she raised her eyes to heaven. The familiar words echoed in the gray morning air and silence fell over us all.

"May God be with us!" Her voice resounded over the battlements and into the city. "Be strong of heart, and Paris will be ours!"

Thousands of soldiers thrust their lances toward the sky. "Paris will be ours!" they shouted over and over as they turned to wave at the king, who sat beneath an open tent far to our right, the same tent in which I had served as a scribe. On that hill he would be safe while his men faced death to regain his kingdom.

"Never will Paris fall," the enemy archers chanted from the wall. They spat at Jeanne and called her Satan's whore. "He wants you back in hell with him."

The shouting match continued on both sides, but Jeanne paid no heed as she conferred with Alençon.

"Remember, keep the water pitchers filled," Hersende bade Georges and me, pointing to the row of barrels.

"If the vinegar runs out, tap the wine barrels," Etienne reminded us for the third time that morning. All the healers turned to the wall, their faces grim as they prepared for their battle to save lives. The taunting grew louder, and soon a quick succession of drumbeats accompanied it.

"To the wall!" Jeanne's battle cry arched over the din. The bells of Paris tolled again, drowning out her voice and the jeering of the two armies. Arrows began to fly, and horses screamed. The earth trembled from the firing of cannons one after the other. Thick black smoke spewed across the meadow, choking everyone. A dark object whizzed overhead and thudded into the ground in front of Georges and me. I ran from it, covering my head and waiting for an explosion.

Georges grabbed my arm. "Just a misfired catapult," he shouted over the noise.

We returned to Hersende and found her stocking a wheelbarrow with supplies. "Follow me with this wheelbarrow," she commanded.

She led us toward the road where old men had gathered, their eyes riveted on the battle raging before them. She tried to enlist them to help retrieve wounded men from the wall, and a dozen or so of the sturdier ones complied. They headed toward a caravan of handheld carts lined up along the road.

Other carts bearing the wounded had already returned from the wall. Each of them contained half a dozen men. Their howls and groans interspersed with the battle noise, and they writhed in pain as they were lifted from the cart and distributed among the healers. One of them had a broken leg with the cracked bone exposed. I looked away, fighting the sickness that rose in my belly.

The barbers and other healers swarmed around the carts, scanning the wounded and deciding which ones needed care most urgently and which ones were best suited for each healer. With amazing speed, the wounded were sorted, and the healers worked together to carry them to makeshift pallets.

Through the smoke, a cart approached, coming from the battle. Its driver was a monk with blood and grime streaking his brown robes. Dark shapes were heaped on the cart behind him. The stench of vomit, blood and excrement emanated from them. An arm, its white flesh exposed by a torn tunic, dangled off the side, and a muddy boot thudded to the road. How could so many men be wounded in such a short time?

As the cart drew closer, I saw that the motion of its wheels on the rutted road was causing the arm to move. There were dozens of bodies piled atop one another. Many of them were contorted into grotesque shapes and split open, spilling forth blood, guts and sinews. One man stared wide-eyed over the arrow that pierced his neck. Another man's face was twisted in a grimace of pain beneath charred and smoldering flesh.

I sank to my knees and covered my face with my hands, gagging and heaving last night's supper onto the ground. I rested my head on my knees before my stomach churned again and the second wave spewed up. When I was done, Georges handed me a wet rag, and I wiped my mouth, panting to recover. I lay there, surrounded by the noises of the battle, everything that held me together ripped apart. "Come with me—we can't help them," Georges urged me.

"Bring the wheelbarrow with the supplies for burns," Hersende yelled, "and the forceps."

I quickly obeyed her while Etienne called for Georges. In the smoke he clasped my hand, and then he was gone.

When I reached Hersende, she was scanning a cart of wounded men and looking for those suffering from burns. Finding one, she carried the moaning man to a blanket on the field. She soaked a sponge in a bowl of the poppy brew and handed it to me. "Hold that next to his nose," she ordered me.

"Breathe deeply," I bade the man. "It will ease the pain."

Hersende knelt beside his middle where his tunic had been burned away. She grabbed scissors and cut even more of it.

"Come look," she said.

I dreaded what I would see but obeyed anyway.

"A glass pot filled with burning fat was hurled over the wall and shattered on him," she explained as I took in his blistered flesh pierced with shards of glass.

"The glass has to come out before we can apply the burn ointment. Watch me pull out a shard. Then you pull out the rest while I tend to other wounded men."

She yanked it out, ignoring the man's shriek, and handed me the forceps. "Don't let his screams stop you. Work as quickly as you can."

She disappeared into the smoke. Drawing in a deep breath, I gripped the forceps tightly and set to work. The first piece of glass was lodged so deeply that it took several tugs to get it out. The man's screams pierced the air so loudly that I dropped the forceps and grabbed the poppy-soaked sponge, holding it to his nose.

All around me, healers were hard at work—moving men to surgical tents, setting broken bones, calling for the cart of the dead. I couldn't see Georges through the smoke, but just thinking of him gave me strength.

"I have to do this," I told the man as I picked up the forceps again. He howled in pain each time I pulled out a shard, but by the end the poppy brew had taken him far away. Hersende returned and nodded at my handiwork. She grabbed the crock of onguent des apôtres and smeared it over his chest and belly with the bandage.

"Put these things back in the wheelbarrow," she commanded. "Get a needle and thread and some bandages."

As I hurried back to the wheelbarrow, I glanced at the blankets spread on the ground and the men writhing on them. Their curses and prayers all melded together. One tugged at my leg and begged for water.

Etienne rose from one of the wounded men carrying a bloody arm. Georges held a censer of burning poppy over the man's face while leaning away from him to retch. I started toward him, wanting to bring him a wet cloth.

"Follow me!" Hersende shouted.

With trembling legs, I forced myself to obey her. We walked so far that when I turned, I couldn't see Georges anymore.

As I held a man's leg steady for Hersende to work on it, I glanced toward the battle and prayed that Paris would fall soon. A wheeled scaffold near the wall burst into flames, and yet the dozens of men on each of its four tiers kept climbing up ladders toward the top tiers. There, a few of the soldiers crossed a wooden platform to the parapet. Their swords flashed in the firelight as they cut down the English. Other soldiers scrambled up ladders that were mounted against the wall and joined in their fray. Protected by wooden barriers, gunners fired cannons and catapults hurled stones into the city.

Through the smoke, the iron gate of Saint Honoré drifted in and out of view. A score of soldiers ran at it with the battering ram, yelling a battle cry. It pounded against the gate, but the huge door remained closed.

The battle raged on, and I forgot about watching the attempts to breach the gate or mount the wall. With three other boys, I fetched buckets of vinegar to cleanse wounds and threaded bone needles with woven thread. I restocked the wheelbarrows with verdigris and *poudre-rouge*, cut endless bandages, and filled pitchers with water. Adding logs to the fire used to heat wine and poppy brew and cauterizing irons, I became a creature with legs, arms, and ears but without thoughts or feelings. Over the gunfire, someone called my name. One of the urchins ran toward me, his eyes huge in his narrow face. "Philippe," he panted, "the barber woman told me to fetch you. She is tending to the Maid—"

"What has happened?" I cried.

"She's been wounded."

"How badly?"

The boy had already turned back to the battlefield. "The barberess said to hurry. Follow me."

We ran along the rear of the battle where the rain of arrows couldn't reach us. Though I could no longer see the boy through the smoke, I kept going. Halfway up the hill where the king's tent was pitched, the smoke cleared enough for me to see Jeanne's banner amid a grove of poplar trees and Midnight tethered to one of them.

Before I could reach it, I saw the king's physician kneeling beside a fallen man. A priest held a vial of holy oil and removed the man's helmet to anoint him. Jeanne's squire d'Amboise. An arrow had wedged its way through a gap in his armor and pierced his eye. *Dear Virgin, may he feel no pain.*

Hersende hovered over Jeanne as she sat with her back propped against a tree, her face pale and her eyes closed. When Hersende moved aside, I saw the arrow thrust deep into Jeanne's thigh. I groaned, running toward them. The urchin boy's face was pale as he passed me on his way back to the healers. "Help her," he gasped. "We can't win without her."

"Mama," Jeanne moaned as I knelt beside her. Hersende looked up, her lips pressed together in a grim line. "Hold her hand," she bade me.

I clasped Jeanne's hand in mine, the hand on which she wore the ring her mother had given her. Hersende held a sponge dipped in poppy brew to Jeanne's nose. "Breathe deeply," she urged.

Jeanne turned to Hersende, her eyes wild. "Will it put me to sleep?"

"Yes."

"I don't want it."

"But I have to get the arrow out of your leg," Hersende insisted. "If you don't breathe in the poppy, you will suffer greatly."

Jeanne shook her head. "I must return to the wall."

"If you change your mind, the sponge is right here." Hersende set it down and grabbed a long piece of linen from her satchel, rolling it tight. "Bite this."

Jeanne clenched hold of the linen with her teeth while Hersende removed her leg armor. In the gap between two pieces of it, the mail undergarment had come untied. An arrow was buried deep in her flesh, a purple bruise encircling it. Hersende lifted Jeanne's leg and peered at the back side. "No exit wound," she murmured. "And it's the bolt of a crossbow—without barbs."

Holding the arrow close to its bolt, she wiggled the arrow in a slight circular movement. Jeanne moaned, the sound muffled by the cloth in her mouth. She squeezed my hand tightly.

"I have to loosen it, or I would injure you even more," Hersende said.

She continued to wiggle the arrow, first in one direction and then the other. Jeanne kept moaning and squeezing my hand, but she didn't ask for the poppy sponge. Hersende grasped the shaft and gave it a slight tug and Jeanne moaned louder.

"Get a bandage from my satchel," Hersende told me. "As soon as the arrow comes out, press the bandage to the wound as hard as you can."

She knelt, grasping hold of the shaft with both hands, and pulled with all her might. Jeanne let out a muffled scream and clenched my hand so hard that it hurt. Finally the arrow came loose. I let go of her hand and pressed the bandage against the gushing blood. It soaked the bandage, turning it dark crimson. Tears streamed from her closed eyes and streaked down her muddy face as Hersende replaced the bandage. She gently wiped Jeanne's face with a wet rag.

The king's physician loomed over us, scowling at Jeanne. "You were riding too close to the English archers, foolish girl, and your squire came to take you back to safety. He's dead, and you are to blame."

Jeanne's eyes flew open. "No!" she cried.

"Hush, child," Hersende crooned, combing her fingers through Jeanne's hair. "D'Amboise was a brave man who put your life before his. Any loyal squire would do what he did. Take comfort, for he received the last sacrament."

Jeanne's shoulders heaved with her sobs as I kept pressing on her wound and prayed that the flow of blood would stop.

"Begone, ignorant woman," the physician growled at Hersende. He opened his satchel and drew out a small black book, a *Vade Mecum*, a book of cures written in Latin like the ones I used to copy at the scriptorium. Hersende thought them useless, every one of them. It didn't surprise me that she ignored the physician and kept applying pressure to the wound.

"You dare to defy me," he spluttered, raising his hand.

She didn't flinch. "Strike me if you want, but I won't leave until the bleeding lessens."

"You know nothing of medicine," he muttered, glaring at Hersende.

Jeanne grew suddenly alert, her eyes darting all around until she found mine. "Felise, bring me my horse and help me onto the saddle."

"She'll do nothing of the kind," Hersende answered for me. "Your wound is deep, and you have lost much blood. You must rest."

Jeanne tried to rise to her knees, but Hersende held her down. "Let go," Jeanne pleaded. "We must take Paris by nightfall."

Hersende ignored her. Jeanne kept struggling until she pitched forward in a faint.

Hersende and I were forced to leave Jeanne's side when the physician called for the king's guards. While she was still unconscious, the physician dabbed her wound with goose fat.

"Dear Virgin, may he not thwart her healing," Hersende prayed as we returned to the barbers. It was hard to find a path through the thicket of wounded men lying on blankets, so many of them now, all writhing and screaming on the ground. At last we found Etienne stitching up a gash in a man's foot with Georges beside him, holding the foot in place. We gave them the news about Jeanne.

"May this slaughter not be in vain," Etienne muttered. "And may we keep on fighting even without her."

Hersende and I returned to her section of the healers' makeshift hospital. We plunged into our labor again while the battle continued without respite. My throat was parched, and my muscles ached. Every time I looked at the road, carts kept coming from the wall to deliver more of the wounded and more of the dead.

As dusk fell, Father helped the healers by lighting lanterns and torches up and down the meadow. Carts made countless journeys to retrieve the remaining wounded from the battlefield, while other carts circled around the meadow and halted whenever a weary healer called out, "Come for the dead." The smells of incense and poppy fumes wafted over the meadow, commingling with the bitter smell of gun smoke.

Underneath a row of cedar trees close to the road, many carts were heaped with bodies of the dead. Women clustered around them, wailing when they found their slain men. Even at the hour of death, they were present with their loved ones. I turned to find Georges, saw him bending over a wounded man with Etienne, and I knew my heart.

Far into the night, I was pinning down a man's arm while Hersende applied onguent des apôtres to his burned flesh. A horn blared from somewhere near the wall. One after another, the gunners stopped firing their cannons. My ears rang in the silence, broken only by the cries of the wounded and the neighs of the horses.

"The Maid has been wounded!" a herald shouted. "She will live but cannot return to battle, though she wants to with all her heart."

A groan rose up from the soldiers. Another of the heralds took up the cry. "The king has declared that there can be no victory without the Maid. The attack on Paris is over for this day."

As I surveyed the battlefield strewn with the dead and fallen, tears sprang to my eye. All this suffering had been in vain.

Loud prayers for Jeanne rose up from the ranks, and the king, surrounded by his guards and ministers, led the procession away from the gate of Saint Honoré. Behind him were mounted noblemen. Their visors were raised, revealing their battle-weary eyes. The Duke of Alençon rode next to Jeanne's litter surrounded by the foot soldiers, their armor torn and bloody as they prayed for Jeanne. She struggled to sit up, and Alençon didn't try to stop her.

When she turned to the foot soldiers, their prayers changed at once into loud cheers. "Tomorrow we will return," she cried, "and win Paris once and for all!"

A thunderous applause broke out among the ranks—from soldiers, Alençon and the other mounted nobles, the healers, and the wounded; all except the king and the captains riding closest to him who stared at the road ahead.

As I stumbled back to Hersende, wounded men lying on the meadow flailed their arms, moaning for me to stop and help them. Tears streamed down my face, but I kept going. Hersende was covering a dead patient with a blanket when she saw me coming. I knelt down beside her and threw my arms around her. "Forgive me, but I cannot stay a moment longer," I said.

She hugged me tightly. "You have served me well, Felise. Even longer than I expected you would. Go, child, and take the tanner with you."

Eighteen

The Gift

September 8, 1429

We stayed at the army's encampment only long enough to saddle Mignon. I rode behind Georges, holding him around the middle and leaning my face against his back just as Charlotte had once ridden behind me. Mignon galloped down the road, away from the battle, away from the camp and soldiers who might see us together. We reached a meadow, and Georges steered the mare onto it. Rabbits scattered as we crossed it, heading toward a cluster of beech trees whose gray bark shone silvery in the moonlight.

After we dismounted, he tethered Mignon to a sapling, and we sank into the shadows of the beeches. As he wrapped his arms around me, an invisible current shot through me, rooting me in his embrace.

I gazed at his ashen face, wanting to caress his brow and thread my fingers through his hair. "Now I understand your anguish and weariness of this war," I said. "Never again will I be a part of it, even to help Hersende."

The sound of our breathing filled the air. "I can finally tell you my true story," I murmured. His eyes smiled into mine, encouraging me to speak. "Ever since I first came to your house, I have thought about you night and day."

He held me tighter as I rested my head against his chest and listened to the beating of his heart. I went on, "I believed I had to resist you in order to please my mother and my sister. Your mother's deathbed wish was for you to go on a pilgrimage, but my mother's was for Ameline and me to remain unwed, unless we were certain we had found love.

"Mama confided to us that she had fallen in love with a man before she was forced to marry Father. She didn't want Ameline or me ever to be separated from our true love as she was from hers."

His hands kneaded my shoulders. "But you were only a child when your mother died. How could you have known what love was?"

"I didn't. As we got older, Ameline became convinced that Mama's idea of love was impossible. And we both knew many girls and women who were bound in unhappy marriages."

"My mother was one of them," he murmured. "My father beat her time and again."

I wrapped my arms around his waist, imagining him as a little boy having to endure the sight of such cruelty.

"When Ameline died," I continued, "my desire to follow in her path as a femme sole grew stronger. I dreamed of owning my own bookshop and writing books of my own instead of copying other people's words."

"Do you still have that dream?"

"Very much."

"You already are a femme sole," he said, smiling. "I would never take that away from you. I couldn't even if I wanted to do so."

I sank into the warmth of his embrace.

"One more confession," I said, lifting my face to look at him. "At the cathedral in Reims, I was hiding behind the Virgin's altar with Charlotte when you came in seeking penance. The priest refused you, and you turned toward the Grande Rose. That look of wonder on your face . . . it stirred something within me. I was just about to go to you when the moneylenders entered. By the time they left, you had gone too."

His eyes held mine. "Do you wish to marry me and come on my pilgrimage with me?"

I hugged him more tightly than ever. "Yes, I do."

He drew my hood back and caressed my shorn hair. "By the time we return to France, your hair will have grown back."

"And it will be just as unruly as ever." I laughed and shook my head.

As an owl hooted in the forest beyond, he kissed me in the guise of a boy for the first and last time.

September 11

The autumn wind chilled me to the bone as Hersende and I hurried to the bathhouse. I clutched my satchel, which contained the only dress I had brought with me on my journey. Georges would see me dressed as a woman again this very afternoon.

I gazed up at the sky that filled the narrow cracks between the rooftops. It reminded me of patches of Ameline's blue silk swirling amid thin strands of clouds. And yet the battle smoke that had filled the sky three days before still haunted my dreams, as did bandages that floated in midair, unrolling into bloody streamers as I scurried about trying in vain to catch them.

The bathhouse was smaller than the one in Troyes, but it had the same familiar smell of wood smoke, lye soap, and sweet herbs. Two stocky women, their hands red and rough, lugged a huge cauldron of water to the hearth and attached its handle to a hook above the roaring fire. Women bathed in wooden barrels all around the steamy room.

I settled into the barrel next to Hersende's with warm water up to my neck, lavender sprigs floating around me. Closing my eyes, I let the misty air tingle against my face and the water soothe my aching limbs. I forgot about the battle until I heard women talking about it as they bathed nearby.

"The attack on Paris is over—even though we were close to

breaching the wall," Father had told me bitterly the day after the battle. "The king has declared a truce with the enemy and disbanded the army until spring. Jeanne and Alençon still want to fight, but he refuses. If he let them, I know that we would take Paris this day!

"But the townspeople of Saint Denis say that the king's ministers have convinced him that she won't win. He is further discouraged because yesterday in battle, her mere presence was not enough to incite the Parisians further in their revolt against the English."

"And Jeanne will go back to Domrémy?" I had asked.

He shook his head. "She will go with the king to his castle at Chinon. He's afraid that she will gather an army and break the truce. In effect, she is a prisoner now."

A young woman in a barrel close to mine wagered with another woman that Jeanne and the Duke of Alençon would try to attack Paris again despite the king's efforts to separate them. Their curiosity about her grew the more rumors and questions they shared.

They finished their bath and went to dry off by the hearth. "I used to talk about Jeanne like that," I told Hersende.

"And now you know how she suffered from the wound and how overwrought she is. A winter's rest is the best thing for her."

Taking a long-handled brush in hand, she set to work massaging my back. It felt wonderful.

"Your back is covered with flea bites," Hersende observed. "Tell me, where will you and Georges live once you return from the pilgrimage?"

I cupped water in my hands, savoring the memory of his arms around me. This very afternoon we would be wed, and I could caress him again. "We'll go to Reims to get Charlotte," I said. We wanted to see the Grande Rose together with Juliane and Charlotte. I wondered if she would have changed in her months there. "But after Reims, I don't know. We can't return to Troyes.

The Gift

Maybe we'll live in Bourges with you and Etienne. And I could help you make your book of herbal remedies."

She shook her head. "We are only there in the winter when the weather is too cold for battles. Our home is mostly on the battlefield until the war ends, or we become too feeble to travel with the army."

Sadness about the war cast a pall over me again. When I arose this morning, Father was hard at work preparing for his journey. He was encouraged because some of the war captains assured him that the king's men would try again to win Paris early next spring. Memories of Father swirled within me, forming patterns of anger and love again and again. It would always be so, even if I never saw him again. I loved him, and he loved me, but he had chosen a life that would separate us forever.

When Hersende and I finished bathing, we dried ourselves with thick wool blankets in front of the hearth. Donning my silk undergarments felt strange; even more so the black underdress and blue skirt. Hersende helped me tie on the bodice, which hung more loosely than it had last June. I fingered the sleeve with the ink stain, noticing how Ameline had cut the sleeves short enough for holding a quill, and how she had embroidered them with roses.

"You need fattening up this winter," Hersende teased.

She put on a bodice and skirt of deep green. "Etienne always likes me to wear this color," she said as she braided her hair and pinned it up. For the first time since I met her, she donned a coif. It made her look like a wealthy townswoman and not the unkempt barberess I had known all summer. Her change in appearance was another sign that my journey had ended.

Once my shoes were on, I practiced walking again in women's clothes. I had forgotten about the tightness of the bodice and the weight of the skirt. When I took too big a step, I almost pitched forward. "Better to practice here than on the streets in Saint Denis," Hersende said, laughing.

A Tale of Two Maidens

We sat on a bench in front of the fire, and she set to work untangling the longer patches of my hair. The brush massaged my scalp, but I winced whenever it found a matted clump. When she was done, she tucked it neatly under a white coif that she bought for me and held up a looking glass for me to see. The thin, pale face that stared back at me belonged to a stranger. And yet I smiled at this person whom my journey had helped me to become: a woman who still possessed the freedom she had discovered when dressed as a boy.

Hersende walked over to me and put her hands on my shoulders, leaning close so that I could see her in the looking glass too. "You have changed in ways that cannot be swept away in the autumn wind," she said, echoing my thoughts.

Father and Georges waited for us outside the bathhouse. With his trimmed beard, Father looked more like he did years ago, though his hair was grayer, and he had lost a lot of weight.

The blood and grime on Georges's face had been washed clean, and he had shaved his beard as well. He looked completely different than he had last spring. Then, his jaw was too square and his body too muscular—to my mind, everything was wrong with him. But now his deep-set eyes shone, his body was strong—and he looked handsome.

He stared at me, shaking his head in disbelief. "You look so different. I had gotten used to seeing you dressed as a boy."

"You look different too," I said shyly as Father and Hersende exchanged a knowing glance.

On our way back to the monastery where we were staying, we came to the cathedral square. A throng of people stood there shouting Jeanne's name. In the morning, a crier had announced that she was going to place armor and a sword on the altar. They didn't belong to her, but to an enemy soldier who had been captured at the battle. Such was the custom for wounded warriors to give thanks to Saint Denis, the patron saint of our land, that their lives had been spared. Afterward, she would depart with the king to his castle.

The Gift

People poured out of shops and taverns and surged into the square. Bells tolled loudly as cries for Jeanne resounded above them. Women held up sick children to be healed. "By Saint Denis, may she cure my palsy!" an old man next to us shouted, his body trembling.

The king's guards held the cathedral door open. Carried in a chair litter, Jeanne emerged wearing a pale blue tunic. The crowd rushed toward her in a frenzy to touch her. But the guards were quick, and they pushed people back with their lances. She noticed none of this and continued to stare at something invisible that hovered over the rooftops of Saint Denis.

It was the same scene I had watched several times this summer. These people and so many others would never know the truth about Jeanne. But I did, or at least a part of it. One day I would set it down in writing for others to read. And I would record the story of my journey for me alone.

The morning air was filled with the fragrance of decaying leaves. Inside the monastery's stable, monks were saddling Georges's horses for the journey and yoking them to the cart. Georges and I hadn't wanted to wed at Saint Denis with all its coffins and relics. This morning we would travel a short way to Montmartre, a village on a hill overlooking Paris, where the road to the Shrine of Saint James began. There, we would wed at the Church of Saint Pierre.

Etienne, Father, and Georges carried our satchels to the stable while Hersende and I walked behind them, arm in arm.

"Felise, you have become the daughter that God chose not to give me," Hersende said, her eyes filled with tears. "May he be with you on your journey."

"And with you also," I said, tears trickling down my cheeks.

"Until we see each other again, child."

We hugged each other tightly. Etienne came to stand by us,

and I hugged him too, knowing I would miss him almost as much as her.

Father came over to me and opened his satchel. I thought that he was getting out apples for the horses. As a child, he always let me feed them to the horses the day he left for a journey. Instead he handed me a book with a cover made of pale brown leather.

"For you," he said.

I looked into his eyes and saw his love for me, brimming in them. It made me cry even harder.

"It's beautiful," I said.

"I bought it at a bookseller's in Saint Denis."

I opened the book and saw that it was full of blank parchment. A secret book like the one he used to keep in his desk. As a child, I had tried to read it, but he'd taken it from me and told me it was his private diary.

"You're a storyteller like me, Felise," he said with a smile. "I know that you'll finish your apprenticeship and become a journeywoman and then a master scribe. I know that you'll set many stories in writing."

"Thank you, Father," I whispered, clasping the book to my heart. As he embraced me, his recorder pressed against my book. Later, when the sun rose higher in the sky, I'd check the watermark.

Georges and I grasped each other's hands. It was all that was seemly in such a public place with monks and their guests walking back and forth from the inn to the stable. It took every bit of my will not to throw my arms around him.

"Are you ready?" he asked.

"I've been ready for a long time."

Epilogue

June 1431
Montmartre

The five of us—Charlotte, Hersende Etienne, Georges, and I—stood on the hill of Montmartre overlooking Paris. The River Seine snaked its way through the churches and buildings while the Cathedral of Notre Dame towered over everything else.

The mud of our journey from Rouen sullied our cloaks, and the memory of what had happened there haunted me still. A year ago, the Burgundians and their English allies had captured Jeanne, and two weeks ago they had burned her at the stake as a witch. Charles, our king, had done nothing to rescue her.

Why had I gone to witness her execution? No one had forced me to do so, but after discussing the matter with Georges, I knew I must. I wanted to be present with her in her last moments of life. I also wanted to search for Father in the crowd gathered in the main square of Rouen. I hadn't heard from him since the day he gave me the secret book. But he wasn't there.

The executioner led Jeanne to a platform amid the wood. Charlotte was too short to see, and we had told her only that our purpose was to bid farewell to "Horse Girl." Nonetheless, she huddled against me, understanding in her own way what was about to happen.

"I will pray for my enemies," Jeanne had shouted in that powerful voice I remembered so well. The English soldiers grew silent. A hush fell over the crowd for the last time as she said her prayers with her confessor. The executioner lit the pyre. I squeezed Georges's and Charlotte's hands. Hersende and Etienne joined us in praying the Lord's Prayer.

Keeping my eyes on Jeanne was the most torturous deed I had ever done, but with Georges beside me, I watched her until the flames rose up. I wept along with many others as her cries for Jesus filled the smoky air, until the fire took her voice away.

Charlotte had fixed her gaze in the direction of Jeanne's voice. She hummed her "Horse Girl" song so softly that only people close by could hear it. I prayed that through some miracle, Jeanne could hear it too. I also prayed that she didn't suffer long.

Suddenly Charlotte dropped my hand and pointed to the sky above the flames. "Look!"

I peered intently but all I saw was a wall of fire. "What do you see, Charlotte?"

"A white dove. It's flying away."

I followed her gaze but saw nothing. Neither did Georges, Hersende, or Etienne.

The people around us took up Charlotte's cry. "A dove! The Maid has given us one last miracle."

"The bird of peace."

Standing atop Montmartre, Georges and I turned to one another and smiled. The tormented look that cast shadows beneath his eyes was gone. In our first year of marriage, we had found peace with one another . . . and love and happiness.

Neither of us believed that war should be used as a path toward peace. Yet it pained us to think that Jeanne's martyrdom might have been in vain. In the Church of Saint Pierre where we were wed, we lit a candle. *May Charlotte's omen come true, and may France be at peace,* I prayed.

Felise's story will continue in

Labyrinth of the Spirit
by Anne Echols

COMING SOON!

Historical Note

In 1430, the Burgundians captured Jeanne at Compiègne and sold her to the English. King Charles VII made no attempt to rescue her or raise a ransom for her. In an attempt to discredit him and destroy Jeanne's popularity with the French people, the English claimed that she was a witch. She was put on trial for heresy and witchcraft before the Inquisition. Found guilty after a trial fraught with trickery and irregularities, Jeanne was burned at the stake in May of 1431.

In 1453 Jeanne's military efforts were rewarded as her mission was accomplished at last. The Hundred Years War was over, and France was at peace with Charles VII still on the throne. To strengthen the legitimacy of his rule, Charles wanted to rid himself of any association with a "witch." Therefore, he called for Jeanne's rehabilitation trial. In 1456, Jeanne was cleared of all charges of heresy and witchcraft. The Catholic Church declared her a saint in 1920.

Sources

For general research on women in the Middle Ages, I drew upon my two previously published works, as well as sources listed in their bibliographies:

- Anne Echols and Marty Williams. *An Annotated Index of Medieval Women*. Princeton: Markus Wiener Publishers, 1992.
- Marty Williams and Anne Echols. *Between Pit and Pedestal: Women in the Middle Ages*. Princeton: Markus Wiener Publishers, 1994.

For an in-depth study of Joan of Arc, I gathered additional information from the following sources:

- Bonnie Wheeler, and Charles T. Wood, eds. *Fresh Verdicts on Joan of Arc*. New York: Garland, 1996.
- "Joan of Arc's Letter to the citizens of Rheims" (August 5, 1429). Translated by Allen Williamson. https://archive .joan-of-arc.org/joanofarc_letters.html..
- Marina Warner. *Joan of Arc: The Image of Female Heroism*. New York: Knopf, 1981.
- Nadia Margolis. *Joan of Arc in History, Literature, and Film: A Select, Annotated Bibliography*. New York: Garland, 1990.
- Régine Pernoud. *Joan of Arc by Herself and Her Witnesses*. New York: Stein & Day, 1982.

- Régine Pernoud, trans. J. M. Cohen. *The Retrial of Joan of Arc: The Evidence at the Trial for her Rehabilitation.* London: Harcourt, Brace and Company, 1955.

For additional research about the Hundred Years War, I turned mainly to these sources:

- Christopher Gravett. Richard and Christa Hook, illustrators. *Medieval Siege Warfare.* London: Reed International Books Limited, 1990.
- Edouard Perroy. *The Hundred Years War.* Trans. David C. Douglas. New York: Oxford University Press, 1951.
- Jonathan Sumption. *The Hundred Years War: Trial by Battle.* Philadelphia: University of Pennsylvania Press, 1991.

For specific information about the work of medieval scribes, I consulted Christopher de Hamel's *Scribes and Illuminators.* London: British Museum Press, 1992.

Research on medieval medical practices came from a variety of sources, including Kate Campbell Hurd-Mead's *A History of Women in Medicine.* Haddam, CT: 1938.

Suggested Bibliography for Further Research

France during the Hundred Years War

Allmand, C. T. *The Hundred Years War: England and France at War, c. 1300–c. 1450.* Cambridge: Cambridge University Press, 1988.

Curry, Anne. *The Hundred Years War.* Basingstoke: Macmillan, 1993.

Jacob, Ernst Fraser. *Henry V and the Invasion of France.* New York: Macmillan, 1950.

Lewis, Peter, ed. *The Recovery of France in the Fifteenth Century.* New York: Harper and Row, 1972.

Newhall, Richard A. *The English Conquest of Normandy, 1416–1424.* New York: Russell and Russell, 1971.

Vale, Malcolm. *The Origins of the Hundred Years War.* Oxford: Clarendon Press, 1996.

Joan of Arc

Gies, Frances. *Joan of Arc: The Legend and the Reality.* New York: Harper and Row, 1981.

International Joan of Arc Society. http://joanofarcsociety.org.

Discussion Questions

These discussion questions will help adults as well as teachers and students discuss this book and its meanings.

Questions for Book Clubs

- As the novel unfolds, how will Felise's understanding of Jeanne affect her own choices?

- Compare and contrast the treatment of women in the Middle Ages with their status in various societies today.

- What was the biggest surprise about medieval life for you as described in the novel?

- What would be the hardest aspect to adjust to?

- How was Charlotte both a burden and a gift on Felise's journey?

- Why do Georges and Felise disagree about Jeanne?

- Did your understanding of Jeanne (Joan of Arc) change after reading the book? Why or why not? Did you like Jeanne? Would you follow her?

- Does she remind you of anyone today? Jeanne (Joan of Arc) was a fifteenth-century celebrity. How has being a celebrity changed from then to now?

- Project into Felise and Georges's future. How do you envision their life together?

A *Tale of Two Maidens*

Questions for Teachers and Students

Characters

* How did Felise's relationship with her father shape her decisions during the course of the novel? Her relationship with Ameline?

* Felise and Georges are attracted to one another despite their differences. Discuss those differences as well as any similarities.

* How did Felise's feelings about Jeanne change over the course of the novel?

* Discuss gender issues presented in the novel.

* Discuss diversity issues presented in the book.

Historical

* Merchants, scribes, tanners, and healers are shown at their day-to-day work in *A Tale of Two Maidens*. Describe the most vivid details of medieval work.

* In the culture of twenty-first-century America, strong female characters, such as Katniss and Lisbeth, enjoy popularity, and in real life we have Hilary Clinton and Danica Patrick. How do our popular fictional and historical women differ from Joan of Arc and other famous women of the Middle Ages?

* Jeanne was an atypical woman of the Middle Ages. What does the novel show about more typical roles available for women during the fifteenth century?

* How has warfare changed from the fifteenth century until now?

* Compare religion in the fifteenth century to religion in Europe and the United States today.

Discussion Questions

- What does the novel reveal about the experiences of marginalized people in the Middle Ages?

Personal

- Did Felise's relationship to her father remind you of how you relate to your father?

- Have you ever had to balance ambition and love in your own life? Have any girls or women you know had to do so?

- If you were in Felise's place, would you have made different choices on your journey? Why or why not?

- If you were Felise's friend, what advice would you give her about her confusion about Georges?

Acknowledgments

After coauthoring two nonfiction works about medieval women, I envisioned the story of an obscure woman against the backdrop of a more famous sister. Thus, Felise the Scribe was born—an ordinary girl who crossed paths with Joan of Arc. Many people helped me write Felise's story. Marty Williams, my coauthor for *Between Pit and Pedestal: Women in the Middle Ages* and *An Annotated Index of Medieval Women,* shared in researching Joan's life and helped me to imagine her untold story. Thanks go as well to Patricia Hurd and Sharon Saxton, my traveling companions on our "Joan of Arc" tour of France.

Throughout this project, my writers' group has been my lifeline. Claire Brown, Greg Changnon, Kathryn Legan, Liza Nelson, and Terry Repak—each of you has an eye for different aspects of my writing. Your insights and honest but constructive criticism have helped me hone my craft and produce the best book possible. My words of thanks come nowhere close to describing the gratitude I feel for each of you.

I'm also grateful for the readers of early drafts, my "kitchen table" team of Patricia Hurd, Sharon Saxton, and (posthumously) Rachael Walter. With humor and wit, they helped me transform from a nonfiction writer to a writer of fiction, as did Carol Lee Lorenzo and Sam Zografos. Later readers deserve a big thanks as well: my mother, Patricia Schmidt; my sister Marcella Wilson; my daughter, Melissa Moynahan; and friends Kathy Gerkin, Nancy Hunter, Patricia Hurd, Katie Smillie, and Kathy Zilbermann.

A Tale of Two Maidens

I am thrilled to have found the perfect publishing home with She Writes Press. The communication and organization skills of this press have been amazing throughout the entire publishing process. A big shout out to the whole team, especially to Brooke Warner, publisher extraordinaire, Shannon Green, astute editor and very efficient project manager, and Julie Metz, the talented art director who created the cover of my dreams.

In the final push toward publication, many people stepped forward to assist. My daughter, Melissa Moynahan, offered valuable publicity and technical support along with my son-in-law, Patrick Moynahan. Fellow writer Ryan Hurd graciously shared his social media strategies for attracting new readers.

Thanks to my family for ongoing support: my mother, Patricia, and my father, Frederick (both posthumously); and siblings Michael, Emily, Marcella, Eric, John, and Mary Pat. My children, Melissa and Jarrett, continue to bring me joy, as well as my grandchildren Hannah, Adalise, and Loukas.

Last but certainly not least, I want to thank my husband, Russ. A self-pronounced "book widower," he nonetheless stoically supports me as a writer. After retrieving me from the airport (following a research trip to France), he led me to the backyard at midnight. He had spent the summer remodeling an old garden shed into a writing studio, complete with windows, heating, air conditioning, and lighting! The "shed" continues to be the writer's space of my dreams. Love always to Russ.

About the Author

Anne Echols is the coauthor (with Marty Williams) of two nonfiction books, *Between Pit and Pedestal: Women in the Middle Ages* and *An Annotated Index of Medieval Women.* Her research for those projects inspired her to go beyond historical facts and imagine the fictional stories of ordinary women from the Middle Ages. After earning a BA and master's degree from Emory University in Atlanta, Anne enjoyed a long career of teaching English to high school students with language learning disabilities. Her husband, Russ, and she have two adult children. Recently retired, she is grateful for the opportunity to divide her time between Silver Spring, Maryland, where her grandchildren live, and Atlanta.

You can contact Anne through her website:
annesechols.wixsite.com/atotm/home,
her Facebook page: www.facebook.com/anneecholsauthor,
or Twitter: @anneecholsauthor.

SELECTED TITLES FROM SHE WRITES PRESS

She Writes Press is an independent publishing
company founded to serve women writers everywhere.
Visit us at www.shewritespress.com.

The Nun's Betrothal by Ida Curtis. $16.95, 978-1-63152-685-5. Sister Gilda and Lord Justin are charged to resolve a conflict: Count Cedric wants to annul his marriage to Lady Mariel so he can marry Lady Emma; Mariel believes Cedric's half-brother Phillip, not Cedric, is the man she married at her wedding; and Philip and Emma are in love. Can Gilda and Justin complete their mission before their burgeoning passion for each other overwhelms them?

Song of Isabel by Ida Curtis. $16.95, 978-1-63152-371-7. In ninth-century France, a handsome officer in the King's army rescues twelve-year-old Isabel from an assault by a passing warrior. When the officer returns to her father's estate several years later, sparks fly and emotions tangle.

Dark Lady by Charlene Ball. $16.95, 978-1-63152-228-4. Emilia Bassano Lanyer—poor, beautiful, and intelligent, born to a family of Court musicians and secret Jews, lover to Shakespeare and mistress to an older nobleman—survives to become a published poet in an era when most women's lives are rigidly circumscribed.

Beyond the Ghetto Gates by Michelle Cameron. $16.95, 978-1-63152-850-7. When French troops occupy the Italian port city of Ancona, freeing the city's Jews from their repressive ghetto, two very different cultures collide—and a whirlwind of progressivism and brutal backlash is unleashed.

The Lines Between Us by Rebecca D'Harlingue. $16.95, 978-1-63152-743-2. A young girl flees seventeenth-century Madrid, in fear for her life. Three centuries later and a continent away, a woman comes across old papers long hidden away, and in them discovers the reason for the flight so long ago, and for her own mother's enigmatic dying words.

Finding Napoleon: A Novel by Margaret Rodenberg. $16.95, 978-1-64742-016-1. In an intriguing adaptation of Napoleon Bonaparte's real attempt to write a novel, the defeated emperor and his little-known last love—the audacious, pregnant Albine de Montholon—plot to escape exile and free his young son. To succeed, Napoleon demands loyalty. To survive, Albine plunges into betrayal.